"If yo

Colonel Sheldon turned sideways to give her room to pass, but as she stepped down next to him, he placed his hand against the opposite wall, blocking her descent. One hand on his arm, she steadied herself, gazing up at him, evidently startled by his sudden move.

The colonel was startled himself. Not since his raw youth could he recall accosting with amorous intentions a female in a dark place. Lady Fanny stood as if mesmerized within the circle of his arms, and Derek felt the warmth of her breath in the air between them.

His eyes fixed on her parted lips. All manner of erotic fantasies raced through his mind. He felt himself drawn inexorably toward those lips, and before he realized what he was doing, his head bent down to take the kiss he knew he could not do without. . . .

Scandalous Secrets

Patricia Oliver

A SIGNET BOOK

SIGNET
Published by New American Library, a division of
Penguin Putnam Inc., 375 Hudson Street,
New York, New York 10014, U.S.A.
Penguin Books Ltd, 27 Wrights Lane,
London W8 5TZ, England
Penguin Books Australia Ltd, Ringwood,
Victoria, Australia
Penguin Books Canada Ltd, 10 Alcorn Avenue,
Toronto, Ontario, Canada M4V 3B2
Penguin Books (N.Z.) Ltd, 182–190 Wairau Road,
Auckland 10, New Zealand

Penguin Books Ltd, Registered Offices:
Harmondsworth, Middlesex, England

First published by Signet, an imprint of New American Library,
a division of Penguin Putnam Inc.

First Printing, December 1999
10 9 8 7 6 5 4 3 2 1

REGISTERED TRADEMARK—MARCA REGISTRADA

Printed in the United States of America

PUBLISHER'S NOTE
This is a work of fiction. Names, characters, places, and incidents either are the product of the author's imagination or are used fictitiously, and any resemblance to actual persons, living or dead, business establishments, events, or locales is entirely coincidental.

BOOKS ARE AVAILABLE AT QUANTITY DISCOUNTS WHEN USED TO PROMOTE PRODUCTS OR SERVICES. FOR INFORMATION PLEASE WRITE TO PREMIUM MARKETING DIVISION, PENGUIN PUTNAM INC., 375 HUDSON STREET, NEW YORK, NEW YORK 10014.

Contents

PROLOGUE

Banished

Cornwall, March 1796

As Lady Fanny stood on the deck of the *Flying Falcon*
and watched the green shores of England slip away
into the morning fog, she thought of her mother and a chill
wind touched her heart. She shuddered, suddenly overcome
by a wild desire to run home and bury herself in Lady
Hayle's warm embrace. But that was impossible. The notorious Lady Fanny St. Ives had no home. And worse yet,
she had no mother. A sob rose in her throat and she
glanced down at the smooth dark ocean below her and
wondered what it would feel like to drown. To let herself
fall into the blue-green water and invite the mysterious sea
to invade every part of her body—like an impatient lover—
inside and out, until she was full of it, satiated with the
cold caresses of death. Only in death would she escape the
pain, only death could make her forget the betrayal.

Lady Fanny shuddered again.

A plump arm slipped tenderly around her waist and drew
her close. "Don't dwell upon it, my dear Fanny," her aunt
said bracingly. "You will only make yourself sick, and you
can change nothing."

Fanny glanced at the small woman standing beside her
at the rail and smiled in spite of herself. Lady Clarissa
Wentworth was that kind of person. She could draw laughter from a marble statue.

"I was thinking of Mama," Fanny confessed. "I had the
eerie feeling that I'll never see her again, Aunt. I cannot
bear it." She turned away to catch the last glimpse of Cornwall, the sob building again. "I wish I were dead."

Lady Wentworth hugged her tightly. "You must not wish

for death, my love. You might get your wish, and where would that leave me? I love you like my own daughter, Fanny. As does your Uncle John. He will be impatient to see you again, my dear. I wrote to tell him about your . . . your misfortune."

"Misfortune!" Fanny repeated bitterly. "You are too kind, Aunt. According to those who think they know, I am a scandalous creature, a loose and immoral female, a whore, in fact."

"Don't do this to yourself, love."

"That is what my own husband called me, Aunt. And that heartless monster who sired me did nothing. Nothing!" she repeated, her voice edged with hysteria. "Poor Mama! He *hit* her, you know. The beast! Oh, how I hate him!"

"Your father?"

Fanny went rigid. "Do not call him that! He is no such thing to *me*," she said coldly. "He has disowned me, as you well know, Aunt. As I do him. He actually *stood* there, and watched Cambourne beat me. To within an inch of my life." Fanny paused to control her trembling voice. "It didn't surprise me that the duke should behave like a maniac; he was always so stiff-necked and full of his own consequence. But I thought my fa—I thought that *other* monster really loved me. I was his favourite, he said. His darling little princess. His precious baby girl. His . . . Oh, Aunt, he let Cambourne do those unspeakable things to me. And then he hit poor Mama when she tried to stop them. Oh, I *do* wish I were dead!"

"Hush, dear," Lady Wentworth murmured and patted her distraught niece's arm. "None of them can hurt you again, Fanny. You will be safe in India with us."

"He *hit* her," Lady Fanny choked, tears she thought had all been wept away weeks ago streaming unimpeded down her cheeks. "I still hear her scream at night. I'll never stop hearing my mama scream."

And that was not all she heard—or saw or felt—in her nightmares, Fanny thought, her eyes searching for one last glimpse of the Cornish coastline, knowing it was gone, knowing herself cut off from all those she had loved. She remembered things she dared not tell her aunt that were said and done that dreadful night last December.

* * *

Fanny had started flirting with Gerald before dinner, and later, when her husband joined a game of hazard with some of his guests, she allowed Gerald to kiss her in the conservatory. Only because Cambourne had been so obnoxious, of course. There had been no need to humiliate her before her houseguests. To treat her like a contentious child. And on New Year's Eve, too. All because of some frippery bill that had come to his notice. She had only wanted to punish him for being so disagreeable, but when Gerald slipped into her room later that night, Fanny realized she had made a grave mistake. And then, as Gerald tried to embrace her, they both heard the sound of heavy steps in the hall outside.

And then the crash of the door thrown open with unmistakable violence.

Fanny was conscious of the chill March wind pulling at her bonnet and drying her wet cheeks. Why did the sound of that door crashing against the wall of her bedchamber still haunt her? In retrospect, it seemed innocuous compared to what followed, but in her mind it had presaged the eruption of a violence far more frightening than any she could have imagined.

The Duke of Cambourne stood on the threshold, his lips peeled back in a snarl of rage. Behind her husband, Fanny saw her father's pale, shocked face. The tableau lasted an eternity, before the duke strode over to the bed and glared down at her, his eyes hard and cold as rain-washed marble. When he spoke, his voice cascaded over her thinly clad body in waves of brutally descriptive insults—fully half of which Fanny had never heard before—whose virulence caused her to cringe into the deep feather bed as though there might be some sanctuary there.

It was then Fanny noticed that her husband clutched a quirt in his right fist.

Fanny felt a gentle tug on her arm and looked down to see Lady Wentworth gazing at her, concern in her pale blue eyes. "Let us go down to our cabin, my dear," her aunt suggested cheerfully. "Captain Hawkins warned me that the winds will pick up as soon as we pass Lands End, and we will not want to be on deck when that happens, child, believe me."

Too miserable to care where she was, Fanny meekly followed her aunt down the steep iron gangway to the lower deck. She must have lost consciousness soon after the beating began, Fanny reasoned as she followed Lady Wentworth into the stateroom and threw herself down on one of the narrow bunks. Her heart was beating wildly, as in her nightmares, and her body felt stiff and chilled. She closed her eyes tightly to block out that sound of her father's hand across her mother's face.

"My dear Fanny, you look as though you have seen a ghost." Her aunt's gentle voice cut through the terror that threatened to overwhelm her.

"I see ghosts all the time," she whispered.

Lady Wentworth was at her side instantly, her soft hands loosening the pins from Fanny's hair and smoothing it gently across the pillow. "My dear, sweet child," she crooned, her voice so like her sister's that for a heart-stopping moment, Fanny imagined she was a child again and her mama was sitting on her bed beside her at Hayle Hall.

"Cambourne cannot hurt you, child," Lady Wentworth added with calm common sense, and Fanny felt the terror gradually recede into the dark corner it occupied in her mind. "That devil was in London the last I heard. You must not be afraid, dearest."

"I am often afraid, Aunt," Fanny replied quietly, reaching out to clasp her aunt's plump hand and press it against her cheek. "I am so glad you are here. You have the power to keep the horror at bay. I do not believe I could have survived without you, Aunt."

"Fiddle!" her aunt exclaimed, her expression once more relaxing into its customary cheerfulness. "You are stronger than you think, Fanny. When I was your age, I was a dizzy girl, falling in love with the most ineligible gentleman in London. A half-pay officer, no less. Father would not hear of it, of course, although Mama was on our side. She believed in love, you see."

"Nobody in my family believes in love," Fanny said brusquely. This was not entirely true, of course. As a schoolroom chit she had dreamed of a tall glittering stranger, darkly magnetic and handsome like her father and brothers. It seemed incredible to her now that these brutish, monstrous men had been her childhood ideals of the perfect gentleman who would love and cherish her as they had. Or as she had been duped into believing that they had.

"Forgive me, Aunt. I did not mean to distress you," Fanny said contritely. "You have been like my own mother to me. I only hope Uncle John will not be too shocked when he learns he has acquired an ostracized, shameless watering-pot for a pensioner."

"He will be delighted, my dear," Lady Wentworth exclaimed. "I thank the Lord that I was in England when all this happened, Fanny. I tremble to think what might have become of you had I been in Bombay with John."

Fanny smiled for the second time since they had boarded the *Flying Falcon* at dawn. "Your housekeeper would have let me stay at Wentworth Hall, I don't doubt," she remarked with more calm than she felt.

Wentworth Hall had become her home since that awful night, a refuge where the deep welts on Fanny's back had slowly healed, and the far deeper wounds to her heart had hardened into open sores of resentment. And where Aunt Clarissa—mercifully home from India for a short stay—had been everything Fanny could hope for in a mother. She and Sir John were all the family she had left now, and Fanny felt ungrateful when her thoughts lingered so persistently on Cornwall and on the mother she might never see again.

Later that night, when the deck was relatively deserted and silent, Fanny wrapped herself in a woollen robe and stole up to stand in the moonlight, gazing at the white wake that stretched behind the vessel as far as her eye could see. All the way back to England, she mused, wondering when or if she would ever see Cornwall again. But whether she did or not, she vowed, she would never, never open her heart to men again.

She would never forget. Or forgive.

CHAPTER 1

The Return

Calais, April 1806

Had it not been for the unfamiliar smells that assailed her nostrils as the Wentworth carriage made its laborious way through the crowds on the dock at Calais, Lady Fanny might have imagined herself back in Bombay. One of her chief delights during her Indian rebirth had been to accompany Sir John Wentworth to the Bombay wharves to welcome one of her uncle's many trading ships returning from England. The seemingly insatiable European craving for exotic East Indian luxuries such as silks, spices, tea, and cotton goods had made Sir John's fortune for him many times over, and Fanny's only regret was that the baronet had not lived longer to enjoy it.

It amused Fanny to ponder the eccentricities of her countrymen, who could deny a second son entrance into the sacred ranks of the *ton*, then a few years later overlook his noxious connexion with Trade because he had quite unexpectedly gained not only his brother's title, but an enormous fortune to boot. Or was it Fate? Fanny mused, watching four sweating stevedores with their bulky loads of goods trudge down the swaying gangway of a merchant vessel tied up at the dock. Had Fate metamorphosed the handsome yet highly ineligible half-pay officer her Aunt Clarissa had lost her heart to so many years ago, into one of the wealthiest English traders in India?

Fanny rather thought it had. She liked the idea of Fate exercising a deliberate twist of its implacable wheel in her aunt's favour. For Lady Wentworth had married her half-pay officer in spite of her father's obstreperous opposition to the unequal match. She had loved him in spite of every-

thing and followed her young husband to Bombay when he
obtained a post in the East India Company. She had believed in him when he had invested a modest inheritance
in a cargo of spices, and encouraged him to invest the profits
into other ventures until the name of John Wentworth had—
over the years—become synonymous with wealth, power,
and an incredible nose for profit.

"Isn't that one of Sir John's ships, Fanny?" Her aunt's
gentle voice broke into Fanny's daydreaming.

"The *Fortune Hunter*? Why yes, so it is, Aunt," Fanny
exclaimed, inordinately pleased at the encounter. "One of
uncle's fastest ships, in fact. Perhaps we can obtain passage
home on her instead of waiting for the packet-boat to
Dover," she added with sudden inspiration.

"That will depend on who the master is," Lady Wentworth cautioned. "You know that your uncle did not believe in wasting ship space on passengers, dear. And what
little cabin space there is may well be already booked."

"Are you forgetting, my dear Aunt, that we *own* uncle's
entire fleet, including the *Fortune Hunter*? The captain will
do as you say, like it or not."

Her aunt's face registered reproof. "Surely you do not
expect me to turn some poor traveller out of his cabin on a
whim, Fanny? Would you even do so yourself, I wonder?"

Fanny grinned sheepishly, knowing that her aunt was
right. "Perhaps we will not have to take such drastic measures, Aunt. The *Fortune Hunter* is under the command of
Captain Jack Mansford. Remember Captain Jack? He was
first mate when old Jeb Hawkins got carried off with small-
pox in 1802. He brought the *Fortune Hunter* safely home
and Uncle promoted him to master."

Lady Wentworth sighed. "Ah, yes. Now I remember. An
impertinent rogue he was, too, that young Jack. But my
John was right, as always. Mansford turned out to be one
of his best captains, in spite of his lamentable fondness for
women of dubious virtue and bottles of inferior spirits."

Fanny laughed. "I daresay Captain Mansford is unaware
of our presence in Calais, Aunt. I shall send him a note
immediately," she added, halting the carriage and sum-
moning the groom. "He must think us already in England
weeks ago."

"And so we would have been, Fanny, had you not taken it into your head to leave the ship in Marseilles and drag me all the way to Paris to refurbish our wardrobes. I cannot imagine when I shall wear all the gowns you ordered for me, dear. It is not as though I intend to do much entertaining when we get back to Brighton. It is too soon."

" 'Tis over a year now that Uncle John was taken from us, my dear Aunt," she pointed out gently, pencil poised over the note she was scribbling. "And I cannot believe that he would be pleased to see you going about Brighton in gowns that must be at least ten years out of fashion."

"You are exaggerating, as usual, Fanny," Lady Wentworth scolded gently. "And what do I care if the *ton* thinks I am a dowd. Nobody is likely to notice me at all when you appear in all your Paris finery, which suits me very well, let me tell you. There will be far too much to occupy me at Primrose Court. It has been over ten years since—"

"If you think I am going to allow you to bury yourself in household tasks and ignore the world around you, Aunt, I can assure you it will not happen." She signed her name with a flourish and handed the note to their groom.

"We shall see about that, dear," Lady Wentworth responded in her quiet voice, fingers picking absentmindedly at the fringe of her woollen shawl.

Lady Fanny glanced at her aunt sharply.

Coming home to England had not been an easy decision for either of them. Life in Bombay had been full of grace and charm, and Fanny had quickly adapted to the relaxed social rhythm of the English colonials. Unlike other ladies of her class, however, Fanny had taken a genuine interest in the native culture, discovering an unsuspected affinity for the unselfconscious eroticism of Indian art. Although the blatant sensuality of statues like that of the tree goddess Vrikshaka had initially startled her, Fanny had been captivated by the secret smile on the goddess's perfect face, and envious of her freely displayed breasts. Large as ripe Pippins, Fanny had always thought, all too conscious of her own modest appendages.

There would be nothing in Brighton as provocative as Vrikshaka to delight the eye. There would be no sacred trees and plants believed to be manifestations of one god or another on the Marine Parade or in the gardens of the Regent's Pavilion. No *tulasi*, the basil-like plant regarded as the incarnation of the goddess of beauty and good fortune, to ease the departure of the dying as it had for Fanny's beloved uncle. Fanny could not in her wildest flights of fancy imagine the Church of England countenancing the placement of a *tulasi* root in a dying man's mouth or covering his face with its leaves.

And certainly there would be no snake charmers in Queen's Park or along the Parade. Or elephants. Fanny suddenly realized that she would miss the elephants. She could not say the same for the sacred bulls strolling casually through the shopping district and clogging the streets of Bombay. She smiled to herself at the thought of cows, sacred or otherwise, invading the Royal Pavilion and eating the roses.

Was her aunt thinking these same thoughts and regretting the decision to return home? Lady Wentworth's pale blue eyes gazed out at the bustling crowd, but Fanny was certain her thoughts were far away, either in Brighton, where she had begun her life with Sir John, or back in Bombay, where her beloved husband lay buried in the land he had loved.

Fanny reached out to clasp her aunt's cold fingers, but before she could utter the bracing words that trembled on her lips, a child's cry of anguish broke into their private moment.

"Oh, Prudy, stop him, *stop* him. He stole my reticule!"

Without the slightest consideration for propriety, Fanny grasped her aunt's ebony walking cane, swung open the carriage door, and jumped down.

The voice was a little girl's, and as Fanny turned to survey the scene, she saw a child sprawled on the cobbles where the thief had obviously pushed her. Her pretty face mirrored her distress, and gaily coloured flowers from a bouquet she must have been carrying lay strewn about her.

An ill-dressed youth of about thirteen or fourteen was sprinting towards Fanny, a smug expression on his thin face. Fanny had little doubt that she was confronting the culprit. Without hesitation, she thrust the cane between the lad's legs and brought him down with a loud thump on the cobbles. Although the breath had been knocked out of him, the young thief stubbornly clutched the child's blue silk reticule in one hand.

As he started to get to his feet, Fanny realized that stronger measures were called for. Stepping forward, she raised the cane and brought it down smartly on the lad's shoulders, causing him to collapse on the wharf again.

"Give it up," she commanded harshly, "or you will get another beating, my lad." She raised the cane again to emphasize her threat.

To her chagrin, the urchin merely laughed up at her, showing a large gap where his front teeth should have been. Something in his eyes warned Fanny of danger even before the little girl screamed something unintelligible. She whirled in time to see two older boys, clearly in league with the first thief, circling around behind her.

"Fanny!" Her aunt's frantic scream sounded muffled from inside the coach, and Fanny paid it no heed. She had dealt with street hooligans aplenty in Bombay and knew that to show the least sign of fear would be fatal. So she did not retreat to the carriage, as her aunt begged her to do, but turned to face her attackers, cane held menacingly in front of her.

A small crowd began to gather at the first sign of a dust-up, but Fanny did not delude herself that any one of the onlookers would come to her aid. They seemed to be more interested in egging on the scruffy duo who edged towards her, swaggering and posturing and shouting obscenities for the entertainment of the crowd.

A tremor of apprehension ran through her as the taller of the lads, evidently the ringleader, sprang forward defiantly, one hand waving a short dirk.

Fanny smiled grimly. If this riffraff thought to intimidate her because she was a female armed only with a cane, they were about to be disabused. Not for nothing had Lady Fanny taken fencing lessons long ago with her four brothers, and learned that dexterity more than compensated for her lack of physical strength.

Her smile broadened.

The ringleader appeared to take this as a challenge and sprang forward again, dirk at arm's length. Fanny pressed the concealed button in the handle of her aunt's cane and felt the urge to laugh aloud when the thief's expression changed from cocky bravado to alarm as the eighteen-inch blade slid smoothly out of its sheath.

He came to a standstill, surprised at this new development. Derisive murmurs rose from the crowd, and Fanny saw an angry flush stain the hooligan's face. Although she understood only snatches of the local patois, she sensed that the volatile crowd had shifted its sympathies from the young thief to her.

Evidently stung by this desertion, the scruffy youth lunged forward, but Fanny had anticipated his move and deftly parried with a thrust that pricked his arm and drew blood. He let out a hoarse cry and his weapon clattered to the cobbles amid shrieks of delight from the crowd.

Defeated, the lad turned and fled, racing after his cohort who had already taken to his heels, disappearing into the maze of crates, sacks, baskets, and other goods piled haphazardly on the wharf.

"Fanny!" she heard her aunt call from the safety of the carriage. "Come back here this minute. What would your poor mother say if she could see you behaving like a mannerless hoyden?"

Fanny paid little attention to this stricture. Out of the corner of her eye, she saw the youngest thief scrambling to his feet, the child's reticule still clutched in his grubby hand.

"Oh no, you do not!" she exclaimed sharply, swinging round to point her sword stick at his skinny chest. "Give that back this instant!" When the lad hesitated, Fanny let the point of the blade rest on his grimy shirt, impeding his attempt to flee.

With a guttural curse, the lad dropped the reticule and jumped back. After a murderous glance in her direction, he turned and fled after his fellows.

Fanny felt herself go limp with relief. Ignoring the dissipating crowd, she retracted her blade and looked around for the young girl.

"Charlotte, come here this instant," a female voice commanded shrilly. Before the frightened looking woman, whom Fanny guessed to be the child's governess, could reach her charge, the girl had dashed across the cobbles and retrieved her property. Then she stared at Fanny, eyes round and filled with admiration.

"Oh, how brave of you," she murmured shyly. "I cannot thank you enough. I was afraid I had lost it forever," she added, indicating the blue reticule clutched to her small bosom.

Fanny smiled. "It was lucky I happened by when I did. And also lucky that I know how to deal with these street ragamuffins."

The child approached her hesitantly. "You were splendid," she offered, her eyes fixed apprehensively on Fanny's cane.

"Nonsense," Fanny replied quickly. "You did not expect me to stand by and allow those pestilential hooligans to run off with your pretty reticule, now, did you?"

The little girl smiled, showing two enchanting dimples. "It *is* pretty, is it not? It was a birthday gift from my papa, and I would hate to lose it. He chose it specially for me."

"A birthday gift? No wonder you were so upset at the prospect of losing it," Fanny remarked, amused at the child's evident affection for her father.

Had her own life been different, Fanny thought with a rare spasm of nostalgia, she might have had a daughter of her own by now, perhaps very like the beautiful child who stood beside her with her father's gift held tightly in her arms. Fanny remembered the endless number of pretty gifts her own father had showered upon her—until that dreadful day he had betrayed her. That fatherly love she had imagined invulnerable had been a lie.

What a fool she had been to believe that the men in her life—father, brothers, husband—were her protectors, her champions. They had all turned out to be her enemies. She had been as naive as this pretty child, whose mother she might have been. Fanny prayed that little Charlotte would not suffer the same fate.

The child's voice brought her back from ugly memories. "I shall tell Papa how much he is indebted to you," she was saying. "He will wish to thank you himself."

"The colonel will indeed wish to thank you for coming to his daughter's assistance, ma'am," a flustered voice reiterated from beside her. "Ever so punctilious the colonel is where Charlotte is concerned."

Fanny turned to find herself being regarded by a pair of anxious brown eyes. "I am Miss Grimes, governess to Miss Charlotte Sheldon," this female announced, making a formal curtsy to Fanny. "We are most—"

"You may call me Charlotte," the child interrupted, her sunny smile suggesting that they were already fast friends. "And my papa is a colonel, There have been Sheldons at Sheldon Hall for over four hundred years. Of course, we will probably be the last, since I do not have a brother to inherit."

"And you may call me Fanny, Charlotte," Fanny countered, amused at the pride in the child's voice. "I am Lady Fanny Wentworth, on my way back to England with my aunt, after a long stay in India." She indicated her aunt's face peering at them from the carriage window.

"India?" Charlotte's voice piped up eagerly. "How exciting! I wish my papa had been stationed in India instead of Lisbon. Is it true that cows are sacred there and are allowed to wander in the streets?"

Fanny smiled. "Yes, that is indeed true."

"Were you frightened?" Charlotte demanded in a breathless voice.

Before Fanny could reply, she sensed a disturbance on the wharf and turned to see a tall man coming towards them, trailed by Hutchins, the Wentworth groom.

Fanny's smile broadened. It had been at least eight months since she had laid eyes on the captain of the *Fortune Hunter*, but he had changed little in that time. If anything, striding purposefully through the crowd that gave way before him, Wild Jack looked more like a pirate than ever.

"What the devil is going on here?" he demanded, coming to a halt beside her. "Let me guess. My little girl here," he added, ruffling Charlotte's mop of riotous curls with one large hand, "has got herself into the briars again. Is that it, Poppet?"

"Oh, Captain Jack," Charlotte cried with an enthusiasm and familiarity that surprised Fanny, "you should have seen how we sent those ruffians to the rightabout. They ran like scared rabbits."

"We?" The captain sounded amused.

"Well, actually, it was Lady Fanny who cut them to pieces with her sword. A wonderful sight it was, too." She paused, then continued in a contrite voice, "Oh, I do beg your pardon, my lady. This is Captain Jack of the *Fortune Hunter*—"

"No need to do the pretty, Poppet," the captain interrupted with a laugh. "Lady Fanny and I have been acquainted these many years. How are you, my dear," he added, raising Fanny's fingers to his lips with a flourish. "I am glad to find you as beautiful and bloodthirsty as ever."

"She is *not* bloodthirsty," Charlotte protested instantly.

Jack raised an eyebrow in mock surprise. "Did you not tell me that the lady cut the hoodlums to pieces, Poppet? That ranks as bloodthirsty in my book."

Charlotte pouted prettily. "They stole my reticule. The one Papa gave me."

The captain favoured Fanny with a disarming grin. "There appears to be a fine distinction here that escapes me, but it may exonerate you from the charge, my lady. Fortunate that you were armed, as it happens."

"How do you two know each other?" Fanny enquired, although she suspected she knew the answer.

"Papa and I are travelling on the *Fortune Hunter*," Charlotte announced. "And Miss Prudy, too, of course. We are having a wonderful time, are we not, Prudy?"

"I doubt that Miss Grimes would agree with you, Poppet," the captain argued, acknowledging the governess with a slight bow. "Sea travel does not agree with everyone, you know." He turned to Fanny. "Hutchins tells me you and Lady Wentworth are desirous of taking passage with me."

"Oh, how famous!" Charlotte exclaimed, jumping up and down in her excitement. "We will have such fun, and you will meet Papa."

"Only if the captain has room for us, my dear," Fanny cautioned. "And you are right, we will meet your Papa," she added, wondering whether this paragon of a father would turn out to be as insipid or as predatory as most of the gentlemen of her acquaintance.

"Oh, I am sure we can accommodate you and your aunt, Lady Fanny," Jack drawled, "even though we may have to throw our Poppet overboard."

This brought a delighted howl from Charlotte.

"Although we are not scheduled to dock at Brighton," Jack continued, "no doubt Portsmouth will suit the owner of the *Fortune Hunter* equally well."

Charlotte looked puzzled. "I thought you were the owner, Jack," she said. "You act like it, always telling the sailors what to do."

"I am only the master, and that is what masters do," Jack explained.

"But—"

"And no more questions, young lady. If I am not mistaken, that is your papa now, returning from his errand in town."

Charlotte gave a shriek of delight and, without taking leave of her new friend, raced across the cobbles to where a tall gentleman was descending from a hired coach, ignoring Miss Grimes's admonishments for decorous behaviour.

"Quite a handful your little Poppet, I would say," Fanny remarked as they watched the child throw herself at the tall man, who caught her up and swung her effortlessly in the air. Even at this distance, they could hear the child chattering excitedly and pointing in their direction.

Colonel Sheldon appeared supremely disinterested in his daughter's new acquaintance. After a brief glance at Fanny, he set Charlotte down and, taking her hand in his, marched her firmly up the gangway, followed by Miss Grimes. When they reached the top, the child turned and waved at them before following her father, her hand still clasped in his.

Fanny turned to exchange a questioning glance with Jack. "Not the most sociable man in the world, I take it," she said with a dismissing laugh.

"You might say that," the captain replied. "Perhaps you will work your notorious charm on the gentleman this evening at dinner, my lady," he teased. "Can you and your aunt be aboard by then? We sail at first light tomorrow."

"Of course," Fanny murmured, blithely committing her staff to a frenzy of packing to meet Jack's deadline.

The captain transferred his attention to Lady Wentworth

in the carriage, assuring her that she was more than welcome aboard any ship of his. When he turned back to Lady
Fanny, she realized that her gaze was still fixed on the
gangway where Charlotte and her father had so recently
passed.

Jack grinned wickedly. "I warn you, my dear Fanny, that
the colonel may be a doting father, but he is a veritable
ogre with the petticoat set. You will be sadly disappointed
if you think to charm him out of his sullenness."

"Any desire I may have had to charm gentlemen evaporated years ago. So do not trouble yourself on my account."

After Jack had gone, Fanny stood beside the carriage,
gazing up at the main deck and wondering whether travelling home on the *Fortune Hunter* had been such a brilliant
idea after all.

She had been warned. The surly colonel was immune to
feminine charms. Fanny wondered if she should take this
as a challenge to her powers of seduction, or if she should
ignore the gentleman as he had evidently chosen to ignore her.

Either way she would probably be disappointed, just as
Jack had warned her. Disappointed or bored.

Nevertheless, as Fanny climbed back into the coach and
settled herself next to her aunt, her mind seemed incapable
of ridding itself of the intriguing image of a tall dark gentleman hugging a little girl protectively to his chest.

CHAPTER 2

Fanny and the Colonel

"I should have known it!" Lady Wentworth exclaimed
in frustration as she surveyed the confusion of band-
boxes, valises, travelling cases, portmanteaux, various shawls
and rugs, hat boxes, baskets of fruit, odd-shaped parcels
wrapped in brown paper, a colourful assortment of cush-

ions, and sundry other unidentifiable objects heaped together in no apparent order in the middle of the cabin.

"What should you have known, my dear?" Fanny asked
innocently, knowing full well what had upset her usually
unflappable aunt.

"That it would come to *this*." Lady Wentworth indicated
the mountain of personal belongings with a sweep of her
arm. "I had not realized that travelling home on the *Fortune Hunter* instead of the regular packet-boat would oblige
me to throw my possessions together in less than an hour
and rush over here to find my cabin thus cluttered!" Again
she gestured despairingly around the cramped space.

Sensing that this was not the moment to remind her aunt
that they had had over five hours to pack, pay their shot
at the hotel, and board the *Fortune Hunter* that afternoon,
Fanny placed a comforting arm around her shoulders, mur-
muring soothingly. Furthermore, it would probably be a
mistake to point out that the formidable Chester, her aunt's
personal dresser, and Yvette, Fanny's own abigail, had
taken care of the packing, leaving her aunt the sole task of
taking charge of her jewelry case.

They were startled by an ear-piercing screech coming
from a crate under the bunk.

Lady Wentworth flinched visibly and clapped both hands
over her ears. "I flatly refuse to sleep with a monkey," she
stated in such tones of loathing that Fanny was hard put
not to laugh aloud.

Making her way quickly through the heaps of baggage,
Fanny knelt down beside the bunk and pulled a crate out
into the open. The angry chattering ceased abruptly.

"There, there, Devi, my pet," Fanny crooned to the agitated monkey, scratching the top of his head with one finger. Devi grasped the top bars of his crate with all four
paws and swung from side to side furiously, uttering a low
wail and sounding for all the world like a petulant child.

"You are tired of this silly old cage, are you not, my
lad?" Fanny remarked soothingly. "He is not accustomed
to being cooped up for so long, Aunt. I think he needs a
little exercise."

"I forbid you to let that creature out, Fanny," her aunt

said sharply. "I doubt Captain Mansford would appreciate having a monkey running loose all over his ship."

"Devi is not just any monkey, Aunt," Fanny protested. "He is one of the family. Uncle John took him everywhere."

"I am well aware of your uncle's idiosyncrasies, my dear. But I know John would not expect me to go about with a contentious monkey hanging round my neck." Lady Wentworth stopped abruptly and glanced nervously round the cabin. "Where will you put him, Fanny? Not in here, I sincerely trust. I shall not sleep a wink tonight."

"You are upset with all this bustle, Aunt," Fanny assured her aunt gently. "Let us go into the sitting room and have Yvette bring up a tea-tray. A good cup of strong tea will make you feel much better."

Lady Wentworth looked unconvinced, but before she could reply, there was a knock on the door and Fanny's abigail announced that a Colonel Sheldon and his daughter were asking for Lady Fanny.

"Colonel Sheldon?" Lady Wentworth repeated. "Is this the gentleman we saw briefly on the wharf, Fanny?"

"He is indeed, Aunt, and I am anxious to find out if he is as disagreeable as he appeared this morning. His daughter Charlotte is a delight, so the father cannot be all bad."

"Let us hope so," Lady Wentworth muttered. "But do not get your hopes up, Fanny. Military gentlemen can be so domineering. Now let Yvette arrange your hair, dear. You cannot wish to appear before a stranger with your hair falling down your back."

"I daresay this particular gentleman will not care a fig how I look, Aunt," she replied carelessly. Nevertheless, she submitted to her maid's ministrations, telling herself that regardless of the colonel's opinion of her, she owed it to herself to look presentable.

Lady Fanny ruthlessly suppressed the errant notion that this uncouth gentleman had aroused her curiosity.

Colonel Sir Derek Sheldon stood in the center of the small, cramped sitting room wishing he were anywhere else. He was here solely on Charlotte's account, he reminded himself. Were it his choice, he would have sent a polite note thanking Lady Fanny for her timely assistance this

morning on the wharf. But his daughter had been in high
fidgets, begging him to let her visit her new friend. The
colonel had been quite unable to hold out against her
pleading.

"You will like Lady Fanny excessively, Papa; I know you
will," Charlotte had assured him at least a dozen times.

"I know I will, sweetheart," he had told her, although
Derek was quite sure he would dislike this Lady Fanny
on sight.

The female his daughter had not ceased to chatter about
since their encounter on the wharf that morning sounded
more like a wild, flamboyant Amazon creature than a lady
of quality. This so-called *lady* had whipped out a sword and
scattered a band of street hooligans instead of remaining
in the safety of her carriage and calling for the assistance
of her male servants. If his daughter's account was correct,
one of the thieves had actually been wounded.

The notion that a lady of breeding would participate in
such a bloodthirsty encounter repulsed him. Undoubtedly
Lady Fanny was one of those managing females he most
disliked. The colonel was not looking forward to meeting
her.

At that moment the connecting door opened and two
females entered. The colonel inclined his head as briefly as
possible without being uncivil, and instinctively stepped
back as if to give the ladies room to move about.

Charlotte was nowhere near as reticent. With a joyous
shriek the child threw herself at the younger lady and embraced her as a long-lost friend. "Lady Fanny!" she cried
with such delight that the colonel felt his heart contract.
His daughter evidently missed the companionship of other
females of her class, a reality that was brought home to him
with shattering force when he heard the note of longing in
his child's voice.

He silently cursed her mother for the wrong she had
done to their daughter. And to him, he thought, bitterly
recalling the dark despair following Constance's desertion.
At first he had thought her note a hoax—a particularly
cruel one even for Constance. He had not wanted to believe that his beautiful young wife had run off with a scoun-

drel, a man known the length and breadth of England for his womanizing.

A professional seducer St. Ives had been—probably still was—and Fate had brought him to a neighbouring estate for the autumn pheasant shoot. Derek had even invited the rogue and his party to shoot over his land, he remembered with disgust at his own naiveté; but St. Ives had shot more than pheasants during his visits at Sheldon Hall.

Derek had not believed it at first. His wife's note had seemed so improbable, so very unexpected in a wife of barely three years with a baby daughter of two. But he had been forced to believe it later, of course, when they brought his wife's body back home to him, battered and broken like a rag doll.

So he had buried Constance in the family plot, trying to forgive her trespasses. But not forgetting. Never forgetting. And endured the commiseration of his neighbours, their furtive glances, their whispered speculation. But worst of all, their pity.

And now, as Derek stared at Lady Fanny crouching down cradling his daughter, Charlotte's arms tight around her neck, he experienced a wrenching vision of what life should have been had the Fates not intervened.

Derek felt the breath catch in his throat as he surveyed this tender scene. The instant obsession Charlotte appeared to have formed for this headstrong female caused him no little alarm. What noxious influence might Lady Fanny exert? He shuddered to think what hoydenish starts his daughter might learn from a female who owned—and apparently knew how to use—a sword stick.

As though she had read his mind, Lady Fanny chose that moment to raise her eyes. Their gazes met over his daughter's pale gold head, and the colonel was instantly affronted by the boldness of her stare and the suppressed humour that twinkled in the depths of those astonishing violet eyes.

Could it be that this brazen hussy was laughing at him? And if so, what could it be about him that she found so amusing? The notion made him decidedly uncomfortable, and he cleared his throat.

"I understand that I have you to thank for coming to my daughter's assistance this morning, Lady Fanny," he began stiffly, the informality of her name sitting awkwardly on his tongue. "Or is that Lady Francesca?" he enquired with a hint of censure in his tone.

"Everybody calls her Lady Fanny," Charlotte chimed in with what seemed to her father quite appalling pertness in a six year old.

"When I wish for your opinions, I shall ask for them, child," he remarked dryly, glaring down his long nose at his daughter.

"Everybody does indeed call me Lady Fanny," that lady corroborated, quite ruining the effect of his reprimand. "I cannot abide Francesca, which my aunt reserves for those rare occasions when I misbehave."

"Rare, indeed?" Lady Wentworth scoffed. "What a Banbury story, Fanny. You will have Colonel Sheldon believing that you are above reproach, which is as far from the truth as you can get."

"What is a Banbury story?" Charlotte wanted to know, settling herself beside Lady Fanny on the small settee.

Lady Fanny laughed, and Derek marvelled at the magic radiance of her face when she smiled. "A Banbury tale is one that is not quite as close to the truth as it should be, my dear," she explained, stroking his daughter's fair hair with gentle fingers.

"Oh, you mean like telling a fib?" Charlotte said with more directness, he thought, silently applauding her honesty.

"Yes, you might call it that, although it is more like a little white lie than a truly wicked, sinful one. More wishful thinking than malicious. I believe it all started with that lady who 'rode a white horse to Banbury Cross.' Do you know the nursery rhyme?"

"Oh, yes, yes," Charlotte cried delightedly, clapping her hands. "The lady who had bells on her fingers and rings in her nose?"

Both ladies laughed, and even Derek could not suppress a smile.

"You have that backwards, dear," Lady Fanny corrected her. "She had the rings on her fingers, not her nose, and the bells on her *toes*. Ladies do not wear rings in their noses except in places like India, where customs are different and ladies do wear golden rings in their noses on special occasions, and often bells on their ankles."

"Do you suppose this lady who rode to Banbury Cross was an Indian lady, then?" Charlotte demanded.

"I doubt that very much," Lady Fanny replied with a smile. "Banbury Cross is a long way from India, and she would have ridden an elephant, not a white horse."

"An elephant?" Charlotte gasped, evidently impressed. "How exciting! Have you ever ridden an elephant, Lady Fanny?"

"Enough questions, Charlotte," the colonel cut in firmly. "And drink your tea, child." He indicated the cup Lady Wentworth set before his daughter.

"Have a sandwich, my lord," Lady Fanny said smoothly, offering him the plate.

Hoping to make an early departure, Derek declined, but was chagrined to see his daughter help herself to three. He caught Lady Fanny's amused gaze upon him and realized that she had devised his intention and was laughing at him again.

"Well, did you ever?"

"Ride an elephant? Why yes, dear, many times."

Lady Fanny appeared to have established an easy rapport with his daughter and was deliberately encouraging her to ask questions. Against his express wishes, Derek thought, his dislike of this sword-wielding female growing with every word she uttered.

"Were you afraid?"

"Only at first. When I got used to it, I found it very enjoyable."

"A most unsettling experience, if you ask me," cut in Lady Wentworth vigorously. "The beasts will sway from side to side all the time. It makes one quite dizzy and I refused to be jostled about on the whim of some mindless animal."

"Elephants are hardly mindless, my dear Aunt," Lady Fanny exclaimed with a laugh. "They are said to have exceptional memories. Better than ours, I would wager."

"Rubbish!" her aunt responded. "My niece is full of romantical notions about India, Colonel," she added apologetically.

The colonel doubted that a single romantical notion of
any kind might be found in Lady Fanny's beautiful head.
As he listened with one ear to Lady Wentworth's rambling
reminiscences of her life in Bombay, Derek watched his
daughter's animated expression as she plied her hostess
with questions. Lady Fanny's face was equally unguarded,
and she appeared to enjoy the bantering exchange that,
even as he watched, sent Charlotte into a fit of the giggles
that threatened to bring disaster to the tea-table.

Derek felt an odd mixture of guilt and regret as he listened to his daughter's merriment. Charlotte had never
been a somber child, but all too infrequently did she indulge in the unrestrained laughter that Lady Fanny seemed
to bring out in her. Disturbed more that he would admit,
the colonel put down his half empty cup and rose to his
feet. "Come, Charlotte," he said abruptly, "it is time to
take our leave of these kind ladies."

"Oh, Papa," his daughter protested, as he had anticipated, "I have not yet seen Lady Fanny's monkey."

Before the colonel could remonstrate, Lady Fanny surprised him by supporting his decision.

"You may see Devi tomorrow morning after my aunt
and I are settled," she said. "He gets upset at having his
routine interrupted, you know. And then he is not at his
best. Now, do as your father says, dear. We will have plenty
of time to talk tomorrow."

Surprisingly his daughter did not protest, but leaned forward impetuously and hugged her hostess. "Thank you for
the tea, my lady," she said politely, then rose and placed
her hand in his.

His daughter's simple gesture brought a lump to his
throat. She was without a doubt the most precious thing in
his life and he vowed to set her happiness above all else,
even if this meant putting up with a sword-wielding female
who kept monkeys as pets and indulged in such unladylike
pursuits as riding elephants.

Risking a glance at Lady Fanny as he made his bow,
Derek found her violet eyes fixed upon him, and a faint
smile of amusement upon her lips.

Without another word, he turned and left. Lady Fanny
would probably see his abrupt departure as uncivil. But

then, he reminded himself, listening to his daughter's innocent chatter as they walked down the narrow hall, the opinion of a hoydenish female could not possibly interest him, could it?

CHAPTER 3

Declaration of War

No sooner had the cabin door closed behind their visitors than Lady Fanny dissolved into gales of laughter. Her aunt gazed at her in disapproval.

"Whatever can have occasioned such amusement, dear?" she enquired mildly. "Surely you do not find the colonel in any way a fit object for mirth?"

This observation merely served to increase Fanny's laughter. "Of course, he is, Aunt," she gurgled, dabbing at her streaming eyes with a wisp of lace. "Did you not see the way he pokered up when Charlotte asked to see Devi. Quite as though a monkey might be a pernicious influence on the child."

"What unsettled the colonel was undoubtedly the prospect of travelling back to England with a monkey in the cabin next door, my dear Fanny," her aunt suggested. "I confess I have to agree with the poor man. It was one thing to dodge your uncle's pets in that large house we had in Bombay, but quite another to be cooped up with a beastie in a space no larger than a chicken house."

"Well, it was not only the monkey that set his back up, Aunt. He did not like me either, did you notice? To begin with, he did not approve of my name. Fanny is not good enough for him. 'Or is that Lady Francesca?'" she mimicked. "And then to give that poor child a set-down because she dared to agree with me." She paused, then added with some force, "I wish now I had brought old Ganesha home with me."

Aunt Clarissa uttered a little gasp of dismay. "Whatever would you do with an elephant in Brighton, Fanny? Do be reasonable, dear."

"I would certainly outshine the Regent, if nothing else. Can you imagine how the *ton* would stare were I to wander along the Marine Parade on dear old Ganesha in all his finery? Why did I not think of this before?"

"Because you know it would not be proper, dear," her aunt replied. "And you are mistaken if you believe the colonel disapproves of you, Fanny. He could hardly take his eyes off you."

"Now that is the biggest Banbury tale I have heard in a long time," Fanny retorted with a grimace. "The man was no doubt afraid that his daughter might pick up some of my unladylike habits."

"Now who is talking nonsense? I'll admit that you are not quite in the common way, my dear, but I fail to see how a little spirit could offend."

Lady Fanny smiled indulgently at her aunt. "You are much too kind, Aunt. Admit it, I am often more *spirited*—as you chose to call my headstrong starts—than is becoming in a well-bred female. Quite hoydenish, in fact. You have said so yourself upon occasion."

"Never!" her aunt exclaimed in a shocked voice. "At least, if I did say anything so unkind, which I cannot believe I did, I never meant—"

"I know you do not believe so," Fanny interrupted quickly, sensing that her aunt was upset. "But I am sure the colonel would not hesitate to use that word to describe me. Notice that he made no mention of the sword stick, Aunt. I cannot imagine he was too thrilled to learn that I did not scream for some gentleman to come to my rescue, as any right-thinking female would have done."

"But, Fanny, my dear girl—"

Lady Fanny smiled wryly at her aunt's distraught expression. "There is no denying that I am no wilting violet, Aunt," she said gently, "the type of female most gentlemen seem to prefer. I am often prickly and opinionated. Uncle taught me to manage my own affairs, and I believe he would be proud of the way I have handled his interests in India."

"I do not pretend to have agreed with John in teaching you to think like a man," Lady Wentworth responded calmly. "Trade is no fit occupation for a female, Fanny, and I cannot help wishing . . ."

Fanny glanced sharply at her aunt. "I trust you are not about to suggest that I give up my independence for a husband and family. I thought we had agreed long ago, Aunt, that the idea of tying myself to another man is abhorrent to me."

"But my dear Fanny, when I see you with little Charlotte, I cannot but think how happy you would be with a daughter of your own."

"Perhaps," Fanny replied shortly, refusing to be led down that path. "But since that feat definitely requires the participation of a gentleman, preferably within the bondage of marriage, I cannot promise that it will ever happen, Aunt."

Unless, of course, Fanny thought perversely as she prepared for dinner later that evening, she was willing to risk being ostracized once again by the *haut monde*. She knew how pitiless the *ton* could be to a female who dared to step beyond the boundaries of propriety. How long would it be, she wondered, before the Brighton gossips discovered that Lady Francesca Wentworth—a name she had adopted in lieu of her family name—was actually the scandalous Duchess of Cambourne? Former duchess, she corrected herself ruefully, branded adulteress and divorced by her husband, disowned by her father, abandoned by her brothers. . . . Her aunt's voice pulled her back from these painful memories.

"Marriage to a respectable gentleman would go a long way towards restoring your reputation with the *ton*, my love," Lady Wentworth was saying, as she had many times before.

Having been blessed with Sir John, her aunt was a firm believer in the wedded state. It was the one issue upon which they heartily disagreed, and Fanny had long ago despaired of making her aunt realize that the gentleman she spoke of—respectable or otherwise—who could tempt Fanny into those treacherous waters again did not exist.

Her laugh was brittle. "You know my feelings on this matter, Aunt."

"You are too harsh, Fanny, my love," her aunt replied. "When a gentleman's affections are engaged, he will risk much to please the lady of his choice. Love works miracles, they say."

Fanny laughed again, less bitterly this time. "Whoever recorded that drivel was surely a Bedlamite, if not worse. And you are a hopeless romantic, Aunt. Few if any gentlemen are interested in love, my dear. They care only for rank and fortune, and choose wives as they would brood mares for their stables."

"Fanny!" Lady Wentworth gasped in horror. "How can you say such things? I cannot believe how cynical you have become, dear."

"I still carry the scars of Cambourne's failed expectations of me, Aunt," Fanny replied harshly. "So do not speak to me of a second marriage. One term in hell was quite enough."

She turned away to hide her distress, but immediately felt her aunt's arm around her shoulders. "Forgive me, my darling Fanny. We will speak of it no more. I had hoped that the years spent in India with John and me had given you a different view of what marriage can be. But it is nearly time for dinner, dear. Compose yourself, Fanny. The gong will sound at any moment now."

Even as her aunt spoke, the reverberations of the cook's dinner gong echoed throughout the ship. Fanny followed her aunt towards the officers' mess, but was not surprised to discover that her appetite had fled.

Both Colonel Sheldon and his daughter were with Captain Mansford when the ladies entered. Of Miss Grimes there was no sign, and Fanny suspected that the nervous little governess had not yet recovered from that morning's adventure on the wharf.

Charlotte was the first to greet them, skipping across the room to hug both ladies affectionately. Fanny fully expected to hear a sharp rebuke from the colonel, and when none was forthcoming, she glanced at the two gentlemen standing beside an old-fashioned sideboard covered with decanters. Jack raised his glass to her and grinned wickedly. The colonel might have been the captain's opposite, for he limited himself to a civil nod, allowing not even the flicker of a smile to disturb the classical symmetry of his mouth.

He had a rather attractive mouth. Fanny wondered why she had not noticed this feature before. Perhaps she had been put off by his glacial stare or his chilly civility. If one were to judge by his behaviour towards her, she reasoned, advancing into the room with an excited Charlotte clutching her hand, Fanny would have written him off as a cold fish. But even as she watched, a shadow of a dimple appeared for the briefest moment beside the left corner of his mouth. Fanny blinked. Surely her imagination was playing tricks on her. This taciturn, austere gentleman could not possibly possess anything as irrepressible as a dimple.

Suddenly conscious that she had been staring, Fanny transferred her attention to Charlotte, who pulled impatiently at her hand.

"Well?" she demanded. "Do you not think it beautiful, Lady Fanny?"

"Beautiful?" Fanny repeated. "Is *what* beautiful, dear?"

Charlotte gave a theatrical sigh. "My new dress, silly." She spread her blue muslin skirt with both hands in a charming feminine gesture. "My papa bought it for me yesterday. He has very good taste, has he not?"

"I think the gown very beautiful indeed," Fanny replied, ignoring the last part of the child's question. "You have quite put Lady Wentworth and me in the shade. I am completely cast down, if you want the truth."

Charlotte's giggle was interrupted by her father. "Little girls do not refer to ladies as silly, Charlotte. I want to hear you apologize to her ladyship at once."

"What if they are?" the child responded pertly. "Silly, I mean?"

Jack let out a crack of laughter. "Touché, Colonel! Ladies can often be very silly indeed, Charlotte, but never Lady Fanny. And even if she *were* silly, just for a moment, of course, and not merely distracted, it is not polite to tell her so."

Charlotte appeared to digest this information for a moment, then reached for Fanny's hand again. "I am sorry I

called you silly, Lady Fanny," she said, and smiled so delightfully that Fanny felt her heart swell. "I did not mean
that you were *silly* silly, only a little bit silly."

"That is quite enough, Charlotte," her father cut in
abruptly. "It is time to take your place at the table."

Thankful for the interruption, Lady Fanny followed
her aunt to the long trestle table where several neatly
dressed stewards were placing steaming plates of food.
Although the service was informal, the food was excellent, prompting Lady Wentworth to send her compliments to the cook.

It was after dinner, as the small group gathered in the
captain's sitting room next door, that Fanny discovered that
Sheldon Hall was situated a mere nine miles from Brighton.

"Only consider, my dear Fanny," Lady Wentworth exclaimed, "we will be able to include the colonel in our Wednesday evening card parties. I trust you do play, Colonel?"

"Oh, I am sure he does, Aunt," Fanny said quickly,
afraid that her Aunt would suffer one of the colonel's caustic set-downs. "Most gentlemen enjoy a game of cards. But
are you not forgetting, dear, that those card parties—
delightful as they were—belong to our days in India, where
you and Uncle John had dozens of friends? I doubt any of
them will remove to Brighton to accommodate you, Aunt."

Lady Wentworth blinked, as though she had not considered the matter in that light. "I do believe you are right,
Fanny. I am assuming that life will continue as it was before
your uncle . . . That is, I suppose we must wait to discover
which of my old friends from years ago are still in Brighton
before I start planning card parties and the like."

And which of those old friends will deign to recognize us
after they discovered my identity, Fanny thought cynically.
Unable to bear seeing her beloved aunt downcast, Fanny
spoke impulsively. "I daresay Colonel Sheldon will grace
us with his company for tea one afternoon, Aunt. And I
know Charlotte will want to see how Devi takes to life
in Brighton."

It was Jack's raised eyebrow and quirky grin that warned
Fanny that her suggestion might be misinterpreted.

Unaware of this unspoken exchange, Charlotte responded
with childish delight, as Fanny guessed she would.

"Oh, may I, Papa?" she pleaded. "You *will* take me to visit Lady Fanny, will you not? Please say you will."

The colonel did not appear any too pleased to have his hand forced in this manner. He glared frostily at his daughter before turning his gaze on Fanny without a noticeable warming in his grey eyes. If Jack's knowing grin meant what Fanny thought it did, this arrogant oaf must imagine she was casting out lures to him. The notion appalled her. If she ever felt the remotest desire to use such feminine wiles on a gentleman, it would not be on this starched-up country rudesby with an inflated opinion of himself.

"We are not at all in the habit of going about in society, my lady," he said, addressing himself to Lady Wentworth, to Fanny's chagrin. "I have much to catch up with on my estate after four years abroad, and my daughter is not yet of an age where those frivolous activities are considered *de rigueur*."

Fanny listened to this speech with growing mortification. When Lady Wentworth appeared quite unable to respond to this barrage of incivility, Fanny snapped icily, "I fail to see how an hour spent drinking tea with my aunt can be construed as frivolous, sir."

Jack was looking amused, she noted. After an awkward pause, which Fanny thought Jack would break with one of his irreverent remarks, relief came from another quarter.

Charlotte burst into tears and ran to cling to her father's sleeve. "Oh, Papa," she sobbed. "You have made Lady Fanny angry, and now she will not let me see her monkey."

The four adults stared in silence for a moment at this distressing sight. Then Jack chuckled, and Charlotte looked at him, her face flushed and tear-stained. "You insult Lady Fanny if you believe her to be so poor spirited, my dear Charlotte," he said. "I can guarantee that she would never punish you just because your father refuses to take tea with her, sweetheart. Now come here and let Uncle Jack wipe that beautiful face for you."

The captain stretched out his hand, but the colonel anticipated him by pulling his daughter onto his lap and using his own handkerchief to dry her face with such unselfconscious tenderness that Fanny could only stare. Jack caught her eye and winked, but Fanny was so touched by the loving tableau of father and daughter that she failed to respond.

This unexpectedly gentle facet of the colonel's personality stirred memories of her own father Fanny had tenaciously suppressed for ten years. The Earl of Hayle had been such a father once, before her life went so terribly wrong. Before she had committed that nonsensical, irreversible act of childish revenge that had brought the world down about her ears.

A terrible yearning to share in the tender scene playing out before her made Fanny's throat tighten. Why, oh, why, had Cambourne not been such as man as this? Capable of tenderness, if not love. For the duke had not loved her, Fanny had soon discovered. Her hopes of winning his heart had faltered every time he criticized her for not showing proper respect for his rank and lineage.

Charlotte's father was far from perfect, of course, Fanny reminded herself grimly, but she could have put up with every masculine imperfection on record had she been made to feel cherished as the colonel obviously cherished his daughter.

Fearing that if she had to witness this tender scene a moment longer, she would burst into tears herself, Fanny rose abruptly to her feet.

"Jack is absolutely right, Charlotte," she said in a voice that sounded strangely unlike her own. "I have every intention of introducing you to Devi this very evening." She paused and stared challengingly at the colonel. "That is if your father will allow you to come with me?"

Lady Fanny could only guess at the colonel's thoughts as he returned her stare. She suspected he was searching for an excuse to thwart her without disappointing his daughter.

"Will you, Papa?" Charlotte pleaded. "Please?"

"Very well," he said at length. "But only for half an hour mind you."

"Thank you, Papa," Charlotte cried excitedly, throwing her arms round his neck and giving him a resounding kiss. She scrambled from his lap and took Fanny's hand. Without a backward glance, Fanny took her leave and led the child, all trace of tears now forgotten, out of the room.

A minor victory, she told herself as she marched down the hall. But it did prove that the colonel placed his daughter's happiness above his own dislike for Lady Fanny.

CHAPTER 4

Two of a Kind

Lady Wentworth was not slow to follow her niece to her cabin, and as the door closed behind her comfortable round figure, the colonel let out an audible sigh. He managed a brief smile when he noticed the broad grin on the captain's rugged face.

He had not intended to offend the lady by fobbing off her invitation to tea, but perhaps he had been rather heavy-handed in his choice of words. If he were honest with himself, he would have to admit that he *had* intended to set the niece's back up. Something about that female brought out a surprising aggressive streak in his nature.

Jack fetched the brandy decanter and refilled both their glasses. "I wager you have never met a female quite like our Lady Fanny, Colonel," he remarked after a long pause.

"I cannot say that I have," he replied slowly, wondering exactly what the captain's relationship with the lady might be. They seemed to be on familiar, even intimate terms. Both ladies referred to the captain by his given name, and from their conversation at the dinner table, it was obvious they were acquaintances of long standing.

"A most provoking female from what I have seen of her," he remarked, swirling the amber liquid in his glass. "Not at all comfortable to have around, I should imagine. Managing, too—something I cannot abide in a female." Derek took another long draft from his glass. "And if indeed the lady actually took a sword stick to those thugs this morning on the wharf, I cannot but deplore her lack of delicacy. Swords are weapons, not toys for females to play with."

"Oh, that is true enough," the captain said with a grin. "About Fanny using her sword stick on those thieves, I mean. And it is a good thing she did. Little Charlotte might well have been hurt more seriously had Fanny not shown a little spirit."

"I cannot argue with that. I owe her a debt of gratitude, even though I cannot condone her use of violence. I gather that you are well acquainted with the Wentworths, Captain," he added after a slight pause.

"I have known Sir John and his lady for many years, Colonel, ever since I decided to eschew the Church career my father had intended for me and run off to sea. It was because of Sir John's kindness that I never regretted my choice."

"I assume you have known their niece equally well," Derek said, wondering why he cared what the captain's relationship with that hoydenish female might be.

"Oh, no. Fanny came out to India much later. I only know part of the story, but I understand there was a tragedy in her past. I do know that her mother died, and she came to live with her aunt. Fanny never speaks of the past, so I assume the memories are painful to her."

Derek was tempted to ask why Lady Fanny had never married, but he reminded himself that the lady's life was none of his concern. He tried to focus his thoughts on his immediate plans for Sheldon Hall, but his mind kept returning to the way Lady Fanny's eyes had turned a darker shade of violet upon his unfortunate response to her invitation to take tea with her aunt. She had fairly snapped his head off, he recalled ruefully, and he had deserved it.

But rudely stated or not, his refusal to commit himself to furthering his tenuous acquaintance with the Wentworths was honest enough. Derek had eschewed social contact after Constance's death. Although few of his neighbours knew the exact circumstances of Lady Sheldon's accident, the inevitable rumours had circulated.

Only when he had begun to see that calculating gleam in the eyes of every mother with marriageable daughters, had Derek decided to rejoin his old regiment and escape to Lisbon. Perhaps he should have entrusted Charlotte to his sister Margaret, but he had been quite unable to tear himself away from his daughter. However, it may have been a mistake to deprive little Charlotte of her aunt's presence, for the child obviously delighted in female company. Miss Grimes had proved to be ineffectual in curbing her charge's enthusiasm for Lady Fanny, as he had instructed her to do only this morning.

"We all have our painful memories," he murmured after a while. "But Lady Fanny appears to have found a new life for herself in India."

"As you did for yourself in Lisbon, Colonel?" the captain enquired with one of his engaging smiles. "I daresay you and her ladyship will find you have experiences in common once you cease snapping at each other."

Derek glared at his host, resenting the familiarity that he had allowed to grow between them during the long sea voyage from Lisbon. "I sincerely hope you may be mistaken," he said dryly. "I do not intend to exchange confidences with a complete stranger, however, so the point is moot." He set down his glass with an air of finality. "Are you up to a game of piquet, Captain?"

Jack laughed, and Derek had the distinct impression that the captain had guessed how anxious he was to change the subject. Jack said nothing, however, and got up to fetch the cards.

Two hours later, after Derek had lost yet another game to his opponent, the captain said out of the blue, "You might well be surprised, Colonel."

Perplexed, Derek took a moment to repeat, "Surprised?"

"At our Fanny," the captain clarified. "She is a fascinating female."

"I daresay she is," Derek replied with studied nonchalance. "But she is knocking on the wrong door if she imagines I am to be caught by any lures she might throw out."

Jack threw back his head and laughed uproariously. "Fanny never throws out lures. And if she were to make an exception—which I keep hoping she will—she is unlikely to cast any in your direction, Colonel."

Derek raised an eyebrow in surprise at this plain speaking.

"No offence meant, of course," Jack added hastily. "But if Fanny wanted you, you would not stand a chance, old man. However, it is plain as a pikestaff that she does *not* want you."

Derek digested this frank statement for a moment or two. "I gather her ladyship does not want you either, my friend?" he could not resist saying.

The captain let out another crack of laughter. "You are right on the mark there, Colonel," he confessed, apparently none too cast down at the admission. "The truth is, I am not in Fanny's league. Although I doubt that would deter her if . . . No use repining about that, of course. The trouble is that Fanny has too much of the ready for her own good. Rich as Croesus she is, and my employer into the bargain."

"Your employer?" Derek stared at the captain in amazement.

"Yes," Jack admitted bluntly. "Owns this ship, does our Fanny. Lock, stock, and barrel. And six more like it, if memory serves. Not your common or garden variety of female at all. And if I know anything about Fanny, she will set her heart on a man she cannot have, and there will be hell to pay."

Derek went off to bed wondering if perhaps he had learned more than he wanted to know about Lady Fanny Wentworth. The thought made him uneasy.

In spite of the bulkhead's shelter, gusts of wind occasionally threatened to send Lady Fanny's bonnet skimming across the forecastle, and slipped beneath Charlotte's pink striped muslin gown to turn it into a gaily coloured balloon.

Each time, Charlotte squealed with merriment and Devi, seated between them in the warmest spot, bounced up and down emitting high-pitched, monkey sounds of hilarity and showing his yellow teeth in a grin. Lady Fanny was soon drawn into this unseemly display of mirth, and it was not until a young, red-faced sailor appeared with a rug, courtesy of Captain Jack, that the ladies were able to take control of their skirts.

With tears streaming down their faces, the two ladies looked at each other and giggled. Devi must have felt left out of this new game, for he jumped into Charlotte's lap and flung his long arms about her neck.

"He likes me," Charlotte said happily, cuddling the monkey with both arms.

"You may be sure of it, love," Fanny responded. "Old Devi is not usually so accepting of strangers, but he has taken a real shine to you. It is an honour, believe me."

"He is not old," Charlotte protested, "although his teeth *are* very dirty," she added, gazing with fascination into the monkey's grinning mouth. "Do you not make him brush them every morning as Miss Grimes does to me?"

Fanny laughed at this artless sally. "Devi is at least twice your age, Charlotte. Probably more. My Uncle John already had him for several years before I went to Bombay ten years ago."

"Older than *me*?" The child appeared intrigued by this information about her new friend. "Then he is a grown-up?"

"You might say that," replied Fanny, whose knowledge of monkey longevity was limited.

"Is Devi as old as my papa, do you suppose?"

"Now that I cannot say, since I do not know your papa's age."

"Thirty-eight," Charlotte answered without hesitation. "But he will soon be older, because his birthday is in June. The fifteenth. Do you think Devi is *that* old?"

Lady Fanny hid a smile, amused that Charlotte considered her starched up father to be *that* old. Perhaps it was not exactly fair of her to encourage the child to divulge details about that gentleman she was sure he would never reveal himself. But what did it really matter? The rude oaf was determined to sever all connection between the two families.

"Well," Charlotte repeated with childish insistence, "is he?"

"As old as your papa? I think he is probably a few years younger, but not much," Fanny invented blithely.

"Then he must have a wife," Charlotte said with conviction. "All grown-ups have wives or husbands. Did he leave her in India?"

"You are mistaken, my dear," Fanny answered hurriedly.

"Some grown-ups never marry at all, and I know for a fact that Devi never had a wife."

"So he has no children either?"

"None that I know of," Fanny replied shortly, wondering how she could change the subject.

"Do you, Lady Fanny?" Charlotte demanded, voicing the question Fanny had been dreading. "Have any children, I mean."

"No, dear. But if I did, they would be just like you, love," she improvised, reaching to tuck a stray curl under the child's pink bonnet. "Now, let us turn our attention to how we are to convince your father to allow you to visit me in Brighton. What do you say?"

Charlotte gazed at her, her blue eyes opening wide. "Oh, we cannot do that, Lady Fanny. Once Papa says no, he never changes his mind."

Fanny threw the child a pitying look. "I see. Once the Great Buddha has spoken, we mortals must bow to his command? Is that it?"

"Papa is not a Buddha," Charlotte said with a giggle.

"No, of course not, but he is as intransigent as one," Fanny responded.

"Intra-what?"

"Intransigent," Fanny explained. "It means pig-headed. Stubborn to the point of never changing his mind. You said so yourself, Charlotte."

The child looked dubious. "Are you calling my papa pig-headed?"

"Of course I am, dear. Anyone who never changes his mind is definitely pig-headed. I am pig-headed myself at times. But perhaps we can convince your papa to allow Miss Grimes to accompany you into Brighton one afternoon to visit me. What do you think?"

Charlotte gave a dismissive wave of her hand. "Miss Pru is scared of Papa. Besides, she is always seasick."

"Surely she will not be seasick on dry land," Fanny protested. "And what about your Aunt Margaret? I understand she lives at Sheldon Hall, too. Perhaps she would be willing to accompany you."

"I cannot say what my aunt would do," Charlotte replied

rather forlornly. "I hardly remember her at all, you see. I was very little when Papa took me away from England."

Fanny felt an almost irresistible urge to ask Charlotte if she remembered her mother. Jack had confided that Lady Sheldon had been killed in an accident long ago. He did not know the details, or if he did, had not seen fit to tell her.

"In that case," Fanny said bracingly, "we shall just have to persuade your papa to bring you to Primrose Court himself."

"Oh, that will not work," Charlotte said with a note of finality in her voice. "You see, Papa will never permit me to—"

"Never permit you to do what, you little scamp?"

Fanny flinched as the colonel's voice cut into her cosy conversation with his daughter. Glancing up at him from under her lashes, she decided that he did not appear particularly combative this morning, but she instinctively prepared herself to do battle nonetheless.

"Charlotte and I were debating how best to induce you to permit her an occasional visit to Primrose Court, Colonel," she said brightly. Seeing the creases of a frown begin to form on his aristocratic forehead, Fanny threw herself into the fray. "Of course, we realize that, having formed an unaccountable aversion for the Wentworths, you are determined never to set foot on my aunt's threshold—"

"I said no such thing, madam," the colonel cut in angrily. "All I remember is some mention of Lady Wentworth's card-party, later amended to a tea-party—"

"Yes, indeed. Your memory is faultless there, Colonel." She calmly ignored the hiss of indignation that issued from the colonel's lips. "However, I distinctly recall you voicing the opinion—doubtless valid enough but hardly appropriate under the circumstances—that such harmless activities as tea-drinking were, at best, frivolous—"

"I beg to differ, my lady," Colonel Sheldon intervened frostily but with considerable force. "You have misconstrued my words. I enjoy a cup of China brew as much as anyone, so I cannot imagine where you got this nonsensical notion that I harbour an aversion for the habit."

"But Papa," Charlotte began, looking at her father with

a puzzled expression on her gamine face, "I heard you say—"

Lady Fanny laid a warning hand on the child's arm. "Hush, dear. We both heard what your father has just said. He enjoys drinking tea as much as we do." She threw a challenging glance into the grey eyes that glared furiously down at her, before continuing gaily. "And you know what that means, Charlotte? It means that your Papa was only funning last night when he refused my aunt's invitation. I confess he had me fooled for a moment, but now I see it was all a hum."

Charlotte looked from Lady Fanny to her father skeptically. "Are you sure? Does that mean that I can visit Devi, Papa?" She hugged the monkey to her and gazed imploringly up at her father, who looked nonplussed.

Fanny gave a little tinkle of laughter. Those who knew her well would have recognized this sign of victory, but the colonel ground his teeth in frustration.

"I sincerely hope it does, Poppet," she said gaily. "Devi will be cast down for weeks if you do not."

"Aunt Margaret will accompany me if you cannot do so, Papa."

"What makes you so sure your Aunt Margaret wishes to make the acquaintance of this . . . this monkey, whatever his name is?" the colonel demanded, but Fanny noticed that the fire had gone out of his voice.

"Devi," Charlotte offered, tickling the monkey under his chin until he chattered at her, baring his yellow teeth in a friendly grin. "You will behave yourself when Aunt Margaret comes to visit you, will you not, Devi?" she cajoled. "You need not be afraid, Papa. Lady Fanny says that Devi loves me, and although his teeth are very yellow—he never brushes them, you see—he will not bite you if he loves you."

"I sincerely hope that is true, Poppet. And I shall hold you entirely responsible," he added, turning a cool grey stare on Lady Fanny, "if anything happens to my daughter."

CHAPTER 5

A Glimpse of the Past

Derek awoke the next morning to the sounds of feet shuffling on the deck above his head and the shouts of the crew as they prepared the ship for docking. He felt the *Fortune Hunter* shudder and wallow as the great sails came down with a swoosh, flapping in the brisk offshore breeze before being quickly rolled and fastened by invisible hands.

Home, he thought, throwing back the covers and reaching for his robe. They were home in England at last. A wave of nostalgia washed over him with such bittersweet joy that he felt his throat tighten. He had dreamed of this moment almost from the instant he set foot on Portuguese soil over four years ago.

Four years was too long to be away from home.

Derek thrust his fingers through his unruly thatch of black hair and asked himself—not for the first time—whether he had done the right thing in leaving England in such haste. Perhaps he should have stayed to face down the curious glances, the ugly speculation, the onslaught of simpering misses with matrimony on their minds. Perhaps, he thought, with a flash of whimsy, he might even have found another mother for Charlotte.

The notion of taking another wife had been abhorrent to him. Even now the thought of exposing himself to another betrayal made him shudder. He had put too much of himself into his first marriage. And lost too much of himself, he admitted wryly.

He stood up and stretched. There might be no need for him to take on another wife after all. Margaret had doted on Charlotte as a baby; the child had seemed to fill a void in his sister's life. Perhaps she would be happy to step into the role of surrogate mother again. Always providing, of course, that Sir Joshua Comfrey had not finally come up to scratch.

Derek smiled to himself as he rang for his valet. Cheerful, steadfast, predictable Sir Joshua had a small but prosperous estate that marched with Derek's own, and his family had been friends and neighbours of the Sheldons for generations. Derek had hoped that Margaret and Sir Joshua would make a match of it; but the years had passed, and the baronet remained nothing more permanent than the assiduous admirer and favoured escort he had always been. Derek wondered if his own absence from Sheldon Hall and four more years to make up her suitor's mind had wrought any changes in his sister's relationship with Sir Joshua.

Half an hour later, Derek stepped out on deck and was enveloped in a misty rain that blurred the Hampshire coastline and turned the Isle of Wight into a dark bulk to their left. As he watched, the ship veered sharply to the right and slid through the narrow straits into the Portsmouth harbour.

He glanced around for Charlotte, who had run out of their suite earlier to watch the docking with Lady Fanny, but failed to see her until she called to him from the bridge, where the ladies had taken shelter with Captain Mansford and his first mate.

"I trust my daughter is not in the way, Jack," he murmured after exchanging greetings and receiving an impulsive hug from Charlotte.

"Captain Jack says that Lady Fanny could take the *Fortune Hunter* into port herself, Papa," Charlotte exclaimed, obviously delighted with the notion that her new friend was able to sail a ship. "He is going to teach me how to do it, too, if I am good and learn my lessons. That is if you agree, Papa."

Distracted by this new addition to Lady Fanny's list of extraordinary talents, Derek did not answer. He was busy devising ways of diverting his daughter's interest from a lady whose accomplishments were definitely not those one expected to find in a young, impressionable girl of six summers.

Lady Fanny laughed gaily at his daughter's enthusiasm and tweaked her nose. "You will also have to grow a little taller, Charlotte, or you will not be able to see where you are going. I can barely do so myself. Besides, steering a ship requires much more than turning the wheel one way or another."

Derek listened with only half an ear to his daughter's excited chatter and Lady Fanny's responses. Occasionally the captain would be called upon to lend his authority to the discussion, but the colonel's attention was drawn to the shimmer of raindrops that misted the lady's hair and eyelashes, turning her into a mythical creature of impossible dreams. Charlotte's hair, flying loose about her face, was also damp with rain, but lacked the allure of her companion's diamond-sparkled curls.

Before he could avert his gaze, Lady Fanny turned her head, and Derek found himself staring into her faintly amused violet eyes. Mortified for allowing himself to be caught gawking like some raw lad down from Oxford, Derek frowned down at her.

"I see you are none too pleased at your daughter's ambitions to become a dashing sea captain, Colonel. I imagine there is little likelihood of that ever coming to pass, but there can be no harm in allowing a little girl to dream." She paused, and Derek saw her amusement fade. "Life will take care of turning all those dreams to ashes soon enough," she added, so softly that Derek wondered if it had been meant for his ears.

She turned away to join Charlotte in watching the rapidly approaching Portsmouth wharf. Derek was left to ponder the irony of a female possessed of all those attributes which were universally held to make any woman happy, but who had, in one unguarded moment, revealed a disillusionment with life that matched his own.

Derek pulled himself up abruptly. What was he thinking? How could he be mad enough to consider, even for a instant, any similarity between Lady Fanny's secret sorrow—however devastating it might be—and the shattering scandal in his own life?

Nevertheless, throughout the bustle of disembarking later that morning, the colonel could not quite banish from his mind that bleak look in Lady Fanny's eyes when she had spoken of unfulfilled dreams.

That evening, as Fanny settled into the best accommodations the popular Blue Parrot Inn had to offer, she regretted that moment of weakness on the bridge of the *Fortune Hunter*. She had been inexplicably outraged at Colonel Sheldon's consistent attempts to suppress his daughter's high spirits. True, Charlotte's momentary enthusiasm over learning to steer a ship on the high seas had been childish and impractical, but there had been no excuse for squashing her joy with silent disapproval, as the colonel had done.

Fanny knew all about silent disapproval. It had dogged her throughout her young life at Hayle House in Cornwall, growing up the only daughter in a family of boys. First with her father, who had tried unsuccessfully to change his daughter from the tomboy she was fast becoming, into a prim, well-behaved young lady suitable to become a nobleman's wife. Fanny grimaced at the memory of the countless scoldings she had endured in Lord Hayle's study overlooking her mother's rose garden. She had amused herself during those tirades in counting the full-blown blossoms and those still tightly furled with the promise of beauty to come.

In her fantasies, Fanny was one of those buds, those unfulfilled promises waiting for that precious moment when the gentleman of her dreams would seek her out and show her the way to happiness. Secretly, she had been confident that man would be Gerald Humphries, Viscount Penryn. Had not Gerald, whom she had known all her life, kissed her behind the laburnum bushes on that glorious summer of her sixteenth birthday? Had he not called her his sweetheart, the prettiest girl in all of Cornwall?

When she had been summoned to her father's study, two months after her seventeenth birthday, she was ecstatic to learn from old Foster, the family butler, that Viscount Penryn was with his lordship. So, she thought as she raced upstairs to tidy her hair and change her plain round gown for one in pale lilac muslin, Gerald had come for her at last. Finally the waiting was over; she would unfurl in the warmth of his love and fulfill her destiny.

Later, she stood on the dark rose-patterned Axminster

carpet in her father's study and listened with mounting dismay to Lord Hayle's complacent announcement that the Duke of Cambourne, the largest landowner in the district and Gerald's cousin, sought Lady Fanny's hand in marriage.

Why then was Gerald here and not the Duke? Fanny remembered thinking. And why would he not meet her stricken gaze? Had she heard aright?

When she had demurred, Gerald had explained curtly that his cousin had been called away to London on the King's business, and would not return for a month. Gerald was here at the Duke's express command, having been entrusted with the delicate mission of securing Lady Fanny's consent to his flattering offer.

Fanny had been aghast. When she protested that she hardly knew the Duke of Cambourne, her father had told her, in tones that brooked no argument, that she could count herself lucky to have attracted the attention of a gentleman of the Duke's stature. But what of love? she had thought, not daring to say so. What of dreams? Of kisses stolen behind the laburnums?

Gerald, his face pale, had talked of settlements and other details with her father, dismissing her as though he had never called her his sweetheart. As though he did not care that she was to wed another.

With an angry shrug, Fanny pushed such thoughts from her mind. She could not afford to fall into a melancholy mood over what was over and done with, past repair. She had rebuilt her life, and had nothing to regret, had she? After all, she had been innocent of those ugly charges brought against her. In her youthful ignorance, she had acted rashly; Fanny could not deny it. But she had been innocent. *Innocent!* And she had been found guilty by those whose love and protection she had taken for granted. She had been branded a—

Fanny felt her aunt's arm slip round her waist, give her an affectionate squeeze. "Do not brood upon it, love. I can see the memories of the past are haunting you now that we are back in England, but ten years is a long time, dear. You are a different woman now. No one can touch you." She paused, and Fanny saw her aunt's eyes twinkle with amusement. "Unless you allow it, of course."

Fanny bristled. "I am not brooding, Aunt. And why would I allow anyone to *touch* me, as you put it?"

"Touch your heart, I meant to say, Fanny. It is high time you let a man into your life, dear. A husband can be a great comfort to a woman. I can testify to that. And I am not blind, dear. You might do a lot worse than admit that our prickly colonel has a soft heart under that gruff shell he wears. If only you would shed your own shell once in a while. . . ."

Fanny put up a hand in protest. "You have said quite enough, Aunt. For one thing, I think you are entirely mistaken about the colonel. There is nothing soft about him at all. Quite the contrary, he is hard-nosed, authoritarian, inflexible, and mulish. He reminds me of—" She stopped abruptly, unwilling to dredge up painful memories of the men in her past.

"He reminds me of *you*, my dear," Lady Wentworth murmured, her eyes twinkling again. "And I am sure the colonel would agree with me. You are barely civil to the poor man."

Fanny gasped. "I cannot believe you said that, Aunt."

"Think on it, Fanny."

"He is such a bore, Aunt," Fanny protested. "Besides, he scowls at me all the time. It is as plain as a pikestaff that he disapproves heartily of me, so why should I be civil to the man?"

"Because it is polite to do so," Lady Wentworth said severely. "Furthermore, Fanny, the colonel is a fine—"

"If you are about to tell me that Colonel Sheldon is a fine figure of a man, you may save your breath, my dear Aunt," Fanny interrupted brusquely. "I am not blind, and I can see that he is passably attractive, if one overlooks his stiff, dictatorial manner and his lack of charm. He has none whatsoever, have you not noticed?" Fanny glared at her aunt as if daring her to dismiss these damning faults.

Lady Wentworth merely smiled as she tucked a stray curl of her niece's silver-blond hair into her chignon. "I agree that the colonel is more reserved than your average gentleman, and he is not lavish with his charm."

"His non-existent charm, I suppose you mean, Aunt."

"He does not toss it around indiscriminately, of course,"

her aunt continued as though she had not been interrupted, "as so many of our young bucks do nowadays. One knows they cannot possibly mean all the pretty nonsense they spill into a lady's ear. But if you think the colonel has no charm, my dear, you cannot have seen his smile. It is quite delightful, I can assure you. And his dimples, when he forgets to suppress them, quite make my old heart flutter."

"Aunt Clarissa!" Fanny exclaimed, half shocked, half amused.

"Oh, I know it is shameless of me, dear," her aunt murmured, cheeks turning rosy with embarrassment, "but I do confess I find the colonel most admirable. And that stiffness and reserve you complain of, dear, is all part of his military training, of course." She sighed. "Even in mufti, your uncle John could never be mistaken for anything other than a military gentleman. He quite stole my heart away from the moment I set eyes on him. Your colonel has the same magnetic aura about him."

"He is not *my* colonel," Fanny corrected her, "and I fail to detect this magnetism you speak of, Aunt."

But this was not quite true, Fanny admitted to herself as she dressed for dinner and submitted to Yvette's efforts to tease her rebellious curls into an elaborate cascade of ringlets. She had certainly glimpsed the colonel's elusive dimples on more than one occasion. Although directed at his daughter rather than at her, Fanny had felt her own heart flutter.

Brushing such absurd thoughts aside, Fanny accompanied her aunt down to the private parlour they were to share with the colonel and his daughter. She had been unable to find an excuse to refuse his invitation to dine with him, particularly since the alternative had been to have trays sent up to their room.

Her aunt had been delighted by the invitation, and chattered happily as they descended the narrow staircase. Fanny considered it an encroachment on so slight an acquaintance, but refrained from voicing her displeasure. She entered the parlour in one of her aggressive moods, prepared to find fault with everything.

As soon as she crossed the threshold her annoyance was

quite deflated by an eager cry from Charlotte, who cata-
pulted across the room to greet her.

"I am so glad you could come," Charlotte piped, quite
as though she were the hostess. "Papa said you might be
too tired, but I knew you would come."

Fanny bent to embrace the child, then raised her eyes to
the gentleman standing before the crackling fire, faintly disturbed by the colonel's astute judgment of her feelings.

She smiled coolly and was surprised to be treated to a
rare glimpse of the dimples her aunt found so delightful.
For the first time she could remember, she recognized open
admiration in his slate grey eyes, which startled her into a
warmer smile.

Annoyed that her defences had been so easily breached,
Fanny declined the sherry he offered and took her place at
the table.

Lady Wentworth glanced at her in surprise. "Are you
sure you will not have a glass, my dear? I know how much
you enjoy it."

"And excellent sherry it is, too," the colonel added, a
hint of laughter in his eyes, which caused Fanny an uneasy
start. "Perhaps if I served you a glass, my lady, and placed
it here beside your plate, you might change your mind."
He suited action to words, and Fanny had to endure the
brush of his sleeve on her shoulder as he reached over to
set the sherry down.

Had she not known any better, she might have concluded
that the rogue was flirting with her, Fanny realized with a
shock. He was wasting his time, of course. Such highhanded methods would not work on Lady Francesca Wentworth. She was immune to the lures of flirtation—although
she indulged occasionally, Fanny never, *never* took them
seriously. This gentleman, however delightful his dimples
might be, would be no exception.

Later that night, however, as she tossed about in the
unfamiliar bed, Fanny could not pry her mind away from
her aunt's words. When he chose, as he obviously had that
evening, the colonel could be both charming and attractive.
But like any other gentleman, Fanny reminded herself dog-
gedly, once Sheldon caught a hint of the scandal in her

past, that rare charm would freeze up faster than the cat could lick her whiskers.

It would cause less disappointment in the future if she remembered that inescapable fact.

CHAPTER 6

Parting of the Ways

After a restless night, Derek rose early and partook of a hasty breakfast in the taproom. He was impatient to see Sheldon Hall again. He regretted his impulsive invitation of the night before, and had mixed feelings about sharing his coach with the Wentworth ladies. Particularly with Lady Fanny, who had made no secret of her disinterest in him. But he had been unable to disappoint his daughter, who had innocently assumed that the parties would proceed to Brighton together. Lady Wentworth had immediately seconded the plan, while her niece sat staring absently into the amber depths of her untouched sherry.

Too top-lofty by half was Lady Fanny, but he was intrigued in spite of himself. Had she fawned over him, as did half the females of his acquaintance, Derek would have felt nothing but contempt for her. But to ignore him deliberately, or worse yet consider him beneath her notice, was a new experience, which piqued his pride.

The devil fly away with contentious females, he thought disgustedly, draining the last of his ale and setting the tankard down on the table with a satisfying thump. Once he had deposited the Wentworth ladies in Brighton, he would be able to forget that Lady Fanny had ever touched his life. With this comforting thought uppermost in his mind, the colonel paid his shot and started up the narrow stairs, intent upon rousing his daughter.

Halfway up the dimly lit stairs, Derek realized that he was not about to escape so easily. For there she was, a

shadowy figure in rustling silk and a halo of fragrance that
enveloped him as she paused on the step above him, waiting for him to step aside to allow her to pass. Some perverse quirk of nature kept him there, his gaze caught in
the depths of her violet eyes, which were level with his own.

So close were they in fact that Derek caught her flash of
apprehension, concealed immediately by the imperious arch
of her eyebrows. If she had been momentarily disconcerted,
he thought, strangely elated at the possibility, Lady Fanny
was an expert in hiding her emotions.

Instead of demanding, in her faintly supercilious tone,
that he remove himself from her path instantly, Lady Fanny
surprised him. "How fortunate that we meet so early, Colonel. I wish to thank you for your generous offer to escort
my aunt and me to Brighton."

"My pleasure, my lady," he responded stiffly.

Miraculously she smiled. A brilliant, dazzling smile that
made his knees weak but also caused bells of alarm to
ring furiously in his head. Could it be that, despite Captain
Mansford's assurances to the contrary, the top-lofty Lady
Fanny was throwing out lures to him? It seemed unlikely,
but the notion that he had broken through the lady's icy
reserve caused Derek's blood to surge.

In the dimness of the stair her eyes were inscrutable. Or
was that a glimmer of encouragement there? The prospect
of an amorous liaison with Lady Fanny had, in the natural
order of things, occurred to him before, but it had seemed
so improbable that he had discarded it as absurd. Now,
Derek was not so sure, and his awareness of her—of her
flowery perfume, her glowing eyes, and the warmth of her
presence on the cramped stair—sharpened.

"Unfortunately, I will be unable to accept your generous offer."

He heard her speak through a haze of desire, and felt a
sharp stab of disappointment and anger overwhelm him as
the import of her words sank in. Should he not be over-
joyed to see the last of this woman? Could it be that he had
entertained, even for an instant, the possibility of intimacy
between them? Not marriage, of course. Lady Fanny possessed none of those qualities he would expect in a wife.
But he would not be averse to a less formal arrangement.

He let the thought taper off. The feeling that he had been duped, played for a fool, clouded his judgement.

"I see," he said tersely, not trusting himself further.

Lady Fanny laughed softly. "I doubt you see anything at all, Colonel. I cannot accept your offer simply because I intend to remain in Portsmouth. There is business I must attend to. Now, if you will allow me, sir," she said, gesturing towards the bottom of the stairs.

Derek turned sideways to give her room to pass, but as she stepped down next to him, her skirt brushing against his leg, he placed his left hand against the opposite wall, effectively blocking her descent. One hand on his arm, she steadied herself, gazing up at him, evidently startled by his sudden move.

The colonel was startled himself. Not since his raw youth could he recall accosting with amorous intentions a female in a dark place. Lady Fanny stood as if mesmerized within the circle of his arm, and Derek felt the warmth of her breath in the air between them.

"I see," he repeated mindlessly, his eyes fixed on her parted lips. All manner of erotic fantasies raced through his mind. He felt himself drawn inexorably towards those lips, and before he realized what he was doing, his head bent down to take the kiss he suddenly knew he could not do without.

Before he could do so, however, Lady Fanny surprised him again. Or had his fevered brain only imagined that she swayed towards him, her face lifted to receive his kiss?

The colonel was never to recall exactly what happened on the stairs that morning because by then his lips touched hers, and the shock of their warmth and softness drove every rational thought from his mind.

Later that morning, the departure from the Blue Parrot was delayed by an incipient argument between Lady Wentworth and Charlotte over whether or not Devi should travel with them in the chaise or with the Wentworth groom in the wagon. The monkey did not help his case, choosing that moment to escape from Charlotte's grasp and race up an old oak tree in the inn yard, chattering wildly and showing a mouthful of yellow teeth. Fanny usually endured these delays philosophically; today she experienced a mounting impatience to see the whole party on the road.

The colonel remained aloof during this noisy altercation, limiting himself to ordering the still weak Miss Grimes to make sure that all his daughter's belongings were safely stowed on the roof of the travelling coach. Even Charlotte's plea to her father to get the monkey down was met with stony silence.

"The more attention we give him, Charlotte," Fanny cautioned, hiding a smile at the notion of the colonel climbing a tree to catch a monkey, "the less he will want to come down. The best thing to do is to pretend you will leave him behind."

"Oh! We cannot do that," Charlotte exclaimed.

"We most certainly can," her father snapped, evidently running out of patience. "Now get into the coach at once, child. We are about to depart." He made a gesture to the Wentworth coachman, who climbed into the driver's seat and gathered up the reins.

Charlotte promptly burst into tears and flung herself into Fanny's arms.

"Hush, dear," Fanny said gently, pulling the distraught child against her bosom. "Devi can come home with me later this week if he insists upon being stubborn."

"But I wish him to come with *me*," Charlotte cried, now thoroughly overset, her wails competing with the monkey's shrieks.

Lady Fanny risked her first glance at the colonel since their morning encounter, and was not surprised to find his cool grey eyes fixed upon her. To her intense mortification, she felt herself blush. The memory of that quite inexplicable kiss on the stairs that morning had rattled her composure more than she would admit. What had he been thinking of? And what had she herself been thinking to allow such inappropriate intimacy?

The frosty colonel aroused nothing but disdain in her; had he not made it clear that she was too much the hoyden for his starched-up perception of females? His unfavourable opinion mattered not a jot to Fanny, whose ideal gentleman was a combination of intelligence, charm, and passion. Colonel Sheldon had not fit that ideal by any stretch of her imagination. Why was it then, she asked herself for the umpteenth time, that his kiss had caused her to lose her composure?

Fanny embraced her aunt, promising to be in Brighton within a sennight, and gave Charlotte a warm kiss that the little girl returned with enthusiasm. She stepped back as the driver gave his horses the office to go, and waved at Charlotte's tear-stained face as the coach rocked forward, leaving the monkey chattering and swinging around in the top of the oak tree.

"Devi," she called to her pet, "you may come down now, old man, they have all left." At the first sound of her voice, the monkey leapt lightly down from branch to branch until he reached the ground beside her. Taking the monkey by the hand, Fanny turned to enter the inn.

"Not quite all of us, my lady," a masculine voice said softly, causing Fanny to pause. Had she forgotten that the colonel was riding beside the coach, or had she deliberately cast it from her mind? She looked at him over her shoulder, but said nothing.

"I wished for a moment alone with you, Lady Fanny," he began, moving across the yard to stand beside her, "but you have been elusive this morning. Deliberately so, I fear, and perhaps with good reason."

"I have nothing to say to you, Colonel," she said flatly.

The colonel smiled faintly, and Fanny was disconcerted to see those rare dimples appear beside his mouth. "I can well believe you, but I have something I wish to say to you, my dear, if you will allow me."

The sound of the endearment on his lips struck Fanny as incongruous in the extreme, but also oddly tender. Before she could gather her scattered wits to give him the set-down he deserved, he hurried on.

"I most sincerely regret the . . . the incident this morning," he began, his deep voice betraying his nervousness and touching an unprotected corner of Fanny's heart. "My behaviour was execrable, and I cannot expect your forgiveness. Indeed, I dare not hope for any such thing. I behaved like a callow youth with a . . . with a . . ." He paused, a slow flush mounting his cheeks.

The sight nearly undid Fanny, who experienced a wild

and quite improper urge to cradle his head on her bosom as she had recently done with a distraught Charlotte. To quell this unseemly temptation Fanny resorted to sarcasm.

"With a chambermaid, I suppose you mean, sirrah," she said acidly. "Not a very flattering comparison, needless to say."

His blush deepened. "I did not mean to imply—"

"I know very well what you meant to imply, Colonel," she snapped, suddenly furious "You wish to blame me for what occurred, no doubt. Well, let me tell you—"

"Not at all," he interrupted, closing the gap between them and obliging Fanny to step back. "No such thought entered my head. I merely wished to assure you that I meant no disrespect. Please believe it was not my intention to insult you, my lady." He gazed down at her so intently that Fanny's heart gave a lurch. Surely he would not dare to repeat the offence here in the middle of the crowded inn yard.

She turned away. "You have said quite enough on the matter, Colonel," she said curtly. "I have already dismissed the entire incident from my mind, and I would advise you to do the same."

"You are indeed fortunate, my lady," he murmured before she could retreat.

Intrigued, Fanny paused to glance at him, one eyebrow raised in surprise. "Oh? And why is that?"

"If you have truly dismissed the kiss we shared, you are more fortunate than I, Fanny," he murmured, the dimples reappearing briefly.

It was Fanny's turn to feel her cheeks grow warm. How dare the rogue make free with her name? And to broadcast that they had shared a kiss to anyone who cared to listen was beyond bearing. She drew herself up to her full height and glared at him.

"You are being deliberately perverse, Colonel," she said between clenched teeth. "I had thought you a man of good sense, but apparently I was mistaken. Perhaps I should have slapped your face for you."

Fanny thought she saw a glimmer of laughter in his curious grey eyes. "I was surprised you did not do so, my lady. I deserved no less. Unless, of course . . ." he paused, and

Fanny was fascinated to see the dimple show itself as if to soften the words that followed. "Unless our kiss was not as unwelcome as you would have me believe."

Fanny stiffened with mortification and fury. *Our kiss*, indeed! Was there no limit to this rogue's impertinence? She opened her mouth to give him the biggest set-down of his life, but no words came. How could she deny that it *had* been their kiss and that it had been far from unwelcome? Had she not enjoyed it utterly, even encouraged it? Had she not lifted her lips to his? Leaned into him quite shamelessly?

Fanny let out her breath in a long sigh, and watched the stirring of passion in his eyes. Heaven help her, how could she admit that she had wanted that kiss to go on forever? Dared she confess that she wanted to kiss him again?

Unaccustomed to denying herself anything within reason, Fanny was hard put to convince herself that embracing Colonel Sheldon in the yard of the Blue Parrot went far beyond what was reasonable. Even for her. Even if he seemed to be willing. Even if the prospect of shocking the stiff-necked colonel out of his complacency was well nigh irresistible.

Dredging up the last of her self control, and suppressing her libidinous impulses, Fanny threw him one of her glittering smiles. "You delude yourself, Colonel," she said coolly.

Gathering her skirts about her, she turned and swept into the inn without a backward glance.

CHAPTER 7

Encounter on the Cliffs

Determined not to allow her last encounter with Colonel Sir Derek Sheldon and his provocative dimples to encroach upon her peace of mind, Lady Fanny resolutely threw herself into the business of reading the stacks of reports submitted by her Portsmouth agent, Mr. Johnathan Cunningham. She made the pleasant discovery that her uncle's shipping business had prospered considerably under her stewardship. Fanny relished the thought of sharing this good news with her Aunt Clarissa, who had initially begged her niece to leave all such tiresome matters of business in the capable hands of Sir John's assistant.

Although her waking hours in the week that followed the colonel's departure were filled with long intervals spent in Mr. Cunningham's musty office near the wharves discussing the future direction of the company, and in more lively meetings with Captain Jack Mansford over dinner, her nights were invaded by memories of that clandestine encounter on the dim stairs at the Blue Parrot Inn.

"You look blue-devilled tonight, my dear," Jack remarked one evening as she sat picking dispiritedly at a plate of sweetmeats. "Why not tell your Uncle Jack what ails you, lass. I can tell something is wrong with you when you refuse a second glass of this excellent sherry our host laid in especially for you, Fanny."

Fanny merely smiled and nibbled on a sugared plum.

"Ah, I have it!" Jack exclaimed, slapping his forehead in mock surprise. "How could I not see which way the wind was blowing?" His voice dropped to a more intimate level. "You miss the scintillating conversation of our Colonel Sheldon. Am I not correct, love?"

"Absolutely not!" Fanny responded emphatically. "Have you taken leave of your senses, Jack? What a preposterous notion."

"You do not think him scintillating, then?"

"Of course not! You have spent more time with him than I, Jack, and must know that the colonel wears a black frown most of the time, but more particularly when he addresses me. He is a veritable ogre to everyone but his sweet daughter. And when he does speak to me, which is not often, he invariably has something cutting to say."

"Ah, I see the problem now. You are miffed because the gentleman failed to cast his heart at your feet, like the rest of us poor mortals."

Fanny stared at him in astonishment. There was something in her friend's tone of voice that she had not heard before. Since their very first meeting in her Uncle John's house years ago, Captain Jack Mansford had stood her friend. He had teased her and made her laugh, and Jack's carefree and uncritical acceptance had become precious to her. Her uncle and aunt were supportive and loving, but it was Jack's friendship and brotherly camaraderie that helped Fanny climb out of the pit of despair into which she had fallen.

"This is utter rubbish, Jack, and you know it," she said unsteadily. "The last thing I want is to listen to a string of charming lies from every fortune hunter within range. I endured that once and paid dearly for my stupidity. I will not do so again."

Jack poured himself another glass of sherry, then looked at Fanny across the littered table, his eyes devoid of their usual twinkle.

"So you label all men fortune hunters and turn yourself into a dragon to discourage them. An effective way of ending up on the shelf for life, my dear." He smiled crookedly. "But perhaps that is what you want, Fanny. Is it?"

Fanny opened her mouth to deny Jack's accusation vehemently, but then closed it with a snap, suddenly sure that she did not want to live her life as a childless spinster, without a family of her own.

"I thought not," Jack said. "Then I suggest you take a closer look at the men who cross your path, love, before you scare them away en masse with your Amazonian starts."

"How unkind you are, Jack," she retorted sharply, truly hurt by her friend's words.

Jack laughed. "If you want me to be kind, then let me ressure you that our Colonel Sheldon is no fortune hunter, Fanny. Very plump in the pocket is the colonel, let me tell you. Nothing underhand or devious about him. His interest in you is purely physical, my dear. But I am sure you know that too, Fanny," he added with a sly wink.

"I know nothing of the sort," Fanny replied, dismissing the embrace she had shared with the colonel. "And furthermore, I have no interest whatsoever in the gentleman, regardless of the state of his finances. Neither do I wish to discuss it with you," she added, all too conscious of her heightened colour.

"Sheldon is not the kind of man to hang around kicking his heels while you decide whether or not to notice him, Fanny. If you want him—and you could do a lot worse, let me tell you—you will have to come down off your high horse and make a push to catch him. I know for a fact he is not interested in taking a second wife, but I wager you might change his mind—"

"But I do not *wish* to change his mind," she exclaimed. "And do stop teasing me, Jack, you know how much I hate it."

"Whatever you say, love," the captain responded, his generous mouth curling into a laugh. "Now let me serve you another glass of sherry."

Fanny moved her glass in acquiescence, but she was not thinking of wine. Jack's smile, devoid of dimples, had conjured up another she had dismissed almost a sennight ago. And that other smile instantly brought back the memory of warm lips on hers and the tenderness of a clandestine kiss she had thought—mistakenly it now seemed—consigned to oblivion.

Two days later, as Lady Fanny sat in her hired chaise gazing out through a misty rain at the green fields and thatched cottages lining the coastal road, Jack's words returned to haunt her. Was she the dragon he had painted her? She absently ran her hand over Devi's coarse fur. The monkey did not like rain, and he had protested loudly at being removed from the warm inn. To pacify him, Fanny had allowed him to curl up on her lap, and now as she stroked his chin, she noticed, with a touch of dismay, that her pet's muzzle was turning grey, a sure sign of age.

Age? She felt a tremor run through her. Naturally, she knew herself to be far beyond the acceptable age for young ladies to wed; but since Fanny had no intention of venturing into those waters again, the thought of aging had never bothered her before.

Idly, Fanny wondered if her life would have been any different had her father given her to Lord Penryn instead of to his exalted cousin. Gerald, whom she had known all her life, had been her idol. Only later had she discovered that he was dependent upon the duke's largesse to support the lavish lifestyle his own income did not begin to cover.

What had Jack been trying to tell her that evening over dinner? For a moment there she had thought he had included himself among her many admirers, but this did not sound like the Jack she had known for the past ten years. No, she thought, dismissing the notion of a romantic liaison with the captain, he was a true friend worth more to her than ten suitors; one of the few friends she had left now that Uncle John was gone.

After a short stop for refreshments, Fanny was relieved when the chaise passed the village of Hove and entered Brighton. Dusk was falling as they approached the select part of town where Sir John had purchased a fashionable house for his bride so many years ago, and the lights glowing in all the front windows told her clearer than words that she was expected.

Lady Wentworth tripped down to the hall in a flutter of ribbons and laces and little cries of joy to welcome her. Fanny was unexpectedly touched, and when she felt her aunt's arms around her, she choked back a sob. Jack had been right, she thought, clutching convulsively at the comforting warmth of her aunt; she had been blue-devilled. But now she was back home, and her dear Aunt Clarissa would set things to rights again.

"Now, now, my love." Her aunt patted Fanny reassuringly, pulling a lacy handkerchief from her sleeve to wipe her niece's wet cheeks. "Come upstairs and have a nice cup of tea with your old auntie. Harvey," she called to the butler who was supervising the unloading of the chaise. "You remember Harvey, Fanny? He is still with us, thank goodness. Harvey, please help Yvette take her ladyship's things upstairs, and then ask Mrs. Crumbly to send us up a fresh pot of tea."

"Welcome home, milady," Harvey said with a bow. "Good to have you back in England again. Your ladyship's chamber is ready, and we shall have the trunks upstairs in no time."

It was not only her aunt's effusive welcome that had overset Fanny's composure upon entering Primrose Court again after so many years. She could not forget that this house had been her mother's last shelter. It was with mixed feelings that Fanny followed her aunt up the staircase to the drawing room. She sensed her mother's presence everywhere, and although she knew that after ten years, no trace of Lady Hayle could possibly remain, Fanny could swear she caught a whiff of her mother's perfume.

Listening with only half an ear to her aunt's seamless flow of chatter, Fanny could not stop her mind from slipping back to the past. What had her mother felt, arriving at Primrose Court a scant month after her daughter had been banished forever from Cambourne Abbey? What must have been her distress upon finding the knockers removed and the shutters closed? Luckily the servants had recognized her and taken her in, but Fanny shuddered at the thought of her mother's panic when she discovered that her sister and her disgraced daughter had embarked for Bombay barely a sennight before.

". . . and you will never guess who it was, dear."

Fanny emerged from her reverie in time to catch her aunt's last words. "Who are you taking about, Aunt?"

"Why, the gentleman who came calling last Wednesday, dear. Can you guess who it was?"

"You know I am no good at guessing, Aunt," Fanny said mechanically, unable to pretend a burning interest in her aunt's callers. "And in any case, I know no gentleman in Brighton except Colonel Sheldon, and I wager it was not that odious creature."

Lady Wentworth shook her head. "No, it was not the colonel, dear, although he did promise to bring Charlotte to visit Devi just as soon as the beast arrived from Portsmouth, which I admit surprised me."

"He will not do so, Aunt, you may count upon it," Fanny said calmly. "Undoubtedly he said that to pacify his daughter."

"Are you not dying to know who this gentleman caller was, Fanny?"

"Of course, I am, Aunt," Fanny protested mildly, although in truth she cared little for any gentleman other than the one who had rudely refused to call at all. "Please do not keep me in suspense." After her aunt whispered a name with bated breath, Fanny wished she had kept silent.

"Who?" she hissed in disbelief. "Surely you are mistaken, Aunt. That is impossible."

"Indeed it is not, my dear Fanny," her aunt responded nervously. "Bold as brass. Harvey brought up his card after I sent down to say we were not receiving. Here it is," she insisted, drawing the offending piece of evidence from among a number of other cards in a silver dish. "See for yourself."

With fingers that shook only slightly, Fanny reached for the card. She held it in her lap for a long moment, staring blindly into her aunt's anxious blue eyes.

When she finally lowered her gaze, the elegant black script leaped out at her aggressively, dispelling any lingering hope that there had been a mistake.

What could Gerald Humphries possibly want with her after all this time? And how did he know she was back in England? The past seemed to be closing in uncomfortably around Fanny.

"I told him I never wanted to see him again," she said harshly, crushing the card in her fist.

"You do not have to see him, love, so do not fret yourself into ribbons. I shall tell Harvey that Viscount Penryn is not welcome in this house, and that will be an end to it."

Fanny smiled weakly. It was one thing to ban a gentleman from one's home, but if she knew anything at all about this particular gentleman, Fanny knew that if he wanted to see her, Gerald would certainly contrive a way to do so.

The misty drizzle that started as soon as the chaise left Brighton turned into a steady shower two miles short of the gates of Sheldon Hall. Derek was glad that he had not driven himself in his curricle, as he originally intended. Although perhaps a good drenching was what he needed to wash the lingering memories of a certain lady out of his head, he thought wryly.

Derek had been restless ever since returning home three weeks ago, and had put it down to lack of exercise. Estate affairs kept him busy every morning, but the colonel liked to spend his afternoons riding with his daughter—who was inseparable from Bubbles, her new pony—or driving with her into Brighton on errands for her Aunt Margaret.

Today had been different, and he was glad that Charlotte was not with him. He felt guilty, but he wished to avoid her insistence that they pay the promised visit to the Wentworths. Derek was not yet ready to take that step. Sooner or later he would, of course, but today he would only leave his card. A small peace offering. Should he send flowers, too? Or would, they be taken as a sign of interest on his part? He decided against flowers, and when his coachman stopped in front of 17 Primrose Court, Derek was prepared to hand his card to the butler with only a perfunctory enquiry about the health of the Wentworth ladies.

"Lady Fanny is not home at the moment, Colonel," the butler surprised him by announcing, after a glance at Derek's card. "Do you wish me to announce you to her ladyship?"

The colonel declined the honour and climbed back into his carriage. The butler had obviously been instructed to admit him regardless of the day he called. This set off warning bells in his head. Having been in similar situations before, Derek followed what experience had taught him was the safest course of action. He fled the scene.

Only later did it occur to him that half an hour spent in Lady Wentworth's company might have saved him from an uncomfortable meeting with her niece. Later still he brought himself to admit that perhaps he did not wish to avoid such an encounter with the lady he had kissed on the stairs at the Blue Parrot Inn.

Lost in these confusing speculations, the colonel was unprepared when the carriage came to an abrupt halt, and the florid face of his coachman appeared at the window, rain dripping from his oilcloth.

"Beg pardon, Colonel," Carruthers stammered, obviously shaken out of his habitual calm, "but another frippery female is about to jump off the same cliff where t'other one kilt 'erself that time."

The colonel stared into the horror-stricken eyes of his coachman for a full five seconds before grasping the door handle. Carruthers yanked it open from the outside, and Derek was pulled unceremoniously from the coach. Regaining his balance in the muddy road, he squinted in the direction of the coachman's trembling finger.

The man was right. Derek automatically pulled his heavy cloak around him against the cold slanting rain, and with a muttered oath, sloshed through the mud and puddles towards the foolish female on the cliff edge less than twenty feet away, who seemed to have chosen the worst possible weather in which to end her life.

And end it—willingly or otherwise—she most certainly would, he thought fatalistically, if she moved an inch closer to the edge of the cliff. Even as he closed in on her, Derek fancied she teetered unsteadily. With a burst of speed, he surged forward and jerked her back, his hands clamped like vises on her slender arms.

With a choked cry of alarm, she collapsed against him, struggling frantically. Derek subdued her easily enough, and after shouting at her to be still, he felt the dead weight of her against his chest as she swooned.

Backing away to a safer distance, Derek swung her up in his arms and made his way laboriously back to the carriage. His hair was soaking when he came up to Carruthers, still holding the door open as if paralyzed in that position.

Derek wrestled the woman's limp form into the carriage and laid her out on a seat. He removed his own damp cloak and used it to cover her. He turned to order Carruthers to make all possible speed back to Sheldon Hall, when the coachman forestalled him.

"What do ye wish me to do with the lady's 'orse, sir?"

"What horse?"

"That big bay yonder under the pine."

Derek stuck his head out of the door and verified that there was indeed an unhappy looking horse tied to a scraggly tree. He cursed under his breath at the improvident female who had ventured out in such weather bent on apparent self-destruction with no thought to the convenience of others. "Or the well being of her mount," he added aloud.

"Beg pardon, sir?"

"Tie the damned horse behind the carriage, Carruthers," he responded curtly, "and then spring those slugs you have up there before we all succumb to the chills."

An amazingly short time later, the coach lurched forward, and the colonel was forced to hold his unconscious passenger with both hands to prevent her from sliding onto the floor at his feet.

When the carriage settled into a steadier pace, Derek reached to untie the wet ribbons of the lady's ruined bonnet. He was curious to see what manner of female would ride all the way out to this particular cliff site to commit such a desperate act.

Gingerly he pulled the bonnet away from the lady's face, allowing damp strands of pale hair to fall across her cheek. He brushed the hair aside with gentle fingers and marvelled at the smoothness of her skin under his touch. His eyes were drawn to the mouth, full and rosy in spite of the chill in the air. A mouth that was strangely familiar, he suddenly realized. A mouth whose texture and softness he remembered all too well.

Even as he watched, the lips opened, and she tried to say something, but he could not catch the words over the rattle of the carriage. He leaned forward to hear better, a smile on his own lips at the thought of the liberties he might take had he a mind to do so.

"That is quite close enough, Colonel," Lady Fanny exclaimed weakly, her violet eyes wide open now and filled with anything but gratitude. "Unless you are asking for that slap I should have given you back at the Blue Parrot?"

Before Derek was conscious of what he was about, he had leaned forward and pressed the lady's mouth with his own, as if in defiance of her threat.

More quickly than he had thought possible, her hand shot out, and Derek was barely able to grasp it mere inches from his face.

"Not so fast, my lady," he said softly, smiling down into her angry eyes. "This is no way to treat a man who has braved wind, and rain, and muddied his best boots to save you from your own foolishness."

She blinked up at him, and Derek had a flash of misgiving. Had he perhaps misjudged her actions on the cliff? But no, he had seen the figure about to jump to her death and had taken immediate action to prevent the disaster.

"Any foolishness here is entirely of your making, Colonel," Lady Fanny retorted contemptuously. "Do I look to you like a female with so little sense as to take her own life?"

Derek had to admit that suicide did not immediately come to mind when he thought of Lady Fanny. But the scene on the cliff had etched itself into his brain. He could not easily put it aside.

"Well?" Her tone was impatient.

"I only know what I saw, my lady," he replied calmly. "And if you were not trying to jump, perhaps you have a better explanation of your presence there."

He heard her gasp and knew that she would defy him to the end. "I have nothing to explain to you, Colonel. My affairs are none of your business, and I will thank you to keep out of them."

"I will be happy to do so, my lady," he said, anger overcoming his patience. "In fact, I am of half a mind to set you down in the rain and let you ride back to Brighton on your own."

"An excellent idea," she snapped, scrambling into a sitting position, her body trembling visibly. "What a pity you did not think of it sooner."

Before Derek could think of a suitable reply to such feminine nonsense, Lady Fanny had pulled the cord and brought the carriage to a standstill.

When Carruthers's face appeared at the window, she requested that her horse be brought forward. "I intend to r-ride back to Brighton," she said unsteadily. "I refuse to be subjected to this manhandling any longer."

Carruthers looked perplexed and glanced at his master for further instructions, rivulets of rain running down his face.

"Her ladyship has taken this idiotic notion into her head," Derek explained with a shrug. "Tell her how nonsensical she is, Carruthers."

The coachman glanced at Lady Fanny in disgust. "Balmy, I call it, Colonel. Plain balmy, the Bedlam kind of balmy. This ain't no night for a lady to be riding around loose."

"Indeed?" Lady Fanny snapped frostily. "We shall see about that. Bring up my horse, Coachman."

When Carruthers made no move to obey, she reached

for the door handle and had it halfway open before the coachman pushed it shut again from the outside. At the same time, Derek caught her by the waist and jerked her back into his lap.

"Home, Carruthers," he ordered, "and quick about it. Her ladyship is delirious."

Expecting a violent reaction to his words, Derek reached for his cloak, which had fallen to the floor, and wrapped it around her shaking shoulders.

To his utter amazement, Lady Fanny gave a little sob and huddled against him, trembling convulsively.

"Foolish girl," he chided her, settling her more firmly on his lap. "Do you want to catch your death of cold?"

"If I d-do," she muttered into his chest, "it will b-be all your f-fault. I'm so c-cold."

Derek cradled the shivering woman more closely against him. "I trust it will not come to that, Fanny," he murmured into the damp curls snuggled under his chin. I dearly hope it does not come to that, he repeated to himself, appalled at the idea.

At that moment, Derek would have given anything to protect this female who had nothing but insults to say to him. He was the bedlamite, he thought, marvelling at the extent of his blindness.

CHAPTER 8

Unwelcome Houseguest

Later that afternoon, Lady Fanny vaguely recollected being carried, teeth chattering, and shivering uncontrollably, up a curving staircase by someone strong and gentle. She remembered murmurs of reassurance but the words escaped her.

The comfort she derived from those cradling arms took her back to her childhood. Had she fallen off her pony again? she wondered, half in and out of consciousness. Was this her dear Papa carrying her up to her room with a scraped knee or a bruised ankle? Or was it Harry, her eldest brother, who was big and protective as brothers should be? It would not be Roger, who would be off in a barn somewhere playing silly games with one of the maids. Nor Willy, who was the only one of the St. Ives boys to take an interest in books. Her youngest brother Freddy seemed to be the most likely choice, but Freddy would be bounding up the stairs two at a time, pretending to be a runaway horse to make her giggle.

Besides, this man did not smell at all like Freddy, Fanny mused groggily, burrowing her face against the rough cloth of the coat he wore. Nor would Freddy's heart be thumping so loudly, as the heart beneath her cheek was doing. Her brother usually smelled of horses, but she did not recognize this scent at all. Except that . . . yes, she seemed to recall a similar scent from somewhere. Recently, too. But her mind refused to stay focused, and she felt herself slipping away into a deep, dark, peaceful place.

Now Fanny moaned and opened her eyes.

A fire crackled in the hearth and in its flickering light, Fanny saw she was in a large, comfortably appointed bed-chamber. The heavy green velvet curtains were closed, so she had no idea of the time.

A woman rose abruptly from a chair beside the hearth and approached the bed. "How are you feeling, my lady?" she enquired in a soft voice. "Are you ready for some supper? You slept right through tea-time, but Cook has made some of her special chicken soup for you."

Fanny loathed chicken soup, and had never seen this female before, but the events of the afternoon were beginning to return to her. "You must be Colonel Sheldon's sister," she began, hardly recognizing the faltering sound of her voice. "Charlotte's aunt?" She paused to accept the drink of water offered by the stranger. "I fear I have put you to considerable inconvenience, Miss . . . ," she paused again, feeling tired and inexplicably cross with herself for landing in this ridiculous predicament. Besides which, her face felt clammy and she had a terrible megrim.

"Miss Sheldon. Margaret Sheldon. I am indeed Charlotte's aunt, and she has done nothing but sing your praises ever since my brother brought you to Sheldon Hall during the rainstorm."

"So he brought me *here*, did he?" Fanny repeated with a touch of asperity. "I distinctly told him I wished to go home. But did he listen? No, of course not," she added before Miss Sheldon could reply. "It is exactly the sort of arbitrary decision he would make. Disregarding my wishes entirely."

She closed her eyes, suddenly tired. Her head was throbbing mercilessly, and Fanny wanted nothing more than to be back in her own chamber at Primrose Court drinking one of her Aunt Clarissa's soothing possets. Instead here she was a virtual prisoner in the house of a man who had . . . She gasped weakly as she remembered more details about that encounter on the cliffs.

The rogue had kissed her again. Or had she dreamt it?

Fanny's eyes flew open and she glared at her hostess, who appeared to have been struck speechless by Fanny's outburst. "Where is this odious brother of yours? Tell him I wish to see him this instant."

Miss Sheldon gasped. "Oh, he will not come in here, my lady," she said nervously.

"And may I know why?" Fanny demanded at her most lofty. "I daresay it amuses him to ignore my wishes. Is that it?"

"Oh, no," Miss Sheldon exclaimed in shocked tones. "My brother is the kindest, most generous gentleman in the world," she began, with what Fanny considered a pathetic disregard for the truth. "He would never deliberately do anything to harm a lady."

Unless that lady happens to be me, Fanny thought belligerently. "If you believe that, Miss Sheldon, all I can say is that you know very little about your brother. He is the most intolerant, autocratic, oafish creature I ever hope to meet in this life or the next. Now oblige me by telling him to step up here. I wish to tell him so to his face."

This heated argument exhausted her, and Fanny closed her eyes again, hoping this whole adventure with the colonel would turn out to be an unpleasant dream.

"He will never come into a lady's chamber, my lady,"

Miss Sheldon said, evidently much shocked at the notion. "My brother is a gentleman of unimpeachable honour, and extremely punctilious about observing the proprieties."

"Are you telling me that Colonel Sheldon has never ventured into a lady's chamber?" In spite of her discomfort, or perhaps because she was feeling so miserable, Fanny could not resist taking out her frustration on her naive hostess.

"I am sure he would do no such thing," Miss Sheldon stammered, wringing her hands in mortification.

"Not even if I invite him?" Fanny insisted languidly. "What a dull dog he is to be sure. You may tell him that he is also a fool. Does he know how many gentlemen would jump at the chance to receive such a summons from me?"

"It would be highly improper of you to invite my brother—or any other gentleman for that matter—into your chamber, my lady," Miss Sheldon said faintly. "I am confident that he would not come."

"Then you can have no reservations about conveying my message to him, can you, Miss Sheldon?" she asked sweetly. "And while we are on the subject, I have twenty guineas that say he will. Dare you wager on your brother's honour, I wonder, Miss Sheldon?"

Fanny's hostess gaped at her, mouth open in shock. "I am not a gamester, my lady," she managed to say, her voice faint. "My brother believes such vices are invented by the devil to ruin us."

Fanny stared at her with growing pity, her initial dislike turning to compassion. This female, needed her help if she were not to fade away into old age in the service of a heartless brother.

"The devil fly away with what your brother says, my dear. He is a man and knows nothing of female dreams. What matters is what *you* want in this life. Believe me, if you do not take what you want, it will pass you by, and you will be left to lead apes in hell. Of course," she added with a wry grin, "I may very well end up there myself, but not before I have made the world dance to my tune."

Exhausted by this outburst, Fanny relaxed against the pillows and closed her eyes. She was wasting her time. It would take much more than her radical rantings to infuse some spirit into this dowdy little mouse of a woman. Why did she care if aging Miss Sheldon remained a spinster for the rest of her days anyway? She must concentrate on getting rid of this dreadful megrim and going home to Primrose Court. Let Miss Sheldon fight her own battles—and lose them, too, as the poor creature was sure to do unless she learned to stand up for herself.

A soft exhalation of breath caused Fanny's eyes to flutter open again. "How I wish I h-had your c-courage, my lady," her hostess murmured wistfully, her pale hands fiddling with the ribbons at her breast. "But I have never been able to argue with my brother. I fear he thinks me a hopeless creature who cannot think for herself."

Fanny was startled by this admission. Perhaps there was hope for this mousy creature after all. Ignoring the throbbing of her temples, she sat up straighter and reached for the glass of water.

"Then you must show him that you are perfectly capable of making your own decisions," she said briskly. "As the only female in a family of boys, I learned early that if I did not react forcefully, my wishes would be ignored."

"I doubt I have ever been forceful in my entire life," Miss Sheldon confessed with surprising candor. "I would not know where to begin."

"You may start by telling your brother that I wish to speak to him, And if you are really serious about defying him, you might accept my wager that he will come into my chamber." She saw her hostess's hesitation and added provocatively, "Do you not wish to prove me wrong?"

Miss Sheldon seemed to rally at this challenge. "I *know* he will not come," she said firmly. "It would not be fair to—"

"Then we have a wager?" Fanny pushed her advantage. "Or perhaps you are not as sure of your brother's honour as Petruchio was of Katherine's obedience in that marvellous testing scene at the end of Shakespeare's *Taming of the Shrew*?"

"My brother is *not* a shrew," Miss Sheldon protested faintly.

"No? Are you perchance implying that I am the shrew?" Fanny enquired crossly. She was beginning to feel petulant

and weepy, a sure sign that something was seriously wrong
with her.

"Of course, you are a shrew," a cool voice remarked
from the open doorway. "How can there be any doubt in
your mind about the matter, Lady Fanny?"

Miss Sheldon spun round guiltily and murmured something utterly unintelligible. Fanny could guess without looking that the lady's cheeks were flaming red with
mortification at her brother's outrageous remark.

Fanny experienced no such embarrassment. She felt a
surge of . . . What exactly was it she felt? She returned the
gaze of the gentleman lounging against the door jamb as if
he belonged there. Which of course he did, she reminded
herself. This was his house, after all. But did that give him
the right to call her a shrew?

Unable to put a name to the emotion this tedious man,
a veritable Petruchio, had triggered in her breast, and unequal to the task of coming up with a crushing rejoinder
to put him in his place, Fanny felt herself wilting beneath
the quizzical gaze.

This will never do, she told herself sharply. She had only
now finished telling Miss Sheldon how to stand up to her
brother, and here she was at a loss for words when con-
fronted by the same gentleman.

"Your behaviour this afternoon was abominable, sir,"
she said with as much force as she could muster. The result
was not as scathing as she had intended, in fact the rogue
had the temerity to raise his eyebrows as though the news
was a surprise to him.

"Do not pretend you misunderstand me, Colonel. We
both know that you manhandled me as though I were one
of your lightskirts."

Fanny heard Miss Sheldon gasp at this plain speaking
and grasp the bedpost for support. "My brother does not
consort with fallen women," she said stiffly, her tone implying that the colonel had white wings tucked beneath the
well-fitting blue coat he wore.

Lady Fanny managed a weak laugh, but her acid rejoinder was cut off by the colonel.

"You know nothing at all of the matter, Margaret," he
said tersely. "Now, you had best come downstairs. Sir

Joshua has arrived and from what I could gather, has some new story to relate about his dogs."

"Oh, I cannot abandon our invalid," Miss Sheldon exclaimed, evidently relieved to move on to a less embarrassing topic. "Sir Joshua will have to wait."

"I am *not* an invalid," Fanny protested weakly, although she did feel so thirsty she could have drunk an entire pitcher of lemon water. She reached for the glass, but everything in the room had become fuzzy. She felt hot and disoriented. The glass was taken from her flaccid fingers and pressed to her lips; she took a long drink, then a cool hand touched her forehead.

"Oh, Derek, she is burning up!" Fanny heard Miss Sheldon's voice quaver with distress. "Perhaps we should send for Dr. Mackensie again. What do you think?"

Fanny did not hear the colonel's reply, but before she gave in to the blackness pressing in around her, she remembered quite clearly that she had tried to slap him in the carriage. Because he had kissed her again.

Perhaps next time, she told herself dizzily before slipping into the welcoming darkness.

"Do you suppose the lass really meant to jump?" Sir Joshua Comfrey remarked jovially. "Sounds rather havey-cavey to me. Even for a female. Although it would not be the first time a deranged female took such a step, of course."

The rotund baronet sat at his ease in a green leather armchair before the hearth. He had just consumed a hearty dinner of braised duck, roast partridge, and rabbit pie, and was presently on his second glass of Derek's excellent French brandy.

Derek observed his neighbour with a mixture of amusement and impatience. After four years of absence from Sheldon Hall, the colonel had expected to return to find the lifelong friendship between Sir Joshua and his sister finally crystallized into a betrothal. Such had not been the case, although Sir Joshua had been at Sheldon Hall with Margaret to welcome Derek upon his arrival home. The baronet had also stayed to dinner that evening and almost every evening since, consuming even larger quantities of food—or so it appeared to the colonel—than he had four years earlier.

"I certainly thought so at the time," Derek responded, the scene on the cliff that afternoon still vivid in his mind. "The lady chose to deny it, of course, but my impression was that she contemplated putting an end to herself."

"I am sure you are right, Sheldon," the baronet continued, his interest unabated. "You say her name is Wentworth? I knew Sir John and his lady, of course, but was not aware of any daughter."

"Lady Fanny is their niece, I believe," Derek said shortly. He was reluctant to indulge Sir Joshua's penchant for gossip, particularly about the lady upstairs. He had yet to settle in his own mind whether she had indeed been on the brink of death there on that cliff, or whether he had merely wished—for reasons he refused to examine closely—to play the role of Perseus to her Andromeda.

"Niece, you say? Do you suppose it runs in the family? After all, Sir John's elder brother is rumoured to have died mysteriously. Perhaps there is a darker side to the Wentworths' family tree we know nothing about," he added with a salacious smile.

Derek could almost hear the wheels clicking furiously in the baronet's mind. "There is no hint of any scandal that I know of," he said brusquely.

"I shall have to ask the local gossips," Sir Joshua said complacently.

Derek's lips curled in distaste. He had expected his return home to stir up some old talk about Constance, but if Sir Joshua insisted upon prying into Lady Fanny Wentworth's past, the Sheldon name would inevitably be linked with the Wentworths. He must nip this in the bud instantly.

He cleared his throat. "I doubt Lady Fanny would relish having her name bandied about Town, Sir Joshua. I trust you will reconsider before embarking on a course that is sure to cause harm to an innocent female."

The baronet gaped at him in surprise. "Never thought of it in that light, old man. You are right, of course. Would not wish to harm a lady. No, sir. Joshua Comfrey is a gentleman. Count on me, Sheldon." He paused to quaff another mouthful of brandy. "By the way, when do I meet this paragon?"

The colonel repressed a shudder. He could see nothing but disaster stemming from an encounter between his jovial but inquisitive neighbour and the outspoken Lady Fanny. On the other hand, her ladyship was more than a match for the baronet, and Sir Joshua might well benefit from a few of her caustic remarks. If they managed to pierce his thick hide.

"I daresay her ladyship will be up and about by the end of the week," he replied with deliberate vagueness. "If you care to dine with us on Saturday next, you can make her acquaintance."

"Saturday next?" the baronet repeated, obviously bewildered. "That is *five days* from now. Margaret is accustomed to seeing me here every day, I must tell you, old man. And since when have I needed an invitation to dine at Sheldon Hall?"

The colonel drew himself up to his full height and glared down at his guest. "I beg your pardon, sir?" he said frostily. Margaret had evidently allowed this fool to run loose at the Hall during his absence, and the baronet would never come up to scratch if he could enjoy his meals and her company without putting himself out or spending his own blunt. Derek had returned from Lisbon to find the baronet entrenched at the Hall as though he were master here. It was high time he learned differently.

Sir Joshua's already florid face took on a deeper shade of red. "I am here at our dear Margaret's invitation," he blustered, his chest swelling alarmingly beneath the green embroidered frogs on his waistcoat, causing those garish amphibians to appear ready to leap off the velvet background.

"Then next Saturday you will be here at *my* invitation, Comfrey. Unless, of course, you have a prior engagement," he added.

Before Sir Joshua had a chance to respond, Margaret swept into the room, looking more flustered than usual.

"Her ladyship is awake again," she announced in an agitated voice. "I swear, Derek, neither Mrs. Collins nor I can get her to swallow a spoonful of Cook's chicken soup. She is demanding roast partridge, which of course she cannot have. I am at my wit's end, I can tell you."

"Do not fret yourself over her ladyship, Margaret," the colonel said soothingly. "If she will not eat soup, she will have to go hungry. Would you not agree, Comfrey?"

Sir Joshua had risen upon Miss Sheldon's entrance, a courtesy he often omitted, the colonel had noticed with disapproval.

"You are not leaving yet, are you, Sir Joshua?" Margaret said before Derek could hint her off. "I thought we might enjoy a hand or two of draughts. You had promised me a rematch from last night, remember?"

"Most kind of you, Margaret," the baronet said rather stiffly. "But I fear that will have to wait until Saturday." He glanced accusingly at the colonel.

"Saturday?" Margaret sounded nonplussed. She looked from one gentleman to the other questioningly. "Why Saturday?"

"I have invited Sir Joshua to dine with us on Saturday," Derek announced briefly, staring hard at his sister. "He is anxious to make the acquaintance of our guest, and Lady Fanny should be fully recovered by then. That will call for a celebration. We might include Lord and Lady Marker, the Palmers, perhaps the Beechams if they are in Town, and of course I presume Lady Wentworth will already be here."

There was an awkward pause, during which the colonel stared encouragingly at his sister, willing her to make the correct response. He sighed in relief when she took a gracious leave of Sir Joshua and rang for Collins to escort him out.

No sooner had the door closed behind the baronet's bulky figure than she swung around and faced him, a frown on her normally passive face. "Whatever have you done to Sir Joshua? I have rarely seen him so put out."

The colonel flicked an imaginary speck of dust from his elegant dark blue coat. "I merely wished to remind Comfrey that he does not live at Sheldon Hall, my dear. And that good manners demand that he wait for an invitation before appearing on our doorstep as he has done every afternoon since my return."

"But he *has* my invitation, Derek," Margaret protested, as he had known she would. "He enjoys our company, as you must know. He is lonely over at Cedar Lodge, Sir Joshua has told me so many times."

"The solution to that is simple," Derek retorted ruthlessly. "All he has to do is offer for you, my dear—which he should have done years ago, I might add—and remove you to Cedar Hall as his wife. Presto! No more loneliness. You should have suggested it to him, Margaret."

Miss Sheldon gasped and blushed. "You know I would never do anything so brazen, Derek. You are embarrassing me."

"Am I correct in assuming you would still welcome a declaration, Margaret?" the colonel asked more gently.

His sister's blush deepened and she averted her eyes modestly. "Yes, Derek, I would," she murmured so softly, he had to strain to catch her words.

"Then I shall take it upon myself to suggest it to him, love. It is past the time for dilly-dallying about on the subject."

"Please do not say anything to Sir Joshua, Derek. How very mortifying for me. I could not bear it."

The colonel took pity on her. "If Comfrey is deprived of your sweet company now and then, and has nobody to amuse him in the evening with his favourite game of cards—which he is always allowed to win, do not think I have not noticed, my dear—and if he is forced to dine at home six evenings out of seven, I warrant you will have an offer out of him before the month is out."

His sister collapsed into a chair, very close to tears. "You must not tease me so, Derek. Are you suggesting that Sir Joshua visits us to eat our food and play cards! I do not believe a word of it." She pulled a scrap of lace from her pocket and blew her nose. "And Derek, I do not wish you to introduce Sir Joshua to Lady Fanny. Luckily, she will be long gone from Sheldon Hall by Saturday."

"It would not surprise me if she were to leave tomorrow," Derek replied, "despite the doctor's orders. And if you are worried about your Lothario developing a *tendre* for the lady, you may rest easy, love. Comfrey is not her style at all. On the other hand," he paused, and a rueful grin softened his harsh features, "should Lady Fanny take a fancy to him—unlikely as this may seem—there would be nothing you or I, or even poor Comfrey himself could do about it. I have it on the best authority that Lady Fanny always gets what she wants."

Margaret rose abruptly to her feet. "In that case, Derek, the sooner we can convince her ladyship that she is well enough to go home, the better it will be for all of us."

The colonel stood before the fire for some time after his sister left him pondering her enigmatic words. At first he thought this uncharacteristic outburst was due to incipient jealousy on Margaret's part. The more he turned her words over in his head, however, the clearer it became that she might have meant to include him.

Rather than alarm him, the notion of Lady Fanny throwing out lures to him—which naturally she would never do if Captain Mansford's predictions were true—was not entirely unpleasant. And by the time he blew out his candle and turned over in his feather bed, Derek had thought up several ways he could depress that unsolicited attraction.

Or encourage it, he found himself fantasizing just before sleep overtook him.

CHAPTER 9

The Past Catches Up

Fanny woke to find the fire burning low, and Mrs. Collins snoring gently in an easy chair beside the hearth. She was hot, thirsty, and in a cantankerous mood. She could hear the gilt ormolu clock ticking on the mantel, but as before, she had no idea of the time.

She groped for the glass of lemon water, but her fingers were so unsteady that it slipped from her grasp and fell to the floor, spilling the liquid on the green Axminster carpet. Mrs. Collins continued to snore peacefully.

"Oh, bother!" she exclaimed peevishly. Where was Aunt Clarissa? She should be here, as she always was when Fanny contracted any ailment that required her to stay in bed. She hated being confined like this, she thought, kicking fruitlessly at the covers. It smacked of weakness, and she needed to be strong, to feel in control of her life, not like that pathetic Sheldon female, who dared not draw a breath unless her precious brother said she might.

No, she thought, her head thrashing weakly from side to side to escape the heat of the feather pillow, she was being unfair. Living as she did under the thumb of that despotic brother of hers, poor Miss Sheldon could scarcely have developed into anything but the mousy creature she was. Perhaps even she, Lady Fanny St. Ives, would have suffered a similar fate had she been afflicted with a top-lofty prig for a brother.

As it was, her rambunctious brothers had encouraged her to indulge in the most unladylike adventures. She had, Fanny thought ruefully, been wild to a fault. Had she been more like the perfectly behaved Miss Sheldon, she might have made a more dutiful, less demanding wife. She might have accepted her husband's cool civility as the price of a brilliant, arranged marriage. She might still be a duchess.

The notion filled her with distress and increased her discomfort. She was burning up, and her head throbbed as though half of Wellington's army were marching through it. That her tormentor, the man to blame for her present misfortune, was probably sleeping peacefully somewhere close by, congratulating himself on plucking her off the edge of that cliff, increased her sense of impotence. Fanny felt like shrieking her frustration, but all she could muster was a weak moan.

It was loud enough to rouse Mrs. Collins, who came over to the bed and poured a fresh glass of water, holding it to Fanny's lips while she drank greedily.

"I am so hot," Fanny protested, pushing ineffectually at the covers. "Summon my aunt, Mrs. Collins. Quickly."

"Your ladyship's aunt is not here yet, milady," the housekeeper informed her. "Lady Wentworth sent word that she will come early tomorrow to nurse you back to health." She pulled the bedclothes up to Fanny's chin again and tucked them in. "You must not throw off the covers, mi-lady. The doctor ordered you to keep warm. We cannot have you coming down with pneumonia, now, can we, milady?"

Fanny pushed the covers off impatiently and tried to sit up. "I am too warm. Burning up. I want my mother," she moaned, slipping easily into the pattern of her childhood. "And Freddy. Where is Freddy?"

Too weak to get out of bed, Fanny fell back against the pillows, phantoms from her past crowding round her bed again as they had on that dreadful day of her disgrace. She moaned in anguish and took refuge in unconsciousness.

The colonel's sleep was disturbed by the muffled sounds of voices in the hall outside his room. Unable to go back to sleep, he put on his dressing gown and opened the door in time to catch a flustered Mrs. Collins scurrying down the hall in the direction of Lady Fanny's room.

"What is the commotion about, Mrs. Collins?" he demanded.

"Her ladyship took a turn for the worse, Colonel," the housekeeper replied, bobbing a curtsy. "Started hallucinating, she did, demanding her horse in one breath, and then crying out to someone not to hurt her. The fever is worse, sir, and Miss Margaret is with her now."

At that moment, Margaret appeared in the doorway of their guest's room. "Ah, I am glad you are up, Derek," she said distractedly. "Did you get the fresh lemon water, Mrs. Collins? Do come in quickly."

Derek strode towards his sister. "Let me see," he said brusquely.

Margaret gasped and stepped out to intercept him before he could glance into the sick room. "You cannot come in here, Derek. It is highly improper, and besides, her ladyship is not presentable."

Not for the first time since his return from Lisbon, the colonel experienced a surge of impatience at his sister's excessive punctiliousness. Had she always been this prudish, or was he only now becoming aware of it? Margaret had always seemed to him the ideal of womanhood, self-effacing, obedient, docile, and unobtrusive. She was a gracious hostess and, unlike his late wife, deferred to him in everything. Rarely had he cause to complain until now, when those very qualities he had admired in his sister seemed to put his back up.

He stared down into her anxious face, and felt a stab of guilt at his inexplicable urge to shake her. "We are not in the damned drawing room, Margaret. I must determine if she is ill enough to warrant sending for Dr. Mackensie in the middle of the night."

"It is hardly the middle of the night, dear," he heard Margaret murmur, but he pushed past her and stood in the threshold of the sick room.

Derek's senses somersaulted as he stared at the woman in the bed. He had not expected her to look so small and helpless. The woman lying there so passively, her silvery gold hair spread in shining disarray across the silk pillow, seemed so vulnerable his arms ached to gather her against his chest and assure her that he would make everything right again. Hastily he suppressed those uncharacteristic impulses and addressed himself to his housekeeper, who bent over the bed, bathing the patient's face with a cloth dipped in lemon water.

"Mrs. Collins," he said brusquely, "see that a message is dispatched to Dr. Mackensie immediately. And send up one of the housemaids to assist your mistress."

Lady Fanny moaned softly as soon as the housekeeper ceased her ministrations, and the sound cut into the colonel's heart. He gestured to his sister to take the housekeeper's place.

"Poor thing," she murmured, rinsing out the cloth and reapplying it to Lady Fanny's face. "The fever seems to be worse. When Mrs. Collins came to wake me, her ladyship was calling out for her horse to be brought round. She appeared to think she could ride home in her condition, which is patently absurd. Then she cried out to someone called Edward not to hurt her. She seemed to be reliving a painful experience in her past with this Edward. Do you know who he is, Derek? A jilted lover, perhaps?"

The mere suggestion that Lady Fanny might have had lovers in her past, jilted or otherwise, incensed him. "What rubbish are you blathering about, Margaret? And what do you know about lovers? Only what you read in those vastly overrated novels from the circulating library, I trust. I will thank you to put such immodest thoughts out of your head, dear. It is not seemly for an unmarried female to discuss such things."

"I do wish you would not keep reminding me that I am single," his sister retorted with more sharpness than was her wont.

Derek stared at her in surprise. "But you *are* single, Margaret." It was not like Margaret to be skittish about her unwed state. Privately, Derek vowed to take more decisive measures to see his only sister safely wed, even if it meant removing to London for the Season, a prospect that made him shudder.

These unpleasant thoughts were interrupted by the invalid, who suddenly sat up in bed and let out a pathetic cry. "No m-more, Edward, I b-beg of you. You misjudge me. I have d-done nothing, nothing, I tell you." She reached out a hand in supplication, and it was all Derek could do to stop himself from grasping it in his. "Papa, *please* help me. He will k-kill me . . ." Her voice dropped so low that Derek was no longer able to hear the rest of Lady Fanny's pathetic plea. The tears that streamed silently down her cheeks, however, told their own story louder than words.

"Oh, Derek, you should not be here," Margaret wailed as she pressed Lady Fanny back into bed, quickly pulled the covers up, and wiped her wet cheeks. "What if Lady Fanny should come to her senses and find you in her chamber? What will Mrs. Collins think?"

Derek cared little for what anyone else thought. His senses were entirely captivated by the beautiful woman in the bed. And she was beautiful, regardless of what Margaret had said. The intimate disarray of her long hair curling on the pillow, and the glimpse of her pale neck escaping in an elegant curve from her night-rail played havoc with his self control. He felt a spiral of desire threaten to undo him.

Turning away abruptly, Derek retreated. "I shall await the good doctor in the library downstairs, Margaret," he said stiffly over his shoulder.

He could not have said afterwards how he arrived safely in the front hall below. All the colonel knew was that he had to get Lady Fanny out of his house soon if he hoped to regain his peace of mind.

When Lady Fanny next regained consciousness, the first thing she saw was her pet monkey snuggled on the bed beside her. The second was the anxious face of her beloved aunt bending over her.

"Aunt Clarissa," she said, in a wispy voice that sounded nothing like her own, "how I have missed you." She reached out and felt a wave of relief when Lady Wentworth grasped her hand firmly in both her own. "I needed you so much. And I am so glad you brought Devi to cheer me up."

Her aunt's smile wavered, and her blue eyes filled with tears. "My darling Fanny, you cannot guess how relieved I am to see you so much improved. I have been at my wit's end ever since I learned you had been taken sick here at Sheldon Hall."

Fanny stared at her. "Sheldon Hall? Why am I still at Sheldon Hall? I want to go *home,* Aunt. Please take me home." Her voice trailed off in a plaintive wail that she was sure could not have come from her mouth. She heartily despised females who whined.

"There, there, dearest," her aunt responded, gently stroking Fanny's tangled hair. "And so I shall, Fanny my love, all in good time. The colonel says that you may be strong enough to go home tomorrow. He has kindly offered us his carriage—"

"The devil fly away with the colonel and his odious carriage," Fanny burst out weakly. "Have we not a carriage of our own that we must needs use his?" She had raised herself during this outburst, and now sank back into the pillows, staring accusingly at her aunt. Abruptly the rest of her aunt's words sank in, and Fanny reared up again, eyes snapping.

"So? Do I hear you correctly, Aunt? Did you say that the colonel has taken it upon himself to dictate my actions? I will not hear of it. Who does he think he is?" she sputtered weakly. "I ceased taking orders from gentlemen ten years ago, Aunt. Surely you remember that?" She paused and gasped for breath, fighting a wave of dizziness.

Her aunt gently pushed her back against the pillows, holding a glass of water to her lips. "If you continue to exert yourself, dear," she said reasonably, "you will have a relapse, and we will be here till Michaelmas."

The prospect of becoming a permanent house guest at Sheldon Hall was intolerable. Fanny had to acknowledge that her aunt might be right; she must remain calm if she were to convince her doting relative that she was well enough to leave.

"I am the best judge of my own health, Aunt," she said evenly. "And I know I am well enough to leave this very afternoon. Pay no attention to the colonel, dear, and send for our carriage."

Before Lady Wentworth could reply, there was a tap on the door and Yvette entered, bearing a tray with a steaming bowl of soup. "Word has it in the kitchen that your ladyship is feeling more herself," the abigail said, placing the tray on the dresser. "And it is thankful we all are to have you back with us after so long, milady."

"Yvette?" Fanny said, startled. "Whatever are you doing here?"

"I brought Yvette with me to help nurse you, dear," her aunt responded. "I could not be sure the Sheldons had provided you with a personal maid. Now, would you drink a little of this soup Cook prepared specially for you when she heard you were awake again?"

"What do you mean, awake *again*?" Fanny demanded, ignoring the soup. "Just how long have I slept, Aunt?"

"Why, you have been in and out of consciousness for the three days I have been here, my dear Fanny. The colonel has had the doctor in to see you every day, although I assured him you were as strong as a horse—"

"Three *days*?" Her voice rose shrilly. "Do you mean to tell me I have been here for three days?"

"Four actually," her aunt said calmly, "if you count the afternoon the colonel found you on the cliffs and brought you here, dear."

"Found me?" Fanny repeated, her temper rising. "Is that what the rogue said? Well, let me tell you, Aunt, I was not lost. That oaf brought me here against my will. I wanted to ride home to Primrose Court, but he would not hear of it. He threw me into his carriage and insisted that he had saved me from jumping over the cliff. I cannot imagine where he got such a totty-headed notion."

"And a good thing he did," Lady Wentworth said sharply. "Really, Fanny, I gave you credit for more common sense. Only a ninny would ride out so far on a rainy afternoon."

"I merely wanted to visit the site where Mama died."

"I know why you went there, Fanny," her aunt said gently, "but I do think you might have chosen a milder day."

"Who sent those lovely flowers?" Fanny asked, noticing the large bouquet of yellow roses for the first time. "My favourites, too."

Lady Wentworth's expression became apprehensive. "You owe that courtesy to an old friend from the past, dear. Viscount Penryn has driven out here every afternoon to enquire after your health—"

"Gerald has been *here*?" Fanny interrupted quickly. "What impertinence the man has. I trust you have not received him, Aunt."

Her aunt looked uncomfortable. "I would not have done so, Fanny, but he was with another gentleman. She smiled tentatively. "One I felt certain you would be not wish me to snub."

"I can think of no gentlemen from my past who would merit the slightest interest, Aunt," she said frostily. A tender heart was one of her aunt's most endearing qualities, but it also occasionally clouded her judgement. "Besides, anyone who frequents the company of that scoundrel has little to recommend him."

"Even your brother Freddy, my dear?" her aunt said gently.

"Freddy!" Fanny exclaimed in surprise. "Are you telling me that Freddy is in Brighton, Aunt?"

"He must be racked up at the White Hart with Penryn, dear, because they have called three days in a row to leave a profusion of flowers and notes." Lady Wentworth gestured towards the low table where the bowl of roses stood. "They are all there, my love, if you care to read them."

"You may burn Gerald's, if you please, Aunt. I have no desire to hear any more of his lies. But Freddy? It is so unlike my brother to write missives of any kind. He was never one for the books, you remember? I lost count of the times he begged me to do his lessons for him, and like a fool I was happy to spend hours pouring over those old tomes of Greek and Latin in Papa's library . . ."

Her voice trailed off as her thoughts drifted back to happier times. "I fear his presence will stir up memories I have tried so hard to forget, Aunt. I want that door to remain closed forever," she added fiercely.

In spite of this resolution, Fanny could not prevent her gaze from lingering on the folded pieces of paper on the table. "On the other hand," she said, promptly contradicting herself, "it might be amusing to see if Freddy's calligraphy has improved with age, and whether his spelling is any closer to normal than it was ten years ago."

When her aunt placed her brother's notes in her hands, Fanny held them close to her heart for a moment, wondering if they would help to heal her wounds or pour salt into them.

Gingerly she opened the first one. The familiar scrawl brought a lump to her throat. Her brother had not changed at all. He was in a bit of a pickle, he wrote, and having learned from Gerald that she was back in England, had rushed to Brighton to seek her help. This had been scratched out and replaced by advice, which made Fanny smile. If her memory served her correctly, that help would entail a substantial loan, another of the many he had never repaid. He hoped that when he next called on her, he would not be turned away like a common tradesman. He looked forward to embracing his dearest sister again, and trusted that she was feeling more the thing.

"How like my careless Freddy," she murmured, refolding the paper, and handing all three back to her aunt. "At least he did remember to ask about my health, Aunt, which is perhaps an improvement. But his first concern is getting himself out of one of his scrapes, and he counts on me to bail him out."

She sighed and felt a tear slip down her cheek. "How can men be so heartless, Aunt? Has he forgotten that he betrayed me with the rest them ten years ago? And now he expects me to . . ."

"Hush, dear," Lady Wentworth said softly, fluffing the pillows and straightening the covers. "And never mind what Freddy expects. He has done very nicely without your help for this long. Let him continue to do so, Fanny. You must consider your own happiness now. It is past time for you to choose a husband and give me some grandnieces and nephews, my love."

"I know of no gentleman I would trust with my life, Aunt, so let us say no more on that subject. Yvette," she added, turning to the abigail hovering in the background, "I think I am ready for that soup now."

CHAPTER 10

Surfeit of Suitors

Colonel Sheldon found himself in a quandary that mild April afternoon as he strode down to the stables, an excited Charlotte skipping beside him. He made a point of riding with his daughter every afternoon, but for the past four days it had been difficult to coax her away from Lady Fanny's bedside. Even then she did nothing but chatter on about their guest and her infamous monkey, installed at Sheldon Hall to cheer up the invalid, according to Lady Wentworth.

He listened absentmindedly as his daughter recounted one of the monkey's latest tricks, but his thoughts were on the two gentlemen who had called at the Hall every afternoon that week, leaving enormous bouquets of yellow roses and endless notes addressed to Lady Fanny which, Collins had confided to him, the lady promptly consigned to the fire.

Since he had plucked Lady Fanny from the edge of the cliff and brought her back to Sheldon Hall as his unwilling house guest, Derek had received nothing but annoyance. That act of chivalry had been a serious mistake. He had ruined a perfectly good pair of Hessians, his coachman had contracted a cold on the chest, and one of the carriage horses had developed a limp. And now his home was being invaded by all manner of visitors, one of whom bore the despised name of his worst enemy. Derek was at a loss to understand the connection between the easygoing, gregarious Hon. Frederick St. Ives and his contentious guest. He could only assume that, like his friend Lord Penryn, St. Ives was another hopeful suitor for the wealthy Lady Fanny Wentworth's hand. Derek told himself he cared little which of these persistent gentlemen won the lady, but was perversely gratified when Lady Fanny had refused to receive either of them.

The colonel heartily wished them all in Jericho, particularly Lady Fanny, whose initial haughty indifference towards him seemed to have developed into an active distaste. He particularly resented her finding fault with his treatment of her in that blunt, unladylike fashion he had come to expect of her. Except for the rare occasions when his cousins invaded Sheldon Hall during the Christmas Season, the colonel was unused to having his peace cut up by houseguests.

He spent far too many of his waking hours thinking of Lady Fanny. He hated to admit it, but when he was not berating her for upsetting his household, Derek often felt strangely elated by her presence under his roof. His daughter was partially responsible, of course. Charlotte had been delighted to learn that the exotic Lady Fanny was to be their guest for a few days, as well as that detestable monkey.

Sometime later the pair rode into the stable yard to find a stable lad rubbing down a lathered mount under the censorious gaze of Jenkins, the head groom.

"In my day, we had more respect for a good 'orse, we did, sir," the old groom remarked morosely. "Like as not, this poor beast has been foundered. That rider deserves to be flogged, and no mistake."

The colonel examined the big-boned chestnut that stood in the yard, head hanging dejectedly. Its legs and belly were spattered with mud, and its flanks still quivered from exhaustion. He nodded in agreement.

"Do what you can with the animal, Jenkins. It does not belong to one of our dandies from Brighton, I gather?"

"Oh, no, Colonel. Those two gents arrive in a curricle, they do. A fancy contraption with yellow wheels and a flashy pair of bays 'itched to it. They left more'n a 'alf hour ago," Jenkins added, throwing his master a knowing look. "Brought the same yeller flowers they always do. For her ladyship, no doubt. I reckon the lady must be particularly fond of them. Only yesterday, old Thomas was saying 'e 'ad better put in more rosebushes this year to keep 'er ladyship 'appy." This last comment was accompanied by a sly grin.

Derek frowned. By now his entire household staff, all his tenants, and most of his neighbours were privy to the presence of an unmarried lady and her aunt at Sheldon Hall. Speculation must be rife as to the nature of the colonel's relationship with his guests, and Derek was sure that fully half the neighbourhood had arrived at the wrong conclusion.

The truth was, he told himself firmly, he had no interest in Lady Fanny at all. The continued attendance of two gentlemen callers should have made this abundantly clear. Apparently it had not, and Derek was more rattled than he cared to admit that his own gardener had presumed to take Lady Fanny's taste into account in planning his spring plantings. He must put a stop to this nonsense immediately.

"Thomas has said nothing to me on the subject," he said nonchalantly, "and in any case, his efforts would be wasted, since Lady Fanny Wentworth is anxious to return to Brighton with her aunt as soon as she is able. It appears that Sheldon Hall is not to her taste."

Neither am I, he added to himself as he strolled up to the house, an impatient Charlotte in tow. Derek had little illusion that he had squashed the speculation of a romantic liaison between him and his guest, but at least he could put his foot down on the subject of yellow roses cluttering his garden.

When he reached the house, Charlotte dashed upstairs, and Derek wondered how Lady Fanny's departure would affect his daughter.

"Colonel," a flustered Collins accosted him on the way to the library, "an urgent message has arrived for her ladyship, which in your absence I have presumed to send upstairs. I trust I did the right thing, sir."

"I am sure you did, Collins," Derek said soothingly. "Have you any idea what the emergency is about?"

"The messenger is a groom employed by a Mr. Johnathan Cunningham in Portsmouth, sir. I gather that this Cunningham fellow is Lady Fanny Wentworth's man of business." Derek watched in amusement as his butler's nose rose perceptibly at the mention of his guest's connection to Trade. "It appears there has been an accident with one of her ladyship's frigates in some foreign port or other."

"Not the *Fortune Hunter*, I trust?" the colonel demanded abruptly. The thought of any misfortune happening to Captain Jack Mansford, caused Derek no little concern. The colonel had come to think of the captain as a friend, even going so far as to invite Jack to Sheldon Hall for some pheasant hunting.

"The lad did not say, sir, but he was in a real pucker to deliver the message to her ladyship. A matter of life or death, I believe he expressed it."

Derek frowned. "How did her ladyship respond? Did she perchance send for her horse to be brought round?"

"Aye, sir, that she did," the butler responded, his lips pursed in disapproval. "I informed her ladyship that no horse would be sent up from the stables except on your express orders, Colonel."

"And she threw a tantrum, I imagine?" he murmured, visions of Lady Fanny in a rage flashing before his eyes.

Collins coughed discreetly. "Well, she was not pleased, sir. Threatened to saddle the horse herself, she did, sir."

"Is her ladyship up yet, Collins?"

"According to that saucy abigail of hers, her ladyship is dressed for riding."

The colonel snorted in disgust. "Then she will have to get undressed again, will she not, Collins?" he said without thinking. His butler's startled expression recalled him to his senses, and he thrust all thoughts of undressing Lady Fanny from his mind. "Her ladyship is not to be allowed out of this house until Dr. Mackensie gives his approval."

"Very well, sir," Collins replied stiffly. "I shall inform her ladyship of your orders."

"On second thought," Derek added, "I shall inform her myself, Collins." He turned toward the stairs but another discreet cough from his butler detained him.

"There is another matter, sir," he said apologetically.

"Well?" Derek said, when the butler hesitated.

"It's that monkey, Colonel. This morning it snatched the upstairs maid's cap and ran down into the formal drawing room with it. Then it broke one of your mother's Dutch figurines," he added nervously. "We could not catch the beast, Colonel. It climbed up the curtains and shredded poor Betsy's cap until there was nothing left of it."

Unaccustomed to hearing long perorations from his sedate butler, the colonel realized that Collins was truly rattled.

"I am sorry about that vase, Colonel. I know how much her ladyship, your mother, treasured it."

The old butler seemed so genuinely distraught that Derek refrained from telling him that those Dutch figurines had offended him since the day his father had brought them back from one of his trips abroad.

"Do not refine too much upon it, Collins," he said kindly. "Accidents happen, and I know my mother would understand were she still with us. I shall tell her ladyship that the monkey must go."

As Derek mounted the marble staircase, his thoughts were not on the monkey, nor on the broken vase, nor, indeed, on the housemaid's mutilated cap. He was relishing his forthcoming encounter with his cantankerous house guest, and savouring the opportunity of laying down the law. After all, this was his house, and she would obey his orders whether she liked it or not.

Derek had a sneaking suspicion that Lady Fanny would not bend easily to his will, and the thought of the upcoming battle of wills caused him to feel ten years younger.

Lady Fanny was not surprised to learn from Yvette that Colonel Sheldon was at the door of the sitting room demanding a word with her. She was fairly sure she knew what this *word* would entail.

"Show him in, Yvette," she said before her aunt could protest. "I have a word or two to say to the colonel myself."

"Please, Fanny," her aunt begged, "do not pick a quarrel with the colonel. He is our host after all, and it is unseemly for you to be at daggers drawn with him every time you meet."

"Is it not unseemly for him to order me around quite as though I were poor Margaret? My brothers never dared to speak to me as that odious creature does to his unfortunate sister."

She had not bothered to lower her voice, and when the colonel stepped into the sitting room, Fanny could tell by his defensive expression that he had heard her last words.

"I am glad to find you in such good spirits, my lady," he said in that dry voice of his that instantly put Fanny's back up.

"How kind of you to concern yourself with my well-being, sir," she replied, traces of sarcasm in her voice. "I would have you know that my spirits are much better than good. I am glad to see you, too, Colonel. Perhaps you will be so kind as to inform those totty-headed servants of yours that when I send for my horse, I expect him to be brought up to the front door without delay."

"Do sit down, Colonel," Lady Wentworth murmured nervously, gesturing vaguely in the direction of a green brocade chair. "I have asked Collins to send up a pot of tea."

Neither of the other two occupants of the room paid her the slightest heed. The colonel ignored the brocade chair, choosing one directly opposite Lady Fanny, and sat down, staring at her so fixedly that Fanny began to wonder at the direction of his thoughts.

"I should warn you, Lady Fanny," he said after a pregnant pause, during which Fanny found herself admiring the rugged angles of his face, "that Dr. Mackensie has yet to pronounce you fit to leave your sickbed, and until he does, I cannot permit you to endanger your health by—"

"Oh, but you do not understand, sir," Fanny interrupted, vaguely disconcerted by the colonel's gaze. "I have received news that the *Fortune Hunter* has been detained in Lisbon, and that Jack has been arrested on suspicion of murder."

"Murder?" The colonel's response was everything she had hoped it would be. Perhaps now he would allow her to ride back to Brighton without any further reference to that stuffy doctor and his old fashioned pronouncements. She was as strong as a horse—always had been. And what if she did tire more easily than before? There was no need for this pompous man to know that.

"Yes, murder," Fanny repeated. "The story I received is that there was a brawl in some tavern—over a woman, no doubt. By the time it was over, an officer of the Guardia Nacionale was dead, and Jack was accused of killing him. Now I trust you will understand why I must leave Sheldon Hall immediately. Another of my ships, the *Peregrine,* arrived in Portsmouth yesterday, and I must make arrangements to send enough funds to purchase Jack's freedom."

"Why did he not set sail and escape from Lisbon?"

"And leave half his cargo behind on the docks? That is not like Jack, Colonel. He must have tried to brazen it out."

"Did the British authorities not intervene in the affair?"

"Yes, they did, I am told, but the Portuguese authorities are being rather sticky about the whole thing because the victim was a Portuguese officer of some note. Now poor Jack is languishing in some dark and dirty dungeon somewhere in Lisbon. I cannot bear to think on it."

The colonel rose abruptly and began to pace around the small room, causing Fanny to be momentarily distracted by the splendid breadth of his shoulders beneath his simple green hunting jacket and the outline of his powerful thighs under his snug buckskin breeches.

Suddenly he paused in front of her, his hands clasped behind his back, a frown on his rugged face. "Am I to understand that you hold Captain Mansford in such high regard that you are prepared to pay an exorbitant sum for his release?" he said bluntly.

Fanny did not hesitate. "Of course, I do. Not only is Jack the best captain in the trade, but he has always been a good friend to me when I needed one most. There is no sum so exorbitant that I will not pay it to bring him home safely."

The colonel stood staring down at her for a moment without speaking. His expression was unfathomable, and Fanny wondered at the sudden bleakness in his grey eyes. She sensed unspoken questions between them, but all he said was, "Mansford is indeed a lucky fellow to have such a steadfast friend."

"I thought he was your friend, too, Colonel," Fanny said briskly. "I trust that now you will understand how imperative it is that I go to Portsmouth immediately. I have been dressed for the ride for over an hour, and I must tell you, sir, I am not accustomed to having my wishes thwarted."

To her amazement, Fanny saw a brief flash of dimples as the colonel smiled, quite as though he was enjoying some private jest at her expense. As if to confirm her words, his eyes dropped to her green velvet riding habit and travelled slowly from hem to neckline, then rose lazily to examine the jaunty little shako she wore on her pale golden head. When their eyes met again, Fanny caught a glimpse of something she had never seen in his gaze before, something to which she hesitated to put a name. It made her suddenly nervous.

"Mansford is indeed a good friend. And because he is, I propose to help you rescue him, my lady," he remarked in that condescending tone Fanny loathed, which implied that females were incapable of acting on their own. "Provided you promise to return to bed and let me take care of things."

This arrogance was not to be tolerated, and Fanny bristled with indignation. "I did not request your help, Colonel," she said in her most quelling accents. "I am perfectly capable of managing my own affairs. If you will be good enough to order my horse to be brought round, I will be gone and trouble you no more."

All she got in return was a condescending male smile without the dimples. "I am sorry to disappoint you, my dear, but you are in no condition to ride out in this weather. In case you had not noticed, it is about to rain."

"You know nothing about my condition, Colonel," she retorted frostily, feeling the heat rise to her cheeks.

He actually laughed at that, as though she had said something too foolish to be taken seriously. "I should remind you, my dear, that I have a six-year-old daughter who is constantly crossing swords with me. I know when I am being bamboozled."

Fanny could not believe her ears. The wretch was implying that she had lied to him. That she had, in fact, stretched the truth a little mattered not a whit. And no amount of endearments—which rattled her more than she would admit—gave this oaf the right to order her about.

To cover her confusion and prove him wrong, Fanny rose abruptly to her feet, then wished she had remained seated. The room appeared to shift beneath her like the deck of the *Fortune Hunter*. She could not afford to fall flat on her face while the colonel was standing there laughing at her. He would have an excuse to keep her in bed for another week.

"Aunt Clarissa," she murmured, wondering why her devoted aunt had not come to her aid. She glanced around the room but that resulted in another bout of dizziness. "Where is my aunt?" She dared not move her head again, but knew she must make a dignified exit if she were to convince this man that she was well enough to leave his house.

"Lady Wentworth has abandoned you," Fanny heard the colonel say in a tone she instantly recognized as dangerously intimate.

Retreat, her mind warned her. Retreat, before she got caught up in a situation like that at the Blue Parrot Inn in Portsmouth. This same man had taken advantage of her weakness then, and would do so again, if she gave him the least encouragement. She saw it in his eyes, as she had seen it then. That dangerous gleam of anticipation, of desire barely restrained, of thinly veiled triumph when a victim appeared within easy reach.

Well, Fanny told herself stoutly, she was *not* a victim. She would march out of here and prove that she was not the weakling Sheldon appeared to think her. Straightening her shoulders, she took a step towards her bedchamber. To her horror, her knees faltered, and she threw up a hand to steady herself. Instantly she felt her fingers encased in a warm grasp. When she tried to tug free, she stumbled, and an arm slipped round her waist to support her.

"Tell me again that you are not trying to bamboozle me, my dear Lady Fanny," a voice murmured close to her ear. "Tell me that you truly believe yourself strong enough to ride all the way to Portsmouth in the rain."

The answer was patently clear, of course, but Fanny would deny it with her dying breath. She tried to stamp her foot in frustration, but the effort only caused her to lose her balance and sway against his chest. The arm about her waist tightened intimately, and she felt her resolve begin to crumble. If she did not break away this instant, there would certainly be a repetition of that improper incident on the dim staircase of the Blue Parrot Inn. She could sense it in her bones, in her befuddled brain, in her wildly beating heart.

Why, then, she wondered, suddenly uneasy at the implications of her inertia, did her limbs refuse to obey her? Could it be that she actually wished him to embrace her? But no, such a notion was absurd. She had disliked this man since the day they met in Calais. Had she not resolved that dilemma after he kissed her at the Blue Parrot? A moment of weakness on her part. Nothing more. And now he had caught her in another moment of weakness. The rogue was a master at the art of stealing kisses from defenceless females. It was his fault, not hers, that she was standing here like some witless ninny, waiting for him to . . .

Fanny jerked her mind out of the treacherous abyss into which it was slipping. "Release me this instant," she said, in a voice she did not recognize as her own.

"Not until you promise me you will return to your bed immediately."

"I promise nothing of the sort," she retorted weakly, unable to summon the outrage she felt at her host's inappropriate behaviour.

"Then I will put you there myself," he said calmly. Before she could guess his intent, Fanny felt herself lifted and carried to her chamber. The door was kicked open, and Fanny heard her aunt gasp and Yvette cry out in shock as the colonel strode into the room and deposited her unceremoniously on the bed.

He stood over her for a long moment, his eyes full of such repressed longing that it was all Fanny could do to keep her arms from reaching out to him. The moment passed, and he turned to Lady Wentworth.

"See to it that this foolish woman is put to bed *now*, and remains there until I say so," he ordered tersely, before striding out of the room without a backward glance.

As her aunt and Yvette removed her riding habit and prepared her for bed, Fanny allowed her imagination to run wild. What might the colonel's actions have been, she wondered daringly, had her aunt and maid not been there to protect her?

The impropriety of his entering her bedchamber at all was dwarfed by the scandal that might have ensued had they been alone. Filled with a sense of malaise and restlessness quite foreign to her, Fanny found herself wishing her aunt and Yvette in Jericho.

CHAPTER 11

Rescue Operation

"I earnestly recommend that you keep to your bed for another two days, my lady," Dr. Mackensie cautioned in a pedantic tone that grated on Fanny's nerves. "You have been seriously ill, and are still dangerously weak. The colonel tells me you were up yesterday, wishing to ride into Brighton. It is a blessing that the colonel had the good sense to prevent you from pursuing such hare-brained starts."

"If I stay in bed much longer," Fanny remarked snappishly, "I shall lose the use of my limbs." She had endured quite enough of this mollycoddling and suspected the doctor of acting on the colonel's orders.

"Now, now, dearest," her aunt fussed at her. "Why must you always exaggerate so?"

"I am already recovered, Aunt," Fanny said shortly, daring the doctor to gainsay her.

"She is a little testy this morning, doctor," her aunt said, turning to regard Mackensie anxiously. "We received some very disturbing news yesterday, and the poor child is at a loss—"

"Balderdash," Fanny exclaimed. "I demand that you allow me to go downstairs this afternoon, doctor, and that you inform the colonel that I am well enough to spend part of the day on my feet. Furthermore, I insist upon being permitted to return home to Brighton no later than Sunday afternoon."

Dr. Mackensie regarded her dubiously. "Well, I suppose a little exercise would do you no harm, my lady. You may certainly spend an hour or two downstairs this afternoon. But as for venturing farther afield, we will have to wait and see."

With this Fanny had to be content. That afternoon Miss Sheldon came to escort her down to the conservatory where Collins had set up the tea-table. Lady Fanny had chosen one of her prettiest afternoon gowns for the occasion, and as she slowly descended the curved marble stairs flanked by her aunt and Miss Sheldon, she began to feel a flicker of her old self again. Her only regret was that Charlotte, who had gone off with Miss Grimes to the village, would not be there to see her.

The glass conservatory allowed an uninterrupted view of the grounds at the back of the house, and Fanny realized with a start that the Sheldon estate was more attractive than she had imagined. Several centennial oaks dotted the Park, spreading their huge branches over the well-tended lawn. Their host awaited them at the far end of the elegant, glass-domed room, staring out at the formal gardens stretching down, on either side of a brick pathway, to a small lake. The view was spectacular, and Fanny could not repress a gasp of pleasure.

At the sound the colonel turned and as their eyes met, Fanny knew that he had seen the delight reflected in her gaze. She made no attempt to hide it and was rewarded with a brief smile.

"You approve of Sheldon Park, I take it, my lady?" His

voice was bland, as though he did not care whether she did or not. But his eyes betrayed him. This man was proud of his home, probably more than he would admit. He had moved towards her, and now stood watching her with an odd expression on his face. In the background Fanny heard her aunt and Margaret settling themselves at the tea-table.

"Yes, I do." She let her gaze stray past the budding roses to the swans floating effortlessly on the surface of the still water. "It is beautiful. So peaceful and inviting.Vastly different from the gardens in India. Those were colourful, of course, flamboyantly so. At dusk the perfume of exotic flowers overwhelmed one, almost like a drug. I found it disconcerting at first, but addictive."

"Do you miss India, then?"

"Oh, yes," she said, her voice soft. "I rediscovered happiness in India. My uncle's house was a place of joy and love. India was the opposite of everything I had left behind in England, and I thrived there. But my heart is in England as is my aunt's. After my uncle died, we felt the need to come back. To come home, to this kind of peace." She gestured at the scene before them.

He said nothing, but Fanny suddenly felt uncomfortable. It was so unlike her to reveal her thoughts to virtual strangers that she blushed, disconcerted at her urge to share them with the colonel. "I seem to be rambling on like some chatterbox. Please forgive me, sir, I have been cooped up too long."

She never knew what he would have replied to that, because Margaret interrupted the intimate moment by demanding that her brother allow their guest to have her tea in peace.

"I was admiring the view," Fanny murmured, accepting a seat on the damask settee beside her aunt. "It is quite beautiful. Would you not agree, Aunt?"

Lady Wentworth agreed. "Indeed, it is, my dear Fanny. But you have yet to see the grotto on the far side of the lake, built by your grandfather, was it not, Margaret?"

"Our great-grandfather," the colonel put in, "after a design by Inigo Jones, or so we were told. In the Greek style, with a shrine to Aphrodite as my grandmother used to call it."

"Our dear mama kept fresh flowers there regularly, although Papa accused her of pagan worship," Margaret remarked with a smile. "It seemed to work though, did it not, Derek? Their match was a happy one. I have always thought it a great pity that Constance did not take up the practice."

"I thought I had forbidden the mention of that name in this house, Margaret."

Miss Sheldon's happy smile faded instantly at the harsh reprimand. "I am so sorry, Derek. I did not mean to . . ." Her voice fell off into embarrassed silence.

"Perhaps you would be kind enough to show me this grotto before I leave, Miss Sheldon," Fanny said brightly into the awkward pause. "I have always admired the Greeks and was an avid reader of their mythology when I was young."

Colonel Sheldon turned to her, his expression relaxing. "I am sure Margaret will be happy to show you the grotto, Lady Fanny," he said coolly. "My sister follows our mother's tradition of leaving flowers for the goddess. Oh, yes, Margaret, I have observed you since my return, my dear, so do not deny it. Perhaps Lady Fanny would like to join you next time. That is if her ladyship aspires to a happy match, which from what I hear is the ambition of most females."

He stood up abruptly, as if to break free of a spell cast by the Greek goddess of love. "Speaking of more serious matters, my lady, I would beg a few moments of your time after tea to discuss the preparations necessary for Captain Mansford's rescue. I shall be in the library."

Lady Fanny opened her mouth to repeat that she did not require his assistance, but thought better of it. She watched him go, then turned to her hostess, a facetious remark on her lips. What she saw on Margaret's face caused her to stay her tongue again.

"Your brother either knows less of female ambitions than he believes, or the females of his acquaintance are dull creatures indeed," she remarked cheerfully. "Personally, I am truly fascinated to learn that you offer flowers to Aphrodite, Miss Sheldon, and I beg you to show me how to do so. Who knows when I might be in need of her superior powers."

So, Fanny thought, passing her cup to her hostess to be refilled, Miss Sheldon had a secret admirer, or one who was taking too long to come up to scratch. Or perhaps her starched-up brother did not approve of his sister's suitor. Something ought to be done to ensure that poor Margaret did not become a confirmed ape-leader. The idea of matchmaker appealed to Fanny, particularly since in solving Margaret's romantic dilemma, Fanny might well disrupt the colonel's plans for his sister.

She leaned towards her hostess, a conspiratorial smile on her lips. "Who is the lucky gentleman, Margaret?"

Colonel Sheldon stood, hands clasped behind him, staring at the tall lime trees bordering the driveway connecting the gatehouse and the main entrance to Sheldon Hall. His great-grandfather had planted those trees, considering them an improvement over the untidy hedge of rhododendrons that his ancestors had allowed to obscure the view of anyone coming up the drive. It was because of his great-grandfather's forethought that the colonel was able to see the bright yellow curricle turn into his gates and bowl smartly up the long driveway.

Derek grimaced in distaste. Had he not made it perfectly clear that these particular callers were not welcome at Sheldon Hall? Margaret had chided him on his surliness only yesterday. Lady Fanny had refused to receive them, which the colonel found oddly gratifying. But the gentlemen continued to call, cluttering the house with roses and innumerable *billet-doux*, which found their way—if Collins was to be believed—into the hearth of the lady's bedchamber, unread.

Matters promised to come to a head this afternoon, he thought, debating whether or not he should warn Lady Fanny of the impending arrival of her two admirers. Part of him wished to save her the annoyance of their company; the other part urged him to accompany the callers to the conservatory himself to confirm the precise relationship between his guest and the assiduous gentlemen from Brighton.

So torn was he between gallantry and curiosity that Derek was vastly relieved when a tap at the door was followed by the entrance of the lady in question. Lady Fanny looked very fetching and the colonel caught himself staring in silent admiration at the expanse of creamy bosom displayed—or so he imagined in a moment of madness—for his enjoyment.

"Colonel?" this vision of loveliness murmured enquiringly, jerking him out of his trance with a faintly raised eyebrow. "You wished to discuss Jack's rescue, I believe?"

The colonel answered on the spur of the moment. "Yes, that is true, unless you prefer to postpone our discussion to receive the two callers now coming up the driveway?" He gestured out of the window.

That was a mistake. Lady Fanny moved across the room to stand beside him, and Derek became acutely aware of her presence. Her perfume, a heady mixture of unfamiliar exotic flowers, more than likely from the Indian gardens she had described so vividly, designed—he was sure of it—expressly to befuddle a man's brain and predispose him to foolishness, reached out seductive tentacles to entrap his senses.

The colonel stared down at the woman beside him. Why was he lusting after a female he did not even like? Was it because this particular female possessed every feminine allure he had ever fantasized about as a young man? Quite aside from the fact that he did not like her, Derek had to admit that Lady Fanny had the ethereal beauty of a Greek goddess. Her profile, as she gazed at the approaching curricle, was flawless, wide brow, delicate nose, delectable mouth that defied a man to maintain his head, small yet determined chin drawing the gaze down the tender column of neck that Derek ached to trace with his finger. To that heavenly bosom.

He felt his palms grow damp.

Derek took a deep breath and forced his eyes away. The exposed mounds awoke memories of his wife, Constance, and of the happiness he had enjoyed before she did the unthinkable. But even during his most happy moments with Constance, he had never been so intimately aware of a woman as he was at this very moment of Lady Fanny Wentworth, a female his every rational instinct warned him to avoid.

"I have no desire to receive either of them," she said, turning to look up at him, a mocking smile on her perfect lips, as though she had read his mind. "May I suggest, Colonel, that you let your sister deal with them. Perhaps a little competition is just what Sir Joshua needs."

The colonel was startled. "What do you know of Sir Joshua?"

"Margaret told me everything," she said. "You must have known she would do so. Secrets are meant to be shared; among women I mean."

"So? Did you share yours, my lady?"

Her smile faded, and she turned away from the window and sat on one of the leather chairs before his desk. "Let us discuss Jack," she said abruptly. "Your sister has begged me to allow you to take charge of his rescue. She assures me that you are particularly efficient at taking charge, which I am inclined to believe. But you must know I cannot agree to that, Colonel. I believe I told you so yesterday."

He allowed himself a small smile. "Yes, you did, my lady," he said. "You also assured me that you were well enough to ride to Portsmouth in the rain. A vastly exaggerated conclusion as it turned out."

"It is you who exaggerate, Colonel," she responded sharply. "I was merely a little dizzy and would have done nicely had you not thrown me on my bed like some . . . some trollop. You behaved insufferably."

"You are right," he admitted, still tingling with the memory of her in his arms. "Perhaps I was somewhat forceful. But my concern was and still is for your welfare, my lady. Now, if you will allow me to explain how I can assist you in—"

"I do not need your assistance, Colonel," Lady Fanny cut in sharply.

"You refuse to listen to my plan for Captain Mansford's release?"

"You are amazingly perspicacious, Colonel," she mocked him, her violet eyes alight with amusement.

The colonel sighed theatrically. "In that case, I shall have no option but to tell Collins to show those two gentlemen

callers into the library when they ask for you, my lady."
He saw the amusement fade from her face, replaced by a
stubborn tightening of the lips.

"Surely you would not be so uncivil, sir," she snapped.
"I do not wish to receive either one of these gentlemen."

"Then hear me out, and we can let Margaret deal with
them."

"No. I will not be blackmailed," Lady Fanny responded,
her expression reminding him of his daughter when she did
not get her way.

He wished there was an easier way to reason with her,
or as with Charlotte, he could command her obedience.
"Very well, my lady, it is your decision."

As if on cue, there was a tap at the door, and Collins
appeared to announce Viscount Penryn and the Hon. Frederick St. Ives.

"Shall I show the gentlemen in here, sir?"

Derek's gaze did not waver from Lady Fanny's face. She
was evidently struggling to control her temper. Finally, she
bowed her head. "Not here, please," she murmured.

After Collins had departed, the colonel moved behind
his desk and picked up a letter he had written earlier.

"As you know, my lady," he began, "I recently returned
from four years in Lisbon. I was attached to the British
troops stationed there under Major-General William Brandon. I still have many friends there, among the ranking
officers in the Portuguese army and government officials.
But I thought it prudent, in such a serious case as Captain
Mansford's, to write directly to General Brandon," he
tapped the letter in his hand, "asking him to use his influence on Jack's behalf."

He paused, hoping that she would not reject his offer out
of hand merely because it came from him. She raised her
head and gazed up at him, her expression unreadable. Had
she realized the advantage of the pressure Brandon could
bring to bear? Or was she thinking up a suitable set-down
for his impertinence at daring to propose a solution for
her dilemma?

"Do you suppose General Brandon would agree to intercede on Jack's behalf?" she asked after a lengthy pause.

"I am sure of it," Derek answered promptly, agreeably

surprised. The lady showed a keen sense of expediency that he could admire.

"If you have the letter ready, I can take it to Lisbon myself," Lady Fanny said, rising to her feet. "I am much obliged to you, Colonel, you have indeed hit upon a way to rescue Jack sooner than I thought possible."

"There is no need to inconvenience yourself, Lady Fanny," he said hastily. "A fellow officer of mine, a Lieutenant Howard, is travelling back to Lisbon next week and would be happy to deliver the letter to General Brandon." He hesitated, half expecting an explosion from the lady at this further meddling in her affairs.

Lady Fanny regarded him steadily, and Derek knew she could not be pleased at the idea of relinquishing all aspects of the rescue operation into his hands. She was a female accustomed to giving orders not following them, and he half expected her to demand her horse be sent up from the stables, a request he would have to deny, setting off another round of bickering between them.

"You appear to have thought of everything," was all she said, her violet eyes opaque as though exhaustion had caught up with her.

"It is my pleasure to be of service, my lady," the colonel replied, cursing himself for sounding so stiff and formal, when he yearned to confess that he would have slain dragons for her. A ridiculous notion in a man his age, of course, but this woman seemed to bring out all his youthful foolishness. He reminded himself again that he abhorred managing females, of which Lady Fanny was most certainly one.

"All that remains is for me to make out a draft for a suitable amount," Lady Fanny murmured, reaching out one slender hand to steady herself on the corner of his desk. "I have not settled on a sum as yet, but I am confident you can also advise me on that, Colonel."

The colonel ignored the veiled sarcasm in her tone; he was more concerned about her obvious weakness. She should be upstairs in bed, he thought, amused that once again he would be instrumental in getting her there. He reached for the bell-pull.

"We can discuss that later, my lady," he said. "Your first

sortie from the sick-room has tired you. I will summon your abigail to help you upstairs to rest."

To his surprise, Lady Fanny made no objection, and it was only after she was gone, leaving a faint trace of exotic perfume in her wake, that the colonel wondered what dark secrets the lady harboured that had chased that mocking smile from her face.

CHAPTER 12

The Grotto

The following afternoon found Fanny and Miss Sheldon strolling through the gardens.

"My brother asked me to assure you that the letter to General Brandon has been forwarded to Lieutenant Howard in Dover early this morning, my lady," Miss Sheldon said after a companionable silence. "In another two weeks, he tells me, at the most three, you should have Captain Mansford safely home again."

Fanny's spirits rose at these glad tidings, tempered only by the thought that she had been obliged once again to bend to her host's judgement. After much argument, Colonel Sheldon had convinced her that General Brandon would be more inclined to accept a couple of barrels of French brandy than any bribe money she might offer.

"I am greatly indebted to your brother for his kindness on my behalf. It was accommodating of him to call upon his own friends to rescue Jack from his latest scrape."

"Gentlemen have their uses, my lady," Margaret murmured, rather self-consciously, Fanny thought. "And Derek is kind and generous to a fault. At least most of the time."

"I imagine he must be a boon to females with little backbone and no brains to speak of," Fanny remarked without thinking. "Of which there are a depressing number out in

Society," she added quickly. "Growing up with four elder brothers, I needed both in order to survive, I can tell you."

"I envy you having so many brothers," Margaret said unexpectedly. "I have often wished we were a larger family. Derek takes his duties so seriously he has little time to talk to me as we used to when we were children."

Fanny sensed the moment was ripe to satisfy her curiosity about the elusive Lady Sheldon. "The loss of your sister-in-law must have affected you both deeply," she murmured encouragingly."

"Constance?" Miss Sheldon's tone was suddenly sharp. "That female was the worst thing that could have happened to my brother," she began, then paused, as if realizing she had said more than was proper. "Let us say that the only good that came out of that union was little Charlotte. I am glad Constance is gone. Derek was besotted with the creature, of course, and I must admit she was gorgeous, the Season's reigning Beauty. But in the end . . ." Her voice faded into silence as they reached the Grecian grotto Fanny had heard so much about.

The structure itself was small, but what it lacked in size it made up in beauty. The white marble columns supporting the roof were elegantly slender, and the steps and floor were of the palest pink marble. The statue of the goddess was of the same pink stone, Fanny noted approvingly, and the rosy blush of her skin seemed alive in the glow of two flickering candles. Two white marble benches with pink velvet cushions invited the visitor to indulge in silent meditation, and Fanny, somewhat out of breath from the walk, sank down on one of them to survey her surroundings. Margaret busied herself in arranging the bouquet of yellow roses that Fanny had contributed from the numerous offerings of her unwelcome visitors.

"I can understand why the females in your family came here to seek help in matters of the heart," Fanny murmured, when her hostess sat down beside her. "The goddess is truly beautiful, and I can well imagine that she listens with pleasure to the requests from the ladies whose ancestor created such a lovely shrine for her."

Margaret smiled shyly, evidently pleased with the compliment. "Our great-grandfather had it built for his young bride, who was a devotee of the classics. They were so immensely happy in their marriage, that the goddess acquired the reputation of granting favours to lovers. Our own mother believed that the presence of the goddess was particularly strong during the days of the full moon."

"And you, Margaret?" Fanny had to ask. She was intrigued that the worship of the ancient Mother Goddess, stifled long ago in Greece by the emergence of the upstart, masculine, Olympian deities, had risen again in a sedate English garden. She stared enthralled at the seductive pink goddess and could have sworn that Aphrodite smiled.

"Oh, I like to think that there is some female force watching over us as we search for happiness," her hostess responded. "I only wish . . ."

"Yes?"

Margaret said nothing for a long moment. "I only wish happiness were not so long in coming."

They sat for several minutes in silence, contemplating the candlelight flickering on the rosy figure of the goddess, giving her the illusion of life and sensuality. Fanny became utterly absorbed by the vision. Margaret's last words kept ringing in her mind, and she knew instinctively that her hostess was thinking of a particular gentleman who seemed in no hurry to come up to scratch.

She searched her own heart to find a suitable candidate worth petitioning the goddess for, but could come up with none, except Colonel Sheldon, whom she dismissed as sadly lacking in romantic possibilities. As far as she was concerned, the yellow roses had been a fruitless offering. Her hostess at least had a gentleman in her sights who might yet be shot down by an arrow from Cupid's bow if his mother so commanded. But what of Lady Fanny Wentworth?

These fanciful meditations were interrupted by the sound of voices approaching the grotto. Gentlemen's voices, Fanny realized, half regretting the intrusion into their feminine seclusion.

She exchanged a glance with Margaret, who shrugged in resignation.

"Gentlemen, going back to my great-grandfather, have always been a little jealous of our connection with the goddess," she said with a smile.

*   *   *

"So, this is where the lasses are hiding, is it, Sheldon?"
Sir Joshua Comfrey boomed out jovially, frightening a flock
of noisy sparrows and a pair of chaffinches that had gathered to beg for crumbs. " 'Tis bored to tears they will be
by now, I wager, and mighty glad to see us, no doubt."
This perspicacious pronouncement was accompanied by a
lusty guffaw that caused Sir Joshua's considerable paunch
to jiggle as if it had a life of its own.

The colonel flinched at his guest's condescending tone.
He followed his talkative neighbour up the steps into the
grotto, marvelling as he always did at the luminosity of
the pink marble statue and the reluctant awe that always
overcame him in the presence of this pagan goddess. He
could understand why the women of his family loved the
shrine. There was a peacefulness here, an otherworldliness
that even he could feel, coupled with a sensuous radiance
from the voluptuous pink figure of the goddess of Love.

Any serenity was now shattered by the blustering voice
of Sir Joshua. "My dear Margaret," he called out, quite as
though he were up in the hills calling for one of his lost
sheep, "Sheldon and I have come to rescue you from this
hocus-pocus that seems to have addled your brains." He
paused in the act of raising Margaret's fingers to his lips as
he noticed Lady Fanny for the first time.

"Aha," he said with such relish that Derek quite expected to hear the baronet smack his lips, "so this is the
elusive nymph who has the whole neighbourhood on its
ears?" He saluted Margaret's fingers perfunctorily, his eyes
glued to the beauty seated beside her.

"Sir Joshua Comfrey, entirely at your service, my dear
lady," he gushed. He would have claimed her fingers, but
Lady Fanny held them tightly clasped in her lap. She inclined her head briefly, her expression frosty.

The colonel lounged against one of the entrance pillars
and regarded the scene with interest. From the frown on
his sister's face Derek guessed that Sir Joshua might well
rue every high-flown compliment he was heaping on Lady
Fanny's head. Would his mild-mannered sister finally put
her foot down with this pusillanimous suitor of hers?

The conversation began to lag when Lady Fanny uttered

not a single word. Her gaze remained fixed on the pink statue of Aphrodite, as though the goddess might release her from Sir Joshua's gushing flattery, none of which was addressed directly to Margaret.

Derek waited for the explosion, but when it came, it was so typically mild that it took him a moment to realize it.

"What brings you to Sheldon Hall, Sir Joshua?" his sister enquired in a deceptively mild voice, putting an abrupt halt to a flowery diatribe comparing Lady Fanny's voice—which Sir Joshua had yet to hear—to the sweet singing of the nightingale in a thicket of climbing roses surrounding the grotto.

"And that is no nightingale, sir," Margaret remarked coolly. "It is merely a blackbird. I am sure there must be dozens of them at Cedar Lodge." Thrown off stride, Sir Joshua gaped at Margaret, his mouth acock, and the colonel was unsure which of his sister's words had rendered the baronet speechless, the challenge to his presence at Sheldon Hall or his ignorance of local birdlife.

The baronet shut his mouth with a snap. "I came over to invite you to ride out with me, Margaret, but naturally Lady Fanny is included in the invitation since it promises to be a warm day. And Charlotte, too, if she is not at her books." He transferred his gaze back to Lady Fanny and was about to continue his fulsome flattery when Margaret again cut him short.

"The gardeners are all saying it will rain again before tea-time. I cannot recommend that either Charlotte or Lady Fanny ride out in the rain. What do you say, brother?" She threw a glance in Derek's direction with a plea in her eyes that he could not ignore. Margaret was either punishing Sir Joshua for fawning over their guest, or she was unwilling to allow him the chance to fill Lady Fanny's ears with his silliness. Quite aside from everything else, Derek knew his sister to be less than enthusiastic about horses, as Sir Joshua was also very well aware. It was a clear indication of the baronet's lack of tact, that he had ridden over instead of bringing his curricle.

The baronet's expression took on a mulish cast. Another sharp glance from Margaret moved Derek to intervene. "No, you are perfectly correct, Margaret. And I know her ladyship will agree that a relapse is the last thing we want. I cannot imagine that she wishes to spend another sennight in bed, much as we are delighted to have her at Sheldon Hall." He shifted his gaze to their house guest and found her eyes fixed upon him, a bemused expression on her face. He wondered if she was remembering, as he was, the afternoon he had returned her unceremoniously to her bed himself.

"But, b-but, my dear Margaret . . ." Sir Joshua spluttered, gesticulating aimlessly, visibly upset at his lady's coolness.

"Not another word, Sir Joshua," Margaret retorted mildly. "I am saddened to think you would place our guest's well-being at risk merely for the sake of an outing on one of those wretched creatures."

"But I d-did not know her ladyship was still indisposed," he protested, glancing from one lady to the other as if to emphasize his innocence of any deliberate slight. Lady Fanny paid him no heed, but returned her gaze to the pink goddess.

"Derek, I believe it is time for you to escort us back to the house," Margaret hinted. "Too much fresh air can be tiring to a recent invalid."

"You are again correct, Margaret. Lady Fanny, permit me." Derek stepped forward, offering his arm.

"I am entirely at your service, my lady," Sir Joshua gushed happily, seizing the opportunity to extend his own arm to Lady Fanny.

For the briefest moment, the party remained frozen as if in some complicated charade: both gentlemen with arms extended, while the ladies exchanged a speaking look that boded no good for the tactless baronet.

Lady Fanny broke the tableau with her usual directness. "I cannot thank you enough for sharing your grotto with me, Miss Sheldon. It has been an uplifting experience, just as you said it would be." She laid a hand on Margaret's arm in silent communication. "I trust you will invite me again."

Without a glance at Sir Joshua, she swept by him, her head tilted regally, and accepted the colonel's arm with a sweet smile that made his heart bounce in his chest.

Vaguely aware that his sister had also ignored Sir Joshua's arm, Derek escorted Lady Fanny down the pink steps, unreasonably elated at the light weight of her fingers on his arm.

"I fail to see what your sister chooses to admire in that country bumpkin," she murmured as they strolled through the stand of aspens towards the lake. "I thought I had met every kind of dolt in the world, but this one takes the cake. Can Margaret be serious about wedding such a blockhead, I wonder?"

"Unfortunately, my sister is infatuated with Sir Joshua. Has been since she was a mere chit. And you know what they say about Cupid's arrows, my lady. They strike at random and without regard for consequences."

"Oh, yes, indeed I do," Lady Fanny murmured, her eyes filled with such sadness that Derek wanted to put his arms about her there in front of everybody and comfort her. With difficulty he restrained this wild impulse, so unlike his usual self that it alarmed him.

"Then Sir Joshua is a lucky man," she continued. "He hardly deserves such a jewel. I cannot say the same about your sister," she added, smiling at him so sweetly that Derek felt she must surely hear his heart pounding. "Although perhaps it is better to wed a doting fool, than a charming rogue."

She sighed, but before the colonel could discover what lay behind this odd remark, Lady Fanny stopped dead in her tracks. "Oh, no," she whispered, half to herself, glancing round as if to find a means of escape from the two figures who had detached themselves from the house and now strolled down the brick path towards the lake. One of them raised an arm when he caught sight of Lady Fanny, and Derek felt her shudder.

Which of his servants had disregarded his order to keep these visitors away from Lady Fanny? he wondered, swearing to wreck vengeance upon that head. Not Collins, he was sure of that. Gently he covered Lady Fanny's hand with his own and found it icy cold. What was it about these two gentlemen that frightened her so?

"Do not worry, my lady," he said, watching the callers increase their pace. "You will be safe with me. I am here

to keep the dragons at bay." He grimaced at his own fanciful choice of words, but Lady Fanny smiled.

"Oh, let them come," she said nonchalantly. "I cannot
escape the past forever."

They stood together, her hand tightly clasping his arm,
watching the advance of the gentlemen Derek had thought
to be Lady Fanny's suitors.

Now he was not so sure.

CHAPTER 13

Poetry Contest

Heartened by the colonel's bracing words, Lady Fanny
smiled up at him, amazed at the genuine concern in
his grey eyes. It was a comfort to have a gentleman to
champion her cause, although she wondered how long the
colonel's support would last if he discovered the scandals
that had rocked her past. She was surprised that neither he
nor his sister had discovered the connection between the
Lady Hayle who had perished on the cliffs ten years ago
and Lady Fanny Wentworth, recently returned from India.
The local gossips must have fresher scandals to occupy
their minds.

Nevertheless, she still felt her heart beat unevenly as the
two well-dressed gentlemen approached. All it would take
to set Brighton tongues awagging would be one careless
word from either of them. It was quite true, as she had just
admitted to the colonel, that she could not expect to shed
her past as though it had never existed, but she wished
these men, who had played such prominent roles in her
disgrace, had remained in Cornwall.

Fanny regarded the gentlemen intently. Her brother
Frederick had changed little with the years; his countenance
was still youthful, although beginning to show signs of de-
bauchery, and his chestnut curls, which had been the envy

of every lady in the neighbourhood, were in perpetual disarray. For a moment her heart warmed to him; remembering how close they had been as children at Hayle Hall. Then she recalled that Freddy had done little to protect her against the wrath of her husband and father. In the end, he had betrayed her as much as Lord Penryn and her other brothers.

Frederick stepped forward, arms eagerly outstretched. "My darling Fanny," he exclaimed in the boisterous voice she remembered all too well. A lump threatened to form in her throat. "What a joy to see you looking so well, my dear," he continued, quite as though the debacle at Cambourne Abbey ten years ago had never happened.

He took her in a bear hug, which Fanny steeled herself not to return. At her evident coolness, Freddy dropped his arms and gazed down at her with a puzzled frown on his handsome face. Had she not known him from childhood, Fanny might have been deceived by this look of contrition. As it was she returned his gaze without a smile.

"Do not tell me you still harbour a grudge, Fanny dearest?" he said in a wheedling tone that she also recognized. Freddy had always been able to talk himself out of scrapes, and he obviously imagined he could do the same now. "I assured Gerald that you never did so, and would be more than willing to let bygones be bygones after all this time. Tell me you have not changed so drastically as to make a liar out of me, Fanny."

Thoroughly disgusted and all too aware of the colonel's presence, Fanny tried to control her anger. "How can you, of all people, talk to me of harbouring grudges, Freddy? What am I supposed to do? Turn the other cheek?" She dared say no more for fear of losing her temper beyond repair, and trusted that her brother would show equal restraint.

Viscount Penryn chose that moment to step up and take her hand, which she gave unwillingly, steeling her heart against the blandishments of the rogue she had once loved to distraction.

He gazed at her a moment, a smile curling the corners of his sensuous mouth. "Fanny, sweetheart," he began caressingly, and Fanny cringed. She had believed this man loved her, and had given her heart as only a sixteen-year-old girl can. That was before he had come to demand her in marriage to another man, a man who could not take the trouble to come himself.

Fanny forced herself to remain impassive under his scrutiny. She could not help wondering if he found her beauty, which he had always praised immoderately, much altered. She fervently hoped so, because she had learned to despise beauty that turned men into fools and deceivers. She wanted no extravagant praise from charming rogues whose every breath was false and every thought self-serving.

"Beautiful as ever, Fanny," he said with practiced charm. "How many broken hearts have you left behind in India, my dear? Not as many as you left here at home, I wager, when you ran off without telling us where you were going. Freddy and I have been worried sick about you, dearest, when we heard you had been taken ill. And since you refused to receive us, we have been reduced to haunting Sheldon Hall in hopes of . . ."

As he spoke, Fanny slowly relaxed. Hearing the same old insincere compliments, Fanny now saw them clearly for what they were. Gerald's charming yet meaningless blandishments may once have turned the head of a romantical young girl, but were little more than annoyances to the Lady Fanny Wentworth of ten years later.

". . . catching a glimpse of our lovely Fanny. We trust that you have not grown too proud to acknowledge old friends from happier times—"

"I have no *old* friends, as you must be fully aware, my lord," she interrupted sharply, her voice rising in anger. "I learned the hard way that whatever friends I imagined I had betrayed me without the least compunction when it suited them. As the principal offender, you will hardly dare to deny it." Impatiently, Fanny pulled her hand free from the viscount's grasp.

Lord Penryn looked nonplussed, but Freddy, never at a loss for words, broke in with a rueful laugh. "I warned you she might fly into a pucker, Gerald," he said lightly, as though humouring a petulant child, raising Fanny's hackles. "Remember how cross Fanny would get when we refused to take her along on our more dangerous escapades, Gerald? Once we escort her back to Primrose Court, she will come around, take my word for it, old man."

"He would be most foolish to take your word for anything, Freddy," Fanny retorted acerbically. "And what makes you believe you will escort me anywhere? I am quite happy here with Margaret and Colonel Sheldon, and do not plan to remove anywhere until I outlive my welcome here." She caught a glimmer of amusement on the colonel's face at this wildly inaccurate statement, and had the grace to blush.

"And that you will never do, my dear Lady Fanny," Miss Sheldon put in at this point, linking her arm companionably through Fanny's and giving her a comforting squeeze. "Is that not so, Derek?"

The colonel, who had remained silent during this exchange, nodded in agreement. "Lady Fanny is welcome to stay at Sheldon Hall as long as she pleases, Margaret, as I am sure she knows."

"Here, here," exclaimed Sir Joshua, who had been standing a little apart, regarding the two gentlemen with keen interest. "I believe we have met, sir," he added suddenly, addressing Freddy. "Only briefly, of course, and your attention was focused on the game of faro you were playing at the time rather than on me. Sir Joshua Comfrey at your service, sir," he added with an elaborate bow directed at both gentlemen.

Freddy turned to look at Sir Joshua, and Fanny fervently hoped he would not make one of his notorious remarks concerning the deplorable manners of yokels. She was relieved when he returned a brief nod.

"Yes, of course, I remember now. You were good enough to warn me that Sir Robert Gardener was not the man to take on at faro if I did not wish to be fleeced." He let out a shout of rueful laughter. "It appears you were on the mark, sir, for I was never trounced so royally in such a short time. Left me without a feather to fly with he did, and that is no lie." He paused for a moment, while Penryn made some flirtatious remark to Miss Sheldon. "Now, had you been with me, Fanny, I know I would have come away with a small fortune." He turned to address the colonel. "You may not know, sir, that Lady Fanny has the devil's own luck when it comes to games of chance. If I had but half her luck, I would be sitting pretty for life."

"It is not luck, Freddy," Fanny protested, "but rather skill based on reason, which is why your pockets are always to let."

"That reminds me, dearest," he added, his expression serious, "did you receive the little missives I sent you?"

Fanny stared at him coldly. Here it comes, she thought dispassionately. Another request for a *small* loan. The more she saw of him, the more she realized that her brother had not changed his profligate ways. To risk playing cards with Sir Robert Gardener was the height of folly. Even Fanny had heard rumours of that gentleman's formidable luck at the tables. But Freddy considered it a challenge to pit his skills, whether at cards, horse racing, dueling, fisticuffs, or such nonsense as balancing marbles on his nose, against all comers. He never heard a wager he would not accept, and Fanny had franked his extravagances for the last time years ago.

"Yes, I did," she responded without enthusiasm. "But they all went into the fire. I have no wish to stir up the past, as you might have known had you given it any thought."

"This has nothing to do with the past, Fanny, I promise you," Frederick said, a hint of anxiety in his voice. "It is all about the present, and I assure you is of the most urgent nature imaginable."

"As I told you," Fanny repeated coldly, "all notes went into the fire."

"You discarded my little verses, Fanny?" Lord Penryn exclaimed in mock horror. "Have you no pity at all, my love? Every word came straight from my heart. What a terrible waste of my little gems. I am quite cast down, Fanny. Can you imagine anything so callous, Miss Sheldon?" he continued, turning a woebegone face to Margaret, "I shall have to address my poems to more receptive ears, I see. Tell me, Miss Sheldon, you would not be so cruel as to burn the outpourings of a gentleman's heart, would you?"

"That would depend upon the poet, my lord, would it not?" a flustered Margaret replied tentatively, throwing a nervous glance at her brother.

"But I can see you are a lover of poetry, are you not, Miss Sheldon?" Penryn cajoled in his honeyed voice. "I can see it written in your eyes." This was said with such feeling that Margaret blushed.

"P-poetry?" Sir Joshua bellowed. "What poppycock! You never told me you liked poetry, Margaret."

"You never asked, Sir Joshua," Margaret pointed out blandly.

"And you have never written any for her, have you now?" Fanny cut in.

"Of course, I have not," Sir Joshua blustered, red in the face. "I am not a blithering idiot, thank you. I have more important things to do than mouth inanities and saccharine phrases, if you must know."

"Ah, but what could be more important than showering praise where praise is due?" Lord Penryn murmured accusingly. "You have been sadly neglected, my dear Miss Sheldon. Tonight I shall pen a sonnet on the beauty of your eyes, my lady. I can hear it already forming in my mind:

> *The starlight in your eyes holds men enthralled,*
> *But little do they know your tender heart*
> *Beats solely for the love that lies installed*
> *And reigns above all others . . .*

He stumbled over the phrase, a frown marring the handsome lines of his face. "Now what rhymes with *heart*, I wonder?" He placed a finger against his forehead and assumed a pensive air, an elaborate pose Fanny had seen often before.

Sir Joshua let out a loud snort of disgust. "The devil fly away with your scribblings, my lord," he stormed. "If Margaret wants a poem to her eyes, she shall have it, but I shall be the one to write it, not you."

Fanny listened to this audacious declaration with amazement. From the little she knew of Sir Joshua Comfrey, she could not imagine him writing a rhyming couplet, much less a sonnet. Evidently Margaret was equally flabbergasted, for she stared at her neighbour with round eyes.

The viscount regarded him with carefully calculated disdain. "My dear Sir Joshua," he said condescendingly, "if you have had no previous practice in penning love poems, 'tis a sorry job you will make of it, no doubt. Miss Sheldon's eyes deserve better, and unless you hold a special place in her affections, I claim the right to address all the poems I wish to her lovely person."

This was clearly a challenge from which Sir Joshua could not back away. He cast so pleading a glance at Margaret that Fanny felt sorry for the poor gentleman. Not only was he outranked by the viscount, but also outclassed in looks, dress, manners, and now the art of words.

Penryn cunningly pushed his advantage. "Miss Sheldon," he enquired softly, recapturing her hand and staring dreamily into her eyes, "has the good Sir Joshua laid claim to your tender heart, my dear? I would not wish to trespass on another man's preserve."

Margaret looked rather nonplussed, but her answer was clear. "No, my lord, he has not done so."

Lord Penryn gave a satisfying laugh while Sir Joshua stared at his hostess as though she had suddenly sprouted two heads. Only the colonel's frown prevented Fanny from giggling.

Freddy was the first to break the silence after Margaret's unexpected admission. "I have it," he cried with malicious glee. "We shall have a poetry writing contest between Penryn and Sir Joshua. He who pens the most feeling lines to Miss Sheldon's beauty will be declared the poet laureate of Brighton. What a lark that will be. We might even place a small wager on the contestants, just to make it interesting. What do you say, Gerald?"

Lord Penryn shrugged his elegant shoulders. "Whatever you say, Freddy," he drawled, a smirk on his face. "Always assuming that Sir Joshua is game, of course."

"And why would I not be game, my lord?" The baronet's florid face showed signs of affront. "Set your time and name your judges."

Fanny felt a surge of admiration for the baronet's show of bravado. He was foolhardy, too, of course, a portly Don Quixote flailing at windmills of words he had no hope of bending to his will; but the gesture moved her. She wished there was something she could do to stave off his ultimate humiliation, but the case of the sonneteering baronet appeared hopeless.

She glanced at the colonel and saw him regarding her as well. "What do you think of this ridiculous wager, Colonel?" she asked. "Is it not foolish beyond reason?"

"All wagers are foolish, my lady," came his calm reply. "But this one more than others, because even poets of renown, like our infamous Byron, cannot be expected to rattle off sonnets at the drop of a hat. Doggerel perhaps, but poetry worthy of the name is more than the mindless counting of words and rhyming of lines."

Fanny stared at her host in astonishment. There were obviously aspects of the colonel's personality than she had not suspected.

"It appears that you are well versed in the intricacies of the craft, Colonel," Lord Penryn remarked with a barely concealed sneer. "I trust you will be willing to act as our judge, sir?"

"Impossible, I am afraid," the colonel replied calmly. "I am not usually a betting man, but I cannot let this occasion pass without venturing a few quid on the outcome."

"A few quid?" Freddy repeated in a startled voice. "Why, that is chicken-stakes, Colonel. I was thinking more in the range of a monkey. I hear you are well able to stand the nonsense."

Enraged at her brother's shyster tactics, Fanny intervened. "And where do you propose to lay hands on five hundred pounds, Freddy? It seems to me that you are already up the River Tick with no prospects of coming about, thanks to Sir Robert Gardener."

"I do not propose to lose this one, my dear Fanny, so stubble it, lass," her brother said rudely. "But tell us, Colonel, which of the contestants will get your blunt?"

"Sir Joshua," the Colonel said shortly.

Fanny sent him a glowing look that she hoped conveyed her appreciation of his support of his friend and neighbour.

At Fanny's insistence, and after some sulking from Freddy, the bets were set at a maximum of five pounds, and the momentous reading set for two days hence in the Sheldon grotto at four o'clock. Lady Clarissa Wentworth, whose love of poetry was well known, would be judge.

Lady Fanny promised to approach her aunt on the subject, although she would have preferred to keep her relative as far away from Freddy as possible, to avoid a possible slip of the tongue from that absentminded lady.

As if aware of the designs being made on her time and expertise, Aunt Clarissa appeared on the terrace and squinted towards the party by the lake with short-sighted eyes.

Fanny saw her chance to escape. "There is my aunt come to remind me that I must rest," she murmured, turning to the colonel, who still stood by her side. "May I impose upon you, sir—" she began, but was interrupted by her brother's anxious voice.

"Fanny, spare me a moment of your time, dearest. I need a word with you—in private."

Fanny ignored him and tucked her hand into the crook of the Colonel's proffered arm.

"Fanny—"

"Not now, Freddy," she murmured, "I confess that I am feeling none too stout. No doubt I have stayed out too long, and my aunt will have something to say about that." She smiled up at the colonel, a silent plea in her eyes.

The colonel responded as she knew he would. "Good afternoon, gentlemen," he said to the two visitors. "And Sir Joshua, I look forward to seeing you in two days' time with poems penned and polished."

As he strolled back to the house with a drooping lady clinging to his arm, the colonel was beset by mixed emotions. On the one hand, he had noticed that the encounter with the two Brighton gentlemen had tired his houseguest beyond what was prudent. Lady Fanny had shown signs of stress from the moment the dandified St. Ives greeted her with an embrace more fitting between close relatives than with gentlemen acquaintances.

On the other hand, Derek had sensed the exact moment Lady Fanny had felt the need to escape from the unwelcome visitors, even before Lady Wentworth's appearance. That Lady Fanny had deliberately used him to effect her escape was not lost on him. But whereas in the normal course of events the colonel would never have allowed himself to be manipulated by a female, beautiful or otherwise, in this case he had actually welcomed Lady Fanny's unexpected dependence upon him.

"Once again, I am much obliged to you, Colonel," she murmured as they trod slowly towards the terrace. "It appears I shall be eternally in your debt."

The poke bonnet she wore prevented him from seeing her eyes, but the tone of her voice was suspiciously meek. What secrets lurked beneath the surface of that beautiful face? Considering that such secrets might well involve the two mysterious gentlemen from Brighton, the colonel was not sure that he wanted to know.

"A slight exaggeration perhaps, my lady," he said. "But in any case, you are more than welcome."

She laughed at this, and the sound of it pleased him inordinately. "I thought it was generous of you to support Sir Joshua in that ridiculous wager, sir. I quite expected you to consign Lord Penryn to the devil for butchering the language. Never did I think you would actually place a wager against him when he went to such pains to prove how excellently he versifies."

"I would never be uncivil to any friend of yours, Lady Fanny," he said, watching her closely.

He saw the amusement fade from her face. "Then you may be as uncivil as you choose, Colonel," she replied, "for he is no friend of mine. Neither gentleman can claim that distinction."

"Then I am amazed that you took an interest in the contest, my lady. Had you shown any displeasure, I would have put a stop to it instantly."

She stopped abruptly and stared up at him. "Was it not apparent to you, sir, how much your sister Margaret enjoyed being the centre of attention? It is not every day that a lady has sonnets written to her eyes, you know. And by an expert, too. Indeed, I cannot remember the last time I endured such a pleasure."

"Are you telling me there are no versifiers in India, then?" he teased.

"Oh, yes, but none worth remembering. False praise is no less false because it is delivered in verse, as I am certain Margaret knows. But to have one's eyes praised in verse has a certain romantic flair not to be despised. However, the chief benefit of this contest will no doubt be to jolt Sir Joshua out of his inexcusable complacency."

"So, the idea is to make poor Sir Joshua jealous?" the colonel remarked. "I cannot say I approve of the plan, my lady. I warn you that my sister has little experience with gentlemen of fashion, and particularly those who are accustomed to dazzling a lady with trivial verse and other wiles."

Lady Fanny laughed softly. "Margaret is in no danger, Colonel, I assure you. I know both these rogues well, and have warned her not to believe a word of their elegant chatter; both are gazetted fortune hunters. Not the kind of husband a decent girl would want by any means."

"You know them well, you say, my lady?"

"We grew up together in Cornwall. The Penryn estate marches with my father's, and at one time I thought—" She paused abruptly, as if realizing she had said too much, then added in a brittle voice, "but that is of little consequence now. You need not fear for your sister, Colonel. For some reason that escapes me, she has her heart set upon Sir Joshua. This poetry contest is just the thing to flush him out into the open."

The Colonel did not share the lady's enthusiasm but held his peace. He did wonder whether Sir Joshua had realized he was being manipulated, and if he had not, if he should be warned what was afoot. Derek sincerely wished to see his sister comfortably settled, but hated to see his friend led down the garden path like a lamb to the slaughter.

CHAPTER 14

Scandalous Secrets

"Come in," Fanny called in answer to the familiar tap on her sitting room door the following morning. She smiled as Margaret entered, followed by Collins with the breakfast tray.

During Fanny's convalescence, Margaret had developed the habit of joining her guests for breakfast in their private sitting room. At first Fanny had considered this an annoying intrusion on her privacy, but as she grew to know her hostess better, she discovered the company of the other young woman rather enjoyable. Her beloved aunt had been her constant companion for so many years that Fanny, an only daughter in a house full of boys, had rarely experienced the simple pleasure of a comfortable coze with a female her own age. Fanny suspected that Margaret enjoyed her company, too.

"I wonder how Sir Joshua is coming along with his sonnet," she remarked, after greeting her hostess warmly. "I shall never forget the look on his face when you told Gerald that Sir Joshua had no claim on your heart."

Margaret's face clouded. "Well, he may imagine he has, but he has yet to say a word on the subject to me. And as for that silly poem, he should not have allowed himself to be teased into accepting Lord Penryn's challenge," she added, handing Fanny her first cup of China brew. "I find the whole idea of a poetry contest rather ridiculous if you want the truth, Fanny."

"Of course, it is, but it is also all the crack for fashionable bucks like those two Town Tulips to indulge in pseudo-literary games." She stifled a giggle. "The notion of poor Sir Joshua perspiring over that sonnet quite doubles me up. Should we offer him some assistance, do you think?"

"That would hardly be fair, would it? Although I would not be surprised if he were to ask you to oversee his efforts, Fanny."

Fanny uttered a snort of disgust. "It was grossly unfair of Lord Penryn to propose so unequal a contest in the first place. Can you imagine your brother agreeing to compete against a rank amateur?"

Margaret laughed. "No, I cannot, of course. Derek is so punctilious about such matters that were he in Lord Penryn's shoes, he would more than likely insist upon some monstrous handicap, such as having one hand tied behind his back or something equally silly. Not that he is any less than a rank amateur himself when it comes to writing verse.

I doubt he has penned a couplet in his entire life, let alone a whole sonnet."

"Not even when he was courting his late wife?" Fanny asked daringly.

Margaret's smile faded, and she refilled her cup before responding. "Now, that I could not say. One never knows what a man in love might do. And Derek was so besotted with Constance. When she died, his heart died with her, and I eventually despaired of seeing a new mistress at Sheldon Hall, especially after he took flight from England so precipitously."

"Your brother's departure from England sounds remarkably like my own," Fanny remarked pensively, "except that I left under such a staggering cloud of unjust accusations that I swore never to return. Yet here I am, and no sooner do I land than I am beset by people from a past I had hoped would be forgiven or at least forgotten." She sighed ruefully and passed her tea-cup to be refilled.

"The *haut monde* forgets nothing, my dear Fanny," Margaret said gently. "Neither does it forgive, as I was saying to my brother only yesterday. Why, in Newhaven last week I was accosted in the street with impertinent questions regarding the *mystery* of Constance's death. There *was* no mystery. What can be mysterious about a carriage accident, can you tell me?"

Fanny professed herself to be at a loss to answer that question, although she did wonder what had given rise to those local rumours.

Margaret must have read her mind, for she added in a somber voice. "The circumstances were unusual in that not only poor Constance, but also the coachman and groom, both died in the accident," she explained, "so there was nobody to tell exactly what happened. The so-called *mystery* was started by farmer Dick Kelly's half-witted lad who was herding his geese along the lane when the Sheldon chaise dashed by. Going *monstrous* fast, as he tells the story. He also insisted he saw a gentleman in the carriage with Lady Sheldon, which is absolute nonsense."

"Perhaps it was the maid he saw," Fanny suggested, intrigued.

"Constance was notorious for travelling about the countryside without her maid. Derek had forbidden her to do so, but Constance paid him no heed. It was quite a sore point with him, and one of the few things they quarreled about. No," she added emphatically, "there was no one in the coach with Constance. Kelly's lad was mistaken."

The possibility that Lady Sheldon might not have been alone in that chaise raised any number of unpleasant questions. But Fanny had had too many of those raised about her own behaviour in the past to condemn the Sheldons' wish to quash the least hint of scandal surrounding Lady Sheldon's death.

"That sounds very likely," she agreed, "particularly if the lad was none too steady in the loft."

Her hostess smiled gratefully, but before she could say more, Collins appeared with a letter for Lady Fanny on his salver.

"The lad from Cedar Lodge is waiting for a reply, my lady," he murmured as he presented the note. "Shall I instruct him to return later?"

Fanny tore open the wafer and spread out the sheet of hastily scribbled writing. After glancing at it, she passed it to Miss Sheldon, who perused it with a smile.

"Just as I told you, Fanny. The poor man is completely at a loss for words. Are you going to help him?"

"Only if you have no objection, Margaret. I think it only fair that I at least hear what Sir Joshua has to say."

With Margaret's approval, Fanny dashed off a note accepting the baronet's frenzied plea to meet him in the grotto that afternoon.

Accompanied by Charlotte, who insisted upon dogging her steps whenever she was not at her lessons with Miss Grimes, Lady Fanny stepped off the terrace soon after nuncheon that afternoon and made her way leisurely down the gentle slope to the lake.

Charlotte had raced ahead, and when Fanny reached the waterside, the little girl was tossing bread crumbs to the six or seven swans who competed, with much splashing and flapping of wings, for the treat. One half-grown cygnet, more aggressive than his companions, had gained the bank and was reaching up his long neck in an attempt to steal the crumbs from Charlotte's fingers. After the last tit-bit was gone, the birds fluffed their plumage and paddled off sedately to the middle of the lake where they sat preening themselves and gazing at their reflections in the water. Fanny envied the tranquillity of their existence.

They traversed the small copse, with Charlotte pointing out the different kinds of birds that made their home there, some of which were unknown to Fanny. As they entered the grotto, a flock of sparrows and several woodpigeons flew out between the slender pillars, but soon drifted back looking for handouts.

"I gave all the bread to the swans, Lady Fanny," Charlotte confessed as the sparrows edged their way closer to her feet, cocking their heads expectantly. "What shall I do?"

"Do not fret, dear," Fanny advised, taking a seat on one of the marble benches facing the goddess. "Aphrodite's birds are not starving, you may be sure of it."

"Do you think I should run back and ask Cook for some more crumbs?"

"Only if you wish to, dear," Fanny replied. "Sir Joshua will not be here for a while yet, so you have time. But I warn you, Charlotte, do not leave me alone too long or the goddess may cast a spell on me."

Charlotte giggled at the notion and scampered off. Fanny sat back in the pink penumbra of the shrine and let her thoughts drift over the death of Lady Sheldon. If there was any truth at all to the rumours about a gentleman in the carriage with the lady, Fanny could understand the colonel's reluctance to have his wife's name mentioned at Sheldon Hall. He had been extremely put out the other afternoon when Margaret lamented the fact that Lady Sheldon had broken with the tradition of offering flowers to Aphrodite.

Perhaps the Beauty had felt no need for supernatural assistance in matters of the heart. Constance Sheldon already had been more than blessed in that area, with a husband who adored her and a baby girl to bring her the joys of motherhood. What more could she have possibly wished for?

The spectre of that mysterious gentleman, who may or

may not have existed, rose again in Fanny's mind. Could it be that the colonel, for all his adoration of his wife, was not the man Lady Sheldon had yearned for? The notion brought Fanny's thoughts to a standstill. There was nothing like a discontented wife to bring disharmony to a marriage. Had not her own mother told her so? Had Fanny not been one herself?

She closed her eyes and let her mind drift back to Cambourne Abbey where she had reigned for so short a time as mistress. Fanny had always blamed the duke for her discontent. He had been too old, too serious, too disinterested in her, and far too inflexible. He could be charming when he wished, but most of the time left her to her own devices. Accustomed to being the centre of attention at Hayle House, Fanny could not adjust to being ignored, so when Gerald had resumed his flirtatious ways, she had responded without considering the consequences.

Had Lady Sheldon's malaise brought about the tragedy, as had Fanny's own? Fanny opened her eyes and gazed at the voluptuous figure of the pink goddess. Had the fault been Constance's rather than the colonel's? A sobering thought if Fanny were to apply the same question to her own marriage.

Fanny had no idea how long she had been sitting lost in thought when the sound of footsteps caught her attention. They were too heavy to be Charlotte's, and Fanny glanced towards the entrance to the grotto, an amused smile of welcome on her face for Sir Joshua. The greeting faded instantly as soon as she saw the gentleman who stood at the entrance, surveying her through his quizzing-glass.

"My darling Fanny, what a charming picture," Lord Penryn drawled, a sensuous smile on his lips as his eyes fixed on her neckline and slid leisurely down to her toes.

"Gerald!" she exclaimed, thoroughly annoyed at the forced tête-à-tête. "Whatever are you doing here? The contest is not until tomorrow afternoon."

He strolled over to stand before her. His eyes were the same clear azure she had so admired as a girl, but the lines around them reminded Fanny that ten years had passed since she had gambled her happiness on this man and lost. A very foolish gamble to be sure, made by an innocent, impulsive, and certainly self-indulgent young girl, with no concern for anyone's comfort but her own.

Penryn smiled down at her and reached for her hand, which he carried to his lips with an exaggerated flourish. Always the poseur, Fanny thought, feeling the warmth of his breath on her fingers. She was glad to see that her old beau's charm no longer had the power to turn her head. She did not return his smile.

"I am well aware of that fact, Fanny dear," he murmured, still holding her hand. "I have my sonnet written already and fully expect to leave poor old Comfrey in the dust when the time comes. What a pathetic creature he is, to be sure. I cannot imagine what Miss Sheldon sees to admire in him. Of course, she is at an age where she may not be too choosy, but her dowry is more than respectable, which leads me to believe she actually wishes to be riveted to the odd codger."

Fanny was startled and suddenly apprehensive. "What do you know about Miss Sheldon's dowry?"

Penryn's grin broadened. "I make it my business to know these things, Fanny, my love. One never knows when such information may be useful. For instance, I have it from a reliable source that your stiff-rumped colonel is a very warm man." His smile became cynical. "Although I cannot imagine why you would need a rich husband, particularly a country bumpkin like Sheldon, when you could choose a man closer to your own rank, my dear. One who knows all your secrets, all the little scandals in your past, and still appreciates you." He paused, then added, his voice dropping to a caressing level that she recognized from long ago, "One who still loves you, Fanny."

Fanny let her gaze drift to the niche where the rosy-skinned goddess stared back at her enigmatically. Was it her imagination, or had Aphrodite's marble face softened in a cynical smile? A little sadly, Fanny wished that Charlotte would return, or that the comforting bulk of Sir Joshua would climb the steps into the grotto. "What nonsense is this you are raving about, Gerald?" she enquired, without much interest.

For answer he dropped to one knee beside her and

grasped her hand. "You were always a sad tease, Fanny, my love," he purred, his voice vibrating with passion.

Fanny was not impressed; she remembered that Gerald had always been able to conjure up passion at the least provocation. He had been as full of tricks as a court jester, and she had fallen for every one of them. Not any more, she told herself, staring impassively into his lordship's azure eyes.

"Do not pretend you have forgotten how much we loved one another, my dearest. How much we still do," he added with an arch look, placing a hot, wet kiss on her palm.

Fanny jerked her hand away and was about to give Lord Penryn a sharp rebuke, when a gasp drew her attention to the entrance.

"Is he sick, Lady Fanny?" a small voice enquired from the doorway.

Fanny breathed a sigh of relief at the sight of Charlotte. "Yes, dear. Very sick indeed. You had best run up to the house and tell Aunt Margaret right away. Do you think you can do that for me, Charlotte?"

"Do not be ridiculous, Fanny," the viscount snapped, evidently put out at the child's interpretation of his amorous posture. "Run away, little girl," he said to Charlotte, "I have something important to say to the lady."

Charlotte stared at Lord Penryn with a puzzled expression on her pixie face. She was obviously considering whether to obey Lady Fanny or stay to see what other entertainment she might derive from the strange gentleman. Finally, she responded to the encouraging nod Lady Fanny gave her and ran back the way she had come.

Fanny sighed and brought her attention back to Lord Penryn, who was still on one knee beside her. "Do get up, Gerald," she said coolly, "you are making quite a cake of yourself." She had an almost irrepressible urge to laugh at the viscount's posturing, but remembered that behind that impeccable address and easy charm, Gerald had an uncertain temper.

"Fanny, my darling," he said in a voice calculated to make widows and orphans render up their last farthing, "whatever happened to that sweet, romantical angel who used to rendezvous with me in the laburnum bushes at

Hayle? Do you remember how you would throw yourself into my arms and beg for my kisses? A saucy little witch you were, dearest, and no mistake." He took up her hand again and feathered kisses on each fingertip.

Fanny squirmed uncomfortably, wondering if Charlotte had reached the house and relayed her message to Margaret. She examined the glossy head of chestnut hair bent over her lap, and tried to speculate what new scheme lay under those carefully windblown curls.

"The girl you speak of no longer exists, Gerald," she pointed out. "You of all men should know that. You helped to destroy her ten years ago."

Lord Penryn raised his head and looked at her reproachfully. "Destroy you, Fanny? How can you say so? It was I who made you a duchess, my sweet. It was I who mentioned your name to Edward when he finally realized he could ignore his duty no longer and must take a wife."

Fanny could not quite believe what she was hearing. "*You*?" she said faintly. "*You* arranged for Cambourne to offer for me? Did it never occur to you that I had no wish to be a duchess?"

He smiled at her tenderly. "Oh, I suspected that you would have preferred quite another arrangement, my love, but that was impossible at the time, you see. Edward needed a wife more urgently than I did, and believe me, sweet," he added when Fanny wrenched her hands away and stood up, shaking with fury, "everything would have worked out splendidly had you practiced a little restraint and not taxed Edward with his lack of lover-like qualities. He tried his best, poor chap, but my little romantic puss wanted passion on a grand scale, which revolted old Edward more than I can tell you."

Fanny stepped back, stunned by this ugly revelation, when the viscount reached to grasp her hands. "You are quite disgusting. All of you." An unpleasant thought struck her. "At least tell me that my father was not a party to this . . . this unspeakable arrangement."

Lord Penryn's smile was coy. "Come now, my darling. You were young and innocent, but not *that* innocent. Of course, Lord Hayle knew of my cousin's—what shall we call it?—*proclivity* I believe is the polite word. And your brothers, too, naturally. How could they not, when it was common knowledge in the village."

"Freddy, too?" Her voice sounded hollow.

"Particularly Freddy," he responded with a sneer. "But do not blame poor Freddy, my love. He was always so short of the ready, and one thing about Edward you must admire, he was always willing to loosen the purse strings when one did him a favour."

"As you no doubt often did," Fanny hissed contemptuously, her stomach roiling in disgust at the things he was insinuating.

"But of course, my dear," he responded smoothly, moving closer so that Fanny had to retreat. "As I said, love, we could have been very comfortable, the two of us at Cambourne Abbey, had you not made unreasonable demands. All poor Edward wanted was a legitimate heir of his blood. And as you know, Edward and I share the same blood." He paused, regarding her from beneath drooping lids, a faint, cynical smile on his lips.

The monstrosity of what the wretch was suggesting was quite beyond Fanny's comprehension. Ruthlessly she repressed her disgust. "Are you doing Edward another favour now, by chance?"

Lord Penryn smiled and shook his handsome head. "Not this time, love. After poor Alice passed, I told Edward—"

"Alice?" Fanny interrupted brusquely.

"Edward's second duchess. Did you not know he had married again? A shy child with no sense of style at all. Totally inappropriate as it turned out. Only imagine, she produced a stillborn babe, but unfortunately died in the undertaking. Edward was quite furious with her. Poor fellow, he has no luck with women at all." He laughed and Fanny cringed at the sound. These men had been as callous with this second duchess as they had been with the first. Except for one important difference.

"At least this Alice was not beaten to within an inch of her life," she said in a frozen voice.

Gerald laughed again, quite as though they had been discussing some amusing social event. "That is because Alice never had the bad taste to make Charles jealous. Whereas you, my love," he added reaching out to stroke her cheek with his knuckles, "you could not leave well enough alone—"

"Charles?"

He looked surprised for a moment, then let out a crack of ribald laughter. "Surely you knew about Charles, my love."

"Do you mean Charles Stone, Edward's secretary?"

"Of course, I mean Charles Stone, my sweet innocent. Who else would I mean?"

The sordid picture Lord Penryn had painted for her began to take on more vivid outlines. She had never liked the handsome, scholarly young secretary, but since he seemed to know how to keep Edward in a good mood, Fanny had ignored the young man's occasional rudeness and impertinence. Gerald's revelations put the secretary's presence at Cambourne Abbey in a different light altogether.

"I wonder that you imagine any of this old gossip would interest me, my lord," she said stiffly. "If that is all you wished to say to me, you might have saved yourself the trouble. Now, if you will excuse me." She turned her back on him and took a step towards the entrance, hoping to see Margaret hurrying to rescue her.

She should have known he would not let her escape so easily. Fanny felt his hands on her shoulders as she was turned about to face him. He held her so close that the ruffles of his elaborately tied cravat almost touched her nose, and she could smell the Holland water he had used that morning.

"Oh, no, Fanny, not so fast, lass. I have left the important surprise for last, my dear. And you are right about the past; that is gone and should be forgotten. We have the future to enjoy, and I propose we enjoy it together, Fanny my love. Only think, dearest, we finally have the opportunity to make all our dreams come true." He held her at arm's length and smiled down at her tenderly. "What do you say to that, my own sweet girl?"

Fanny gazed at him for several moments, wondering how a gentleman with half his wits about him might delude himself into believing that she would accept his cynical proposal.

"And what dreams would these be, Gerald?" she enquired pleasantly, hoping to keep him at bay until Margaret arrived.

His grin faded and Fanny felt his fingers tighten on her shoulders. "This is not the moment for jesting, love. Do not trifle with a man's heart, I beg of you."

"Beg all you wish, my lord," she said coolly. "I cannot stop you, but I have other things to take care of, and must ask you to leave now, sir." She made a motion to escape his grip but his fingers only dug more deeply into the tender flesh of her arms.

"You are hurting me, Gerald," she protested, pressing her palms against his chest to no avail.

"How can I be hurting you, Fanny, you heartless wench? I am asking you to marry me, for God's sake. You ought to be swooning with joy instead of telling me you have other things to do. Other things to do, indeed. I will give you other things to do, lass," he growled menacingly. "How about this, love? I know what you want from me. What you always wanted."

With surprising violence, Fanny felt herself crushed against the viscount's chest and her lips captured in a passionate kiss. Struggle as she might, she could not shake loose of the unwelcome embrace. After what seemed like an age, the viscount raised his head and laughed down at her, clearly convinced that he had won the day.

"Only say you will be my wife, Fanny dearest, and we can be comfortable again."

"Unhand me this instant, Gerald," Fanny cried out, her fists flailing impotently against his chest.

"Nay, love. Only think of all the good times we will have together—"

"The lady said to unhand her," a cold voice broke in sharply. "I recommend you do so, for you have certainly outstayed your welcome here."

Fanny felt her arms released abruptly and reached out to steady herself against the ledge that held—ironically—the bowl of yellow roses contributed by the viscount on a previous visit.

"Lady Fanny and I are having a private conversation and would prefer not to be interrupted," Lord Penryn said in a soft yet dangerous voice intended to put the colonel in his place.

Fanny took heart from the colonel's grim smile. "You are mistaken, my lord," she said icily. "This was no conversation, but an impertinence, and I have nothing further to say to you. Please do not return."

Without another word, but with a furious glare that told Fanny plainly enough that the matter was not closed, Lord Penryn stalked past Colonel Sheldon, descended the marble steps, and strode off in high dudgeon, leaving a heavy silence in his wake.

CHAPTER 15

Unwelcome Offer

As the viscount stalked out in a cold fury, the colonel listened to the heels of the thwarted Lothario's expensive Hessians ringing on the marble steps, followed by the rustling of leaves as he strode away through the wood.

A short silence ensued during which the colonel found himself admiring the slim female figure leaning against the ledge next to a bowl of yellow roses. Suddenly she sighed, a long, drawn-out sound that triggered an instinctive reaction in him. He stepped forward and took her firmly by the elbow.

"Sit down and rest for a while," he said gently, guiding Lady Fanny to the white marble bench facing the niche where the pink goddess flaunted her perfect beauty.

She obeyed without protest, which pleased him. If only she were always this biddable, he thought, Lady Fanny would make someone an excellent wife.

"I owe you an apology, my dear lady," he said at last, after she had smoothed her pale lilac gown and settled herself on the bench, eyes modestly downcast. She presented such a delectable picture of womanhood that the colonel was quite enchanted in spite of himself.

At his words, Lady Fanny raised her eyes to his face, and Derek realized that she had not looked directly at him since Lord Penryn had left. He was once again struck by the violet glow of her eyes in a pale face tinged with a pink aura from the tiles surrounding her. She was truly beautiful. Not in the cool perfection of the Goddess of Love in her pink niche, but in a warm, seductive, intimate manner of a mortal woman who knew her own power to captivate the hearts of men.

It was several moments before the colonel realized that there was something not quite right about this perfect picture. It struck him suddenly, like a dash of icy water in his face, what that blemish was. So blinded had he been by the lady's appearance of womanly modesty and tractability that he had ignored that side of her nature he had encountered so forcibly in Calais. There was no meekness in those violet eyes. Quite the contrary. She was amused.

She shook her head, causing the pale ringlets to bounce delightfully against the pale column of her neck. "Oh, no, Colonel," she murmured, "you owe me nothing. On the contrary, I seem to have caused you an endless amount of trouble, so it is I who should apologize, not you, sir."

The colonel frowned. How typical of her. Instead of accepting his apology gracefully, this contentious female must needs come to points with him. He clasped his hands behind his back and glared down at her as if his gaze alone might mend her manners.

"As a guest in my house, my lady," he explained stiffly, "you are under my protection and should not have to endure unpleasantness from anyone. I hold myself responsible that you were accosted by Lord Penryn without my knowledge. I can only assume he came to the grotto directly from the stables without informing Collins. Why he would commit such a breach of etiquette I cannot imagine. Unless, of course," he frowned at the thought, "he received an invitation from you, my lady."

She met this suggestion with a tinkle of laughter. "Now what makes you think, Colonel, that I would so far forget myself as to invite a rackety Bond Street fribble to a secret assignation? Have I sunk so low in your estimation that you think me capable of such an indiscretion?"

"I could not help overhearing the viscount urging you to become his wife—"

"So you instantly assumed I had enticed the poor fool here to wring an offer from him? Let me assure you, Colonel, that Lord Penryn is the last man on this earth I would wish to wed." She appeared to reconsider, then laughed, her eyes bright. "Perhaps the second to last," she remarked, casting him an arch glance. "In any case, his lordship's offer came ten years too late."

Imagining a hint of regret in her tone, the colonel cleared his throat. He wished she did not look quite so vulnerable sitting there demurely, eyes once more lowered. "I applaud your good sense, my lady. The viscount is not the kind of husband I could wish for any lady of my acquaintance."

Lady Fanny laughed again. "I am glad to hear you say so, Colonel." Her voice dropped into a wistful murmur. "I had quite despaired of gaining your approval in anything."

This confession rattled the colonel because it came perilously close to the truth. He had not approved of Lady Fanny Wentworth since first setting eyes upon her in Calais. Yet here she was, shatteringly beautiful, bewitching him with her eyes, her voice, her very accessibility. For with a sudden flash of masculine intuition that shook him down to the toes of his highly polished boots, Derek realized that this woman was accessible to him. She was within his grasp. He could reach out and she would come to him. The prospect made him giddy with a desire he had not thought to experience again after Constance had left him.

Derek took a deep breath and let it out slowly. His heart had shrivelled and died when he had found evidence of Constance's affair with Roger St. Ives, and again later, when they had brought his wife's battered body back to Sheldon Hall. Now his heart appeared to be very much alive again; he felt it heating his blood, making it sing in his veins. He felt young and reckless as in the days before his marriage, before the perversity of a beautiful woman had destroyed his joy. But would he not be foolish indeed to listen to the rhythm of his heartbeats? To fall into the same trap a second time?

"You are mistaken, my lady," he said, suppressing the wild urge to throw discretion to the winds. "There is much to admire in you besides your common sense."

Lady Fanny smiled up at him, her marvellous eyes shining with amusement. "How very circumspect you are, Colonel. And you are quite right to mistrust me," she added unexpectedly, her expression turning serious. "Actually there is little enough to admire in me, as Lord Penryn was kind enough to remind me. Perhaps he is a more appropriate candidate for my hand than I would like to admit, since he knows about my scandalous past. I had hoped that unhappy time might be forgotten by now, but Gerald managed to bring it all back in every sordid detail, even adding a number of aspects unknown to me that have made me feel positively unclean."

Her gaze strayed to the goddess during this extraordinary confession, and Derek's heart contracted at the sadness on her face.

"I cannot believe things are as black as you paint them, my lady," he said bracingly, wanting more than ever to take up this fragile creature in his arms and shield her from the devils that plagued her. "We often see our own troubles as larger than they are because we are so closely affected by them. To others they might seem less so. But in any case, it is useless to repine over things we cannot change. We all have secrets in our past we would rather forget."

"Even you, Colonel?" Her momentary sadness seemed to have passed, and he was glad to see her smile again.

"Even me." What kind of tragedy could have overtaken such a magnificent creature? She was an enigma to him. Derek had never been entirely comfortable around single females, and the beautiful ones had made him painfully aware of his own shortcomings. He had been petrified when he realized that the celebrated Beauty, Constance Browning, seemed to prefer his company to that of his more polished fellows. Even when she had unmistakably hinted that he approach her father, Derek had not wanted to believe his good fortune.

"Yes," he repeated softly, "even me."

Had he listened to Margaret, who told him bluntly that in Brighton social circles—which neither of them fre-

quented with any regularity—he was considered to be a
very fine matrimonial catch indeed, he might not have married the first woman who irrefutably wanted him. Not even
when Constance herself had admitted that her father was
so far up the River Tick that the chances of his coming
about looked grim indeed, had the colonel stopped to consider that the Beauty's affection might be anything but
genuine.

That rude awakening had come later.

And now, as the colonel stood in the soft pink glow of
Aphrodite's shrine with another beautiful female, he was
beset by similar doubts about his own worth. Even as he
gazed into the violet depths of Lady Fanny's eyes, Derek
caught himself wondering if perhaps that limpid stare was
not another trap set to make a fool of him again. What
troubles did this Beauty need him to take care of?

There were no answers in those lovely eyes, but the colonel suspected that Lady Fanny's scandals were not as innocuous as gaming debts. And if he were not careful, he would
be saddled with them, he realized, suddenly aware that they
had been alone in the grotto far too long for propriety.
Lady Fanny had received one offer of marriage that afternoon. Could it be that she was hoping for another?

"I wonder what is keeping Sir Joshua," she said, breaking into the colonel's meditations. "He seemed most urgent
in his wish for my opinion on the sonnet he is composing
for tomorrow."

"I fear you have been misled, my dear lady," the colonel
responded, grateful that the conversation had deviated to
a less dangerous topic. "It is my belief that Sir Joshua did
not write that note you received this morning. It is quite
unlike him to write notes, my sister informs me, but Collins
claims it was delivered by a lad from Cedar Lodge. It is
my belief that Lord Penryn may have bribed that lad and
set up a clandestine assignation under false pretenses."

"I should have thought of that myself, Colonel. I had
forgotten how devious he can be."

The colonel was about to suggest that they remove themselves from the intimacy of the shrine when Charlotte came
scampering into the grotto, her face alight with curiosity.

"Is he dead?" she demanded, rushing to Lady Fanny and

clasping her hand, glancing around as if she expected to see the viscount's corpse.

"Dead?" Lady Fanny looked at the colonel in bewilderment.

"My daughter is under the misapprehension that Lord Penryn was deathly ill because she saw him kneeling in what she took for prayer," Derek explained, keeping a straight face with difficulty.

"You said he was sick," Charlotte added accusingly.

Lady Fanny laughed. "Yes, I did, sweetheart. And he was indeed as sick as can be, especially when your papa told him to take himself off, which he did like a scared rabbit."

"Did you land him a facer, Papa?" Charlotte demanded eagerly. "I wish I could have seen it. Papa was a famous pugilist when he was young. He has sparred with Gentleman Jackson, my Aunt Margaret told me."

"You have a very bloodthirsty daughter, Colonel."

"Also one with a vivid imagination, I am afraid," he replied. "And Charlotte, have I not told you to refrain from using cant expressions?"

Charlotte merely giggled and hid her face in Lady Fanny's skirts.

"Are you telling me you were not a famous pugilist when you were young? What a crushing disappointment, Colonel. One of my fondest dreams has always been to meet a real live pugilist. Especially one who spars with Gentleman Jackson."

For a moment, Derek forgot that he had vowed to keep his distance from Lady Fanny, a female whose past held shadowy scandals perhaps even more dark than his own.

For another delicious moment he wavered, wondering what it might be like to enjoy this playful bantering on a more intimate level. Then, pulling his thoughts hastily away from such imprudent fantasies, the colonel cleared his throat.

"I am sorry to disappoint you, my lady," he began mildly.

"Aunt Margaret sent me to bring Lady Fanny back to the terrace for tea," Charlotte interrupted, effectively breaking any lingering intimacy.

"Then we must not dawdle, must we?" Lady Fanny

joked, moving towards the steps, his daughter still clinging to her hand. "If I were your age, Charlotte, I would challenge you to a race up to the terrace. I used to be quite good at racing when I was young."

She threw a conspiratorial glance at him over her shoulder as the party left the grotto, and the colonel could have sworn Lady Fanny had winked at him. But that was not possible, was it? Well-bred females did not wink at gentlemen. Unless, of course, they were like Lady Fanny, who might very well wink at anybody if the notion took her.

The colonel thought about that playful gesture all the way up to the house, as he strolled behind the ladies, listening to his daughter chatter on about her new pony, Bubbles. Charlotte and Lady Fanny joined in gales of laughter as his daughter's tales of the pony's antics became increasingly inventive.

This is what a family should be like, the colonel mused, lulled by the happy sounds. Except that there should be a boy—perhaps two—to walk beside him, and another daughter—or even two—to skip beside their mother and fill the air with their childish voices. Except that Lady Fanny was not Charlotte's mother, nor anybody's mother as far as he knew.

And she certainly was not his wife, so the sooner he ceased to include her in this happy make-believe picture, the better it would be for all of them.

CHAPTER 16

Blackmail

Late that evening, after the ladies had gone up to bed, Lady Fanny heard a scratching at her door, which opened to admit her aunt.

"Fanny, my love, I am all a-twitter to hear what *really* occurred in the grotto this afternoon," she announced, settling herself in a brocade chair beside the bed. "I realize your reluctance to discuss such matters with the Sheldons, but surely you can tell *me*, dearest."

Fanny had been expecting this visit, having crossed speaking glances with her aunt over the dinner table, and in the drawing room while Margaret entertained them at the pianoforte. But for some obscure reason she was reluctant to share her intimate encounter with Colonel Sheldon with anyone. More than anything, Fanny wished to curl up in her bed and dream of him, dream of what might have happened in that shrine of the love goddess had he been less reticent, had she been more . . . more . . . more what? she wondered, not for the first time. More flirtatious? More brazen?

She sighed and returned her aunt's smile. "Of course, I can tell you, my dear Aunt. What do you wish to know?"

"What do I wish to know?" Lady Wentworth repeated in a shrill voice. "I do declare child, you are most provoking. What do you think I wish to know? Why, everything, of course. Absolutely *everything*."

"Everything?" Fanny teased. "Why, that would take all night, Aunt, and I confess to being a little tired after all that excitement."

"Now do not, I beg you, Fanny, be so tiresome. Here you are, fresh from encounters with not one, but two gentlemen in the most romantic of circumstances, and all you can say is that you are tired. I swear I did not taste a morsel of that roast duck and sautéed crab Mrs. Collins sent up from the kitchen tonight. And you know how much I love crab, dear. I could barely swallow a spoonful or two of her cabbage soup, which I am also partial to, as you well know. So, do not tell me you are tired, dear, I cannot bear it."

Fanny laughed at her aunt's enthusiasm. Had she not known that Lady Wentworth had her best interests at heart, Fanny would have pleaded a megrim and delayed the confidences until the morning.

"Well," she began, settling herself more comfortably against her feather pillows, "as you know, I went down to the grotto to meet Sir Joshua, but he did not come—"

"Yes, yes," her aunt interrupted, "we all know that Sir

Joshua did not write that note to you this morning. Very improper of Lord Penryn to forge it, I must say, but also so romantic it makes me come out in goosebumps."

"The man is a consummate scoundrel," Fanny protested. "How can you condone his deceitful trick as romantic?"

"I do not condone it, my dear Fanny," her aunt protested. "I merely remarked that it appeared like a romantic gesture."

Fanny snorted disgustedly. "There is nothing romantic about Gerald. The man had the gall to offer me marriage, Aunt. To insist upon it, in fact."

"Marriage?" Lady Wentworth repeated in amazement. "I cannot believe Gerald actually came up to scratch." Fanny could hear the wheels of her aunt's brain turning busily.

"I trust you are not about to suggest that his offer is anything less than insulting, Aunt."

"Of course not, dear," her aunt said quickly. "Although, of course, the title is not to be sneezed at, Fanny," she added cautiously.

"Aunt! How could you? After all the scandal that man has caused in our family. And my poor Mama! No, I will not hear of it."

"So you rejected him, dear?"

"Yes, I certainly did. He did not take it well at all, and had the temerity to maul me in a most vulgar manner. Luckily the colonel appeared at that moment and sent Gerald to the rightabout." She paused, recalling the scene. "He was rather splendid, actually."

"Gerald?" her aunt asked facetiously.

"No, the colonel, of course. Charlotte tells me he was a follower of the Fancy in his youth. To tell the truth, I was disappointed he did not bloody Gerald's pretty nose for him."

Her aunt stared at her in astonishment. "My dear child, it is hardly ladylike to encourage gentlemen in their bloodthirsty pursuits. Besides, poor Gerald is no match for the colonel; I daresay he would be seriously impaired if it came to a dust-up between them."

"Just so," Fanny responded laconically.

"But enough about Gerald," Lady Wentworth exclaimed

impatiently. "Tell me about the colonel. After he came to the conclusion that Sir Joshua was not the author of that letter, he stormed out of the house like a mad bull. I swear, he looked angry enough to chew nails when he left us."

Fanny smiled, oddly gratified that her host had taken her safety so much to heart. "He was cool enough when he reached the grotto."

"But what did he *say*?" her aunt insisted.

Fanny was not quite sure she could explain the undercurrents that had passed between them during that brief encounter, so she stuck to dry facts. "He apologized. As well he might, after allowing stray visitors to sneak into the grounds and assault female guests."

"Oh, Fanny," her aunt wailed, "I see you are quite determined to be secretive about this."

"He accused me of inviting Gerald to a clandestine meeting," Fanny admitted, wishing her aunt would go away and let her go to sleep and dream. "He seemed to think I was eager for an offer from Gerald. Of course, I told him that was nonsensical."

"Did he seem relieved?"

"No, but he did tell me he admired my good sense," she murmured.

"Nothing else?" her aunt demanded, sounding vastly disappointed. "Did he not drop a single hint?"

"Hint? What kind of hint did you expect him to drop, Aunt? Now it is you who is being obtuse," she added, although she had a pretty good notion what her aunt was angling for.

"Why, a hint that he might wish to make you mistress of Sheldon Hall," Lady Wentworth said coyly. "Margaret told me he—"

Lady Fanny was never to hear what Margaret had said, for at that moment there was another scratching at the door and Miss Sheldon herself appeared. On the pretext of not being able to rest without making sure that her guest had not suffered any ill effects from her encounter with Lord Penryn that afternoon, Margaret had brought Fanny a glass of warm milk from the kitchen. Then she settled herself companionably in a spindle-legged chair next to Lady Wentworth, with whom she appeared to be on the most cordial of terms. When the two ladies proceeded to make predictions regarding Fanny's matrimonial prospects, she lost interest and closed her eyes, slipping easily into a deep sleep.

Fanny woke up the following morning in a contentious mood. She had fully expected to savour her encounter with the colonel in her dreams, but on that uninhibited, sensuous level that only deep sleep seemed to make possible. No such dreams had come to titillate her, or if they had, she recalled not even a scrap of them. Not even a kiss, she thought crossly, ringing for Yvette with more force than necessary. Nothing.

Although Fanny was not normally superstitious, she was briefly tempted to take this absence of the colonel in her dreams as an omen before brushing the notion aside as childish. When she burned her tongue on her hot chocolate, and tore the hem of her favourite morning gown, she still refused to credit these contretemps to anything more than coincidence. When Collins brought up the letter on his silver salver addressed to her boldly in Lord Penryn's florid hand, Fanny vividly recalled her mother's favourite explanation for an unusual proliferation of misfortunes. The hobgoblins were on the rampage, Lady Hayle used to say, and could only be appeased by a saucer of milk outside the kitchen door at midnight. This morning, her mother's hobgoblins, real or imagined, appeared to be on a serious campaign to deflate her spirits.

When she had opened the missive and read its elegantly worded, yet venomous contents, Fanny was sure of it. She read it over a second time to make sure her eyes had not misled her, then threw on a Norwich shawl over her pale green bombazine morning gown and marched downstairs in search of the colonel.

She found him in his study and, ignoring Collins's offer to announce her, Fanny knocked briefly and entered before the colonel had a chance to invite her in. She found him ensconced comfortably beside the open window, reading the latest London *Gazette*.

"Lady Fanny," he exclaimed, throwing down the paper

and rising to his feet. "What has happened to send you into the boughs?"

"You might very well ask what has happened, Colonel," she responded, waving the offending letter under his nose. "That wretch Penryn has had the temerity to send me this. He renews his offer, in the most threatening manner, and since some of his remarks indirectly concern you, Colonel, I thought you should see the perversity of which this rogue is capable."

Only after the colonel had begun his perusal of the letter did Fanny regret her hasty decision to share Gerald's missive with her host. She watched his face as he read and then re-read the contents. Fanny could not tell his thoughts, but as she recalled Gerald's poisonous threats to reveal her sordid secrets if she refused his offer a second time, and his mockery of the colonel's character, Fanny wished she had been less hasty in coming to her host.

After staring out of the window for what seemed to Fanny an endless age, the colonel turned to face her. His face was expressionless. "Penryn cannot force you to wed," he said in a clipped voice, "but then you must know that. And as for any damage he might do to your reputation, that is an empty threat; anyone who knows you, Fanny, will not be swayed by malicious gossip."

"What if it is not merely gossip but the truth?" Fanny felt obliged to say, oddly moved by his use of her name.

"Then the messenger will more than likely discredit the tale. This is not London, where the main amusement for many idle minds is to take the slightest hint of scandal and blow it out of all proportion, then pass it along to other equally malicious individuals as gospel truth. I recommend you do not allow yourself to be overset by this attempt to blackmail you, my dear lady."

Fanny returned the colonel's gaze, wondering what thoughts lay behind that cool grey stare. Had he not read Gerald's snide assessment of him or the remark about a possible intimate connection between them?

"What disturbs me more than any threat that Gerald could make to me, is the slander he directs at you, Colonel," she said bluntly, determined to speak her mind. She was delighted to see a single dimple flicker as his mouth curved into a reluctant smile.

"If you mean Lord Penryn's labeling of me as—" he glanced down at the letter in his hand, " 'a paragon of prudence and morality,' then you may rest easy, my lady. I can think of worse things he might have called me." He paused, and his smile disappeared. "Is that how *you* see me, Lady Fanny?"

Fanny started at the unexpected question. She could hardly tell this man that her first impression of him had been entirely unflattering. But their intimate encounter at the Blue Parrot Inn had revealed another side to the colonel's character. There had been a tenderness beneath the rigid exterior that had moved her as she had not expected to be moved by any man ever again.

As a result, her perception of him had changed. Did she now consider him the paragon of prudence and morality Gerald had called him? Suddenly the label did not sound pejorative at all.

Fanny was abruptly reminded of her Uncle John, who had shown her that gentlemen could also be gentle and kind, and Jack Mansford, whose unstinting friendship had helped her adjust to her exile. And now here was Colonel Sir Derek Sheldon, who was nothing like the men in her family, nor quite like Uncle John or Jack either, waiting for her to tell him what she thought of him.

"Aha," he said quietly, when Fanny did not answer, "I see you agree with Lord Penryn—"

"Oh, no!" she exclaimed hastily, "that is not the case at all. I realize Gerald meant to disparage you, Colonel, but I can see nothing wrong with prudence. I often wish I possessed more of it myself." She smiled faintly. "As for morality, having seen how the lack of it has destroyed my family, I can only envy those whose lives are guided by moral standards."

"If you believe I am one of those fortunate individuals, then you have no reason to be upset, my lady," he said. "Lord Penryn has missed his mark."

"It was not precisely your morality that concerned me, Colonel," she began, hoping she might find the correct words to address Gerald's other insinuations. "I know you too little to be able to judge. But I find Gerald's assumption that you are considering . . . that is to say, that I have given you cause to believe . . ." She halted in mid-sentence, at a loss to put it more plainly.

The colonel smiled. "I never thought to see you at a loss for words, my lady," he murmured. "I assume you refer to Penryn's impertinent suggestion that there is an understanding between us?"

"Precisely," she breathed, relieved to have the subject out in the open at last. "And impertinent it certainly was of him. Ridiculous, too, of course, when one considers the circumstances," she added vaguely.

The colonel raised an eyebrow. "And what circumstances might these be?" he murmured, causing the colour to flood Fanny's cheeks.

She stared at him, alarmed at the question. Fanny suspected he might be teasing her, but his grey eyes showed no hint of amusement.

"I thought that would be obvious," she said defensively. "You will not deny, sir, that you have disapproved of me since the day we met. So how Gerald came to imagine otherwise is inexplicable to me."

The colonel looked at her strangely, and Fanny felt her heart leap about erratically in her breast. After a long pause, during which he appeared to be pondering some deep dilemma, the colonel smiled briefly and turned to stare out of the window.

"Yes, I cannot explain it either. The notion is ridiculous, as you have pointed out, my lady. But do not think for a moment that I disapprove of you, at least not entirely." He glanced at her with a faint smile. "In fact, I ask nothing more than to be allowed to help you discourage this scoundrel who would bully you into accepting his ultimatum."

He turned back to the window, and Fanny wanted to protest but could think of nothing to say.

"All unwittingly," the colonel said abruptly, thrusting both hands into his pockets and rocking back on his heels, "Lord Penryn may have given me the means to rid you of his unwelcome attentions."

"I do not follow you, sir."

The colonel smiled then, and Fanny noticed anew that

in his softer moods, this man was surprisingly attractive. "Penryn assumes, or pretends to assume, that there is an understanding between us, am I correct?"

"Yes, indeed," Fanny murmured, still puzzled.

The colonel turned to face her, his eyes bright with a devilment that made him appear ten years younger.

"Then let us pretend that he is correct," he said softly.

Derek could not believe he had actually suggested anything so outrageous. But the words still hung in the air, echoing like a cannon shot. Lady Fanny's eyes widened in consternation, and the pupils turned a darker shade of violet until they were almost black. Lips parted, cheeks pale, she clasped her hands together and stared at him quite as though he had suddenly sprouted an extra head.

She blinked rapidly, and Derek saw a rush of colour return to her face as the enormity of his suggestion began to sink in. "Are you suggesting that we . . . Did I hear you say, Colonel, that we should *pretend* . . . that is to say . . ." Her voice petered out in a sigh, and Derek saw that his proposal had truly taken her breath away.

He relaxed. "What?" he said bracingly, "at a loss for words again, my lady?"

"Can you blame me, sir?" she said in a choked voice. "Have you windmills in your head? What you suggest is beyond anything bizarre and improper."

He raised an eyebrow. "You think me capable of undertaking anything improper, my lady?" he demanded, carefully discounting the very improper fantasies that had plagued his sleep recently. "Believe me, I would never suggest such a plan if I thought it might bring dishonour to you."

She looked skeptical. "Such a pretense as you propose, Colonel, would certainly put Gerald's nose out of joint, but I would not wish to deceive your sister or my aunt into believing there is any truth to it. After all, they both know your true opinion of me," she added with a faint smile.

Derek felt oddly elated. The lady was actually considering going along with his ruse. "Both Margaret and Lady Wentworth would be fully apprised of our plan to thwart Lord Penryn. And as I said before, I do not entirely disapprove of you, my dear," he clarified. "And only consider, you disapprove of me, too. So at least we are in accord on one thing."

Lady Fanny laughed outright at that. "You are impossible, sir. Perhaps you can explain to me how a mutual disapproval can add up to an understanding between us."

Secretly pleased that they could discuss the plan openly, Derek pretended to ponder the question. "Perhaps we might plead our intention of reforming one another," he suggested lightly.

"Oh, that would never work," she argued. "For one thing, I do not believe I am equal to the task of reforming you, Colonel." Her eyes twinkled beguilingly, and Derek knew she was teasing him. "And even if I could get you to admit that you need reforming, which is doubtful, there is no way I would admit to being anything less than perfect."

"I can see we have a lot of serious discussion ahead of us."

She laughed at this sally, then her face became serious, and Derek knew that he was about to learn her real objection to his proposal.

"I appreciate your offer of assistance, Colonel," she said after a long pause. "However, once this scheme reaches Gerald's ears, he will ride out here *ventre-à-terre* to fill your mind full of every scandalous secret he knows about my past. He will be merciless."

Lady Fanny began to pace up and down the room, and Derek saw that she was truly upset. After a while she came over to stand beside him, gazing unseeingly out of the study windows.

"No," she said, after several minutes had elapsed. "It is far more prudent for my aunt and me to return to Primrose Court this afternoon. We have already put a heavy strain on your hospitality, Colonel—"

"Rubbish!" he exclaimed, more disappointed than he cared to admit. "I will not hear of it, Lady Fanny. Only this morning Margaret was telling me how much she enjoys your companionship. And think of how distraught Charlotte would be. Besides, I had thought you more than a match for that Town Tulip and his scurrilous gossip. My sister and I care not a fig for his malicious rumours, and together, you and I, we will call his bluff."

She smiled wanly. "You make it sound so easy, Colonel." She turned to look up at him, and Derek saw the sadness in her eyes. He felt an alarming, irrational urge to take this lovely woman in his arms and assure her that, with him, she would be safe forever.

"It may not be as easy as it sounds, my dear," he said softly, "but it can be done if you stand firm. Running away is out of the question. Your presence at Sheldon Hall with your aunt cannot but support our story."

He saw she was vacillating, so he stepped closer and took both her hands in his. For no clear reason he could see, it was vitally important to him that Lady Fanny agree to play her part in the little drama he had devised.

"Please allow me to do this small thing for you, my dear," he murmured, his voice low and intimate. "I have not forgotten what you did for Charlotte in Calais. It is only fitting that I do this for you now."

She studied him intently, her gaze troubled. Then he felt her tension drain away and knew he had convinced her.

"Very well, you win, Colonel. I will stay and play your game." Her smile was tentative. "But there are two things I must insist upon."

"Anything you wish, my dear." His heart was beating so erratically, Derek was afraid she would hear it.

"This make-believe *understanding* we are about to enter into must be made known to your sister and my aunt. They must not be allowed to think there is a grain of truth in it."

"Agreed," he murmured, still holding her hands against his waistcoat.

"And second, before we even start this deception, you must allow me to reveal to you the scandals that have haunted me for ten years. If you find them too disgraceful to bear, you will tell me honestly, and allow me to return home."

"Your first condition is already granted, my dear," he said. "As for listening to your life's scandals, I do not wish to know them, Fanny, so there is no need to tell me what is obviously painful to you."

Lady Fanny shook her head impatiently. "You will learn

them whether you wish to or not just as soon as Gerald
hears what we are about. I would prefer you to hear them
from me rather than from Lord Penryn.''

Derek looked down at Lady Fanny's beautiful face and
wondered if he would later regret following his instincts.
Then she smiled, a smile of utter sweetness and trust, and
suddenly it did not matter how many scandals this woman
had in her past. He knew such thoughts were irrational,
imprudent, even dangerous, but he did not care. Life, which
had come to a standstill after the funeral of his wife,
seemed to be moving forward again, pulling him into a
whirlwind of emotions that made him feel young and
lightheaded.

"I see no point in such a confession," he insisted. "And
if Lord Penryn so much as opens his mouth to slander you,
my dear, I shall take great pleasure in teaching him a lesson
he will not soon forget."

She smiled at his bravado, but shook her head. "I would
not wish you to be sorry later, Colonel. Or shocked. Allow
me to tell you at least the worst of my sins."

He placed a finger on her lips to silence her, surprised
at his own daring. "Humour me in this, my dear."

When Lady Fanny acquiesced without further protest,
the colonel had a sudden premonition that the lady's sins
would return to haunt him.

Chapter 17

Counterfeit Betrothal

If Miss Sheldon felt any misgivings about the deception
her brother proposed to practice upon Lord Penryn, she
did not share them with Lady Fanny. Lady Wentworth, on
the other hand, had clapped her hands in an unusual display of excitement when the colonel had outlined the plan.
Both ladies threw themselves wholeheartedly into the

game of make-believe, and the next few days passed in a whirl of activity. By the end of the first week, Fanny was beginning to feel rather overwhelmed by the affair. She had never realized that pretending to enjoy a certain under-standing with a gentleman would entail so much work. What might have been expected of her had an actual offer been made and accepted?

"But I do not need more clothes," she protested one morning when Margaret announced that the carriage had been ordered for eleven o'clock to carry the ladies into Brighton to visit the mantua maker.

"Never say so, Fanny, my dear," Margaret cried in dis-may. "This is one of the few times in your life when you may order as many gowns and other fripperies as you wish and no gentleman will accuse you of frivolity."

"I should hope not," Fanny had responded, instantly up in arms. "No gentleman of my acquaintance would dare dictate to me on matters of fashion."

"Fanny, dearest," her aunt remarked soothingly, "be guided by us in this. Fashions are different here in England, and your Indian gowns are sure to appear outmoded. We cannot have that in a newly betrothed lady of your rank and fortune."

"But I have an entirely new French wardrobe. And I am not betrothed, as you insist upon calling it, Aunt. The colo-nel and I have agreed to *pretend* to an understanding. That is all."

"Of course it is, dear," her aunt murmured, although Fanny was sure she had not listened to a word. "The colo-nel has agreed not to send a notice to the *Gazette* until Lord Penryn—"

"Notice to the *Gazette*?" Fanny burst out indignantly, suppressing an uncomfortable fluttering in her chest. "I should hope he has more sense. There was never any talk of notices in the newspapers, Aunt. Was there, Margaret?" she added, turning to her hostess who was poring over the latest issue of *La Belle Assemblée*.

"No, of course not, Fanny," she replied reassuringly. "At least not yet."

Fanny's mouth dropped open in astonishment. "W-what

d-do you m-mean, n-not yet, Margaret," she stammered. "There can be no question of notices of any kind."

Margaret smiled enigmatically. "No one can predict the future, Fanny, so how can we be sure of anything? Now do put on your bonnet and shawl, for we cannot be late for our appointment with Madame Clochard."

The session with the fashionable modiste was fraught with awkwardness for Fanny. Not only did Madame Clochard appear to know exactly who she was and the extent of her fortune, but also the reason Lady Fanny Wentworth was desirous of enhancing her wardrobe.

"This striped silk in emerald green is bound to appeal to a military gentleman," the modiste cooed, displaying an outrageously expensive bolt of watered silk just arrived— or so she claimed—from the Orient.

After Madame had supervised the assistant summoned to take her measurements, Fanny drew her aunt aside. "How does this female know so much about me and the colonel?" she hissed angrily.

"I am afraid Margaret dropped a few hints," Lady Wentworth replied.

"How *could* she?" Fanny fumed, glancing over to where Margaret was deep in a discussion with Madame over the relative merits of Brussels or French lace for the trimming of evening gowns.

The worst moment in Fanny's afternoon occurred when Madame Clochard produced a bolt of beautifully embroidered white silk that, she suggested archly, was all the rage in London for bridal gowns. Quite unable to cope with such impertinence with any degree of serenity, Fanny cast her eyes wildly at Margaret, who gamely came to the rescue.

"I believe her ladyship would prefer to focus on her prenuptial wardrobe," she said with admirable calm. "There will be time to think of bridal gowns later, perhaps in the summer."

"Perhaps by that time you will be ready for a bridal gown yourself, Miss Sheldon," the modiste simpered.

Margaret blushed and murmured some polite rejoinder, but as they left the shop, Fanny was reminded that Sir Joshua had actually completed a poem to Miss Sheldon's beauty—not a masterpiece by any means, but a poem nevertheless. He had been persuaded to read it aloud after dinner one evening, since the infamous poetry contest had been cancelled. He had also brought over flowers for Margaret on several occasions, and only last night the colonel had remarked that he was expecting a formal request from the baronet as soon as Sir Joshua could summon up the courage.

On impulse, Fanny turned back to Madame Clochard and quietly ordered her to reserve the entire bolt of white silk for Miss Sheldon, admonishing the modiste to keep the purchase strictly a secret. If Sir Joshua did come up to scratch, she thought, her friend would have her bridal gown waiting to be made up.

On the drive back to Sheldon Hall, Fanny had to listen to her aunt and Margaret discuss not only each purchase she had made, but also to their plans to introduce Fanny into their circle of friends. Margaret insisted that Fanny and her brother should be seen together in Brighton and attend a few select gatherings in the neighbourhood.

"I have taken the liberty of accepting an invitation from Sir Denis and Lady Palmer to attend their spring card-party next Wednesday," Margaret remarked as their carriage swept up the Sheldon driveway. "It is considered one of the highlights of the Season around here. An affair not to be missed. Lady Palmer thoughtfully included you and Lady Wentworth in her invitation, Fanny, and since Dr. Mackensie has declared you completely restored to health, I see no reason why you need deny yourself amusement."

"You are right, Margaret," Fanny's aunt agreed. "It is high time Fanny started to enjoy life."

"I *am* enjoying life," Fanny protested, feeling slightly overcome by the role she had taken on. "There is nothing so enjoyable to the spirit as an English garden in the springtime."

She was thinking of the soothing atmosphere of the grotto as she spoke, and the intriguing moments she had spent there with the colonel. Had she been rather more brazen during that encounter, perhaps she would not be merely pretending to an attachment with the gentleman. But then again, how could she expect a man of honour to offer his name to a female as tainted as Lady Fanny Wentworth? No, she corrected herself, she was Lady Fanny St. Ives, divorced wife of the powerful Duke of Cambourne, accused adulteress. It was time she admitted her shame openly, and at the first opportunity, she would insist that the colonel allow her to reveal her scandalous past to him. That would put a quick stop to any understanding between them, feigned or otherwise.

"Fanny!" she heard her aunt exclaim, breaking into these unhappy thoughts. "You have not heard a word Margaret has been saying, dearest. Wool gathering is what you are doing, admit it."

Fanny meekly confessed it, but before Margaret could review the list of diversions she had planned, the chaise drew up at the front door. Collins stood ready to assist the ladies out of the carriage, but before he could do so, the colonel appeared in the doorway and hastened to hand the ladies down himself.

"I trust my sister has not overtired you, Fanny," he said solicitously as he escorted her up the steps, her gloved hand snugly caught in the crook of his arm.

"Nothing of the sort, Colonel," she replied, enjoying the attention. "My aunt always says I have the stamina of an elephant."

"Believe me, you are like no such animal I have ever seen," the colonel murmured, his smoky eyes full of amusement.

Fanny laughed, amazed that she had ever considered this gentlemen humourless. "I shall need all my strength if I am to keep up with the engagements your sister has planned for me. Between dinner and card-parties with your neighbours, and excursions to attend select soirées in Town, to say nothing of the musicale Margaret plans to hold before the end of the month, I shall be quite run off my feet."

"I must have a word with my sister," the colonel said with a frown. "We cannot have you suffering a relapse."

"Oh, there is no chance of that, Colonel," Fanny countered. "I am happy to see Margaret and my aunt in such good form." She paused, then added in a more serious tone, "My agent is demanding my presence in Portsmouth before the departure of the *Peregrine* next week. There are decisions to be made regarding the cargo. Cunningham also tells me he has been approached by the agent of the Horton Brothers in Falmouth. They are of a mind to expand their fleet and have an eye on the *Fortune Hunter*."

"And will you sell?"

Fanny laughed. "I doubt that when Jack returns, he would be very happy to learn I have sold his ship out from under him. Besides, I doubt the Hortons could offer me enough to tempt me. The *Fortune Hunter* is my fastest ship and very profitable."

The colonel made no reply, and Fanny glanced at him, noting that his brows were drawn together in a deep frown. She was vividly reminded that this man did not approve of her connection with Trade. They were as far apart as they had ever been. This make-believe betrothal was a sham that had momentarily clouded her judgement and stirred up childish dreams of love and happiness and a family of her own. She had cast such foolishness from her life the day her father had given her to the Duke of Cambourne. Why then was she spinning such nonsensical fantasies around a gentleman so unsuitable, so unattainable, that she felt foolish even pretending to a connection with him that did not exist?

Besides which, she reminded herself as they stepped into the hall and the colonel guided her towards the stairs, he *does not care a fig for me.* This is merely repayment for the slight assistance she rendered Charlotte in Calais. There is nothing between us that the lightest summer breeze could not dissipate in an instant.

This depressing thought followed Fanny up to her room and stayed with her far into the night, robbing her of sleep.

The colonel watched Lady Fanny ascend the stairs, a frown lingering on his face. The light banter between them had evaporated the instant she mentioned her shipping interests in Portsmouth. It was evident that she had no intention of relinquishing that activity now that her health was restored.

That Lady Fanny had not changed back into a respectable lady of quality the moment she set foot on English soil disturbed him more than he cared to admit. He had believed, rather naively he now supposed, that once cut off from the pernicious influence of her uncle's trading activities in Bombay, Lady Fanny would no longer feel the need to manage Sir John's affairs personally. And the information that the Horton Brothers—the shrewdest merchants on the south coast—had made an offer for one of Lady Fanny's ships had raised a brief hope that she would divest herself of this embarrassing connection with Trade.

Her assurance that she could not leave Jack Mansford without a ship had struck another uneasy note in his mind. Had Jack not assured him that there was nothing but friendship between them, the colonel would have chosen the captain as the logical match for Lady Fanny. They shared the same reckless, devil-may-care approach to life, whereas it was as plain as a pikestaff that Derek shared nothing with her.

Not that he wished to share a closer connection with the lady, Derek hastened to remind himself. Lady Fanny Wentworth was as far as any female could get from the ideal he carried in his heart. But perhaps it was foolish of him to believe in ideals after his wife's betrayal. Perhaps that wastrel Penryn came closer to the mark than he imagined when he labeled Derek a paragon of prudence and morality. Perhaps he was a little too rigid in his beliefs.

The colonel's peace of mind was further jolted later that evening as he watched the three ladies descend the curving staircase. He was engaged to escort them to the Palmers' card-party, Lady Fanny's first sortie into *ton* circles since their plan to dupe Lord Penryn had been set in motion. His sister was glowing in a green satin gown, its neckline lower than he had seen her wear before. Lady Wentworth showed to advantage in puce velvet with a lace collar. But his eyes were drawn to Lady Fanny, a vision in deep blue silk that seemed to float around her in shimmering clouds. As he watched her graceful descent, Derek felt his mouth go dry. Although he knew Lady Fanny in no way resembled an angel, he could not help likening her to a celestial apparition as she cast him a radiant smile.

"Egad, what a bevy of beauties," exclaimed Sir Joshua, who had arrived earlier to accompany the Sheldon party. His jovial compliment made Margaret blush, but Lady Fanny laughed.

"You are a heartless flatterer, Sir Joshua," she chided, but her tone belied her pleasure. She looked buoyant with anticipation, and the colonel felt himself returning her smile. How lovely she must have looked as a young girl, he thought, if the passing years have turned her into this stunning woman.

No sooner had their party arrived at Palmer House than the colonel knew his impressions had not been wrong. As the colonel and Sir Joshua stood in conversation with their host, he followed the ladies' progress round the spacious saloon and noted the enthusiasm Lady Fanny's presence elicited, particularly from the male guests.

"A real charmer, that Wentworth gel," Sir Denis declared jovially when it became apparent that several young gentlemen had attached themselves to her train. "Quite the little Beauty, too, if you do not object to my saying so, Sheldon."

The colonel had expected that word of his supposed interest in the lovely lady from Bombay would have leaked out by now, but he was unprepared for Palmer's direct attack.

Quickly regaining his poise, he responded carefully. "And why should I object to whatever you care to say, Sir Denis?"

His host chortled delightedly. " 'Tis no secret that you have a eye for the lass yourself, m'lad," the baronet replied. "Cannot say I blame you, either. A pearl past price she is. And rich as Croesus, too, I hear."

The colonel made no response and both gentlemen turned their attention towards the opposite side of the room where Lady Fanny was laughing gaily, the clear sound of it reaching across the room to tantalize him. Derek felt a twist of emotion. Telling himself that he was not the lady's nursemaid, the colonel settled down to a quiet game of piquet with his host. Unfortunately he remained distracted, and soon discovered that his inattention had placed him in Sir Denis's debt. Mortified at his imprudence, the colonel put Lady Fanny firmly from his mind and set himself to win back his losses.

An hour later, Lady Fanny rose from a game of whist to stretch her legs and wandered into the dining room, where all manner of refreshments had been laid out. She accepted a glass of champagne punch from the footman at the head of the table, collected a few crab patties on a small plate, and was about to return to the card room when she saw her brother standing in the doorway.

He had obviously been awaiting the opportunity to accost her, for he came up to her immediately, a dark frown on his handsome face.

"What a surprise to find you here, Freddy," she remarked coolly. "I seem to remember that, until quite recently, you complained of being under the hatches. Am I to assume that you have come about?"

Her brother answered with a grunt. "Gerald has practically cut me off since you turned down his obliging offer, Fanny," he muttered. "I trust he has enough of the ready to pay the shot at the inn, because—"

"Obliging offer?" Fanny cut in sharply. "Did I hear you aright, Freddy? You cannot mean that you wish to see me tied to that lying, cheating panderer?"

"I care little whom you get yourself hitched to, Fanny," her brother replied, his voice surly, "just as long as the chap has deep pockets. Even this Sheldon fellow you seem to have set your sights on has a respectable fortune, although you could do better than throw yourself at that dry stick." He seemed to think this comment amusing for he let out a cynical laugh. "Of course, it would be better for everybody if you were to accept Gerald. He is practically one of the family in any case, and then we could all be comfortable."

"With my fortune? Is that what you mean?" Fanny shot back, utterly appalled at the callousness of this speech. "You deceive yourself, Freddy; Gerald is no family of mine and never will be. And you may tell him so when you see him."

"Are you threatening to let your favourite brother be sent up for debt?" His voice had dropped back to a cajoling level Fanny recognized from their childhood. For a moment memories of happier times at Hayle House rose up to haunt her, and she was tempted to tell Freddy to send his inn reckoning to Primrose Court. Then she hardened her heart.

"Apply to your brothers or to Father. And stand aside, Freddy, I wish to return to my friends."

He made no move to do so, and Fanny's blood froze at the savage expression that flashed across his face. This was no longer the brother she had known and loved, she realized with a pang of regret.

"You would do well to reconsider, little sister," Freddy said slowly, skewering her with his eyes. "Do you really believe your precious colonel would look twice at you were he to discover, by one of those convenient coincidences"— and here he sneered cynically—"that your past is so riddled with scandal that it would put a hardened criminal to the blush?"

Fanny stared at him, feeling suddenly nauseous. "You would not do anything so perverted. I will not believe it of you. Besides," she added with false bravado, "what could you tell him that he does not already know?"

The grin on Freddy's face was so sinister that Fanny flinched. "My dear innocent, does your pompous colonel know that you are related by blood to the man who seduced his wife and caused her death?"

Fanny thought her heart must have stopped beating. After a pause she managed to whisper, "Roger? Do you mean Roger?"

He laughed, apparently vastly amused at her distress. "Of course, I mean our womanizing brother, my dear. Who else could I possibly mean? I am sure the colonel would be loath to ally himself with such a female, particularly if she has hidden the truth from him." He grinned mirthlessly. "But you would never do that, would you Fanny, my love?"

Carefully, Fanny set her glass and plate down on a nearby table. She was no longer hungry. Briefly overcome by sudden dizziness, she rested one hand on the table to steady herself. "You are blackmailing me?" she said, surprised that her voice sounded so calm.

"Of course, my pet," he smirked, his voice full of false regret. "You give me no choice, Fanny. Now, if only you would be sensible and accept Gerald, none of these ugly secrets have to come out. Nobody in Brighton need know that the rich and top-lofty Lady Fanny Wentworth is actu-

ally Fanny St. Ives, a divorced adulteress, with close connections with wife killers and card sharps."

Fanny felt the bile rise in her throat. "And perverts,"
she hissed so loudly that several guests turned to stare. "Do
not forget the perverts, Freddy. Gerald has told me the
whole sordid story of Cambourne's scandalous secrets,
which includes you."

Her brother went pale at this revelation, and Fanny guessed
that he had imagined his own scandals safe. How she wished
she had insisted upon telling the colonel about her past, although she doubted he would be here with her tonight had
he learned she was the sister of his wife's seducer.

They stared at each other for a long moment. "So do your
worst, Freddy, and I will do mine. Colonel Sheldon is not
the only eligible gentleman in England," she added defiantly,
knowing that she lied. Sheldon was the only man who had
made her feel like a giddy girl again. It dawned on her quite
suddenly, standing there seeing old ghosts rising from her
past, that her heart was lost, quite irrevocably, to a man who
could hold her in nothing but contempt once he discovered—
as he would—that Lady Fanny Wentworth was a fraud.

CHAPTER 18

Secrets Unravel

Out of the corner of his eye, the colonel saw Lady Fanny
rise from her table and move gracefully from the room.
She paused to exchange pleasantries with Squire Masters
and his lady, who were seated near the door with the vicar
and one of Sir Denis's daughters. Derek could not help
thinking what a gracious hostess she would make, and from
there his thoughts wandered back to Sheldon Hall, over
four years without a proper mistress. And soon to be without even his sister's presence if Sir Joshua's new de-
meanour meant what Derek was certain it did.

His own daughter had sensed that Lady Fanny should be the next mistress of Sheldon Hall. Derek wished that he shared Charlotte's trust, but how could he after Constance's betrayal? His heart seemed to be willing, but his mind was still scarred by bitterness.

Why then had he refused to listen to Lady Fanny's confession of her *sins*, as she had called them? Was it possible that he simply did not wish to know that this enchanting female would prove to be no different from the Beauty who had shattered his life once before? A foolishly gallant gesture, he thought wryly, staring unseeingly at the cards in his hand. As much so as this make-believe betrothal he had embarked upon with little thought of the consequences, which he would most likely regret before too long.

"Well, lad, have you gone to sleep at your post again?"

Sir Denis's jocular reprimand jolted the colonel out of his reverie. He grinned sheepishly. "I think it is my empty stomach that is distracting me, Sir Denis," he lied blithely. "What do you say if we sample some of those crab patties Lady Palmer is justly famous for providing?"

His host turned to glance at Lady Fanny's table, then eyed the colonel with a sly grin on his round face. "Ah! I see what ails you, lad. A certain lady has also gone in for refreshments, has she now? Well, you had best run along to see that none of those foppish young bucks steals a march on you." Sir Denis gestured across the room. "Keep a sharp eye on that one, lad," he warned, an expression of distrust marring his cheerful countenance.

The colonel glanced across the room to discover who had attracted Sir Denis's censure, and a feeling of uneasiness assailed him as he recognized the elegantly dressed gentleman in pale yellow pantaloons, exaggerated shirt points, and a cravat tied in a fashionable Trône d'Amour, sauntering from the room. What was Viscount Penryn doing at a country card-party?

The answer seemed to be obvious, and Derek rose to his feet to stride down the hall towards the refreshment room. As he approached the doorway, a man's cynical laughter floated out to greet him, followed by a low remark he did not catch. Then another voice he recognized as St. Ives's rose angrily.

"You would do well to abandon that high and mighty

stance you have picked up in India, Fanny. It does not become you, and besides, as Gerald's wife you would never have to worry about your reputation. As Viscountess Penryn you would be accepted everywhere."

Derek heard Lady Fanny's trill of laughter. "If that is the price I must pay for acceptance, far better I return to India."

"Then this silly rumour I hear about an understanding between you and that gapeseed Sheldon is all a hum?" Penryn demanded. "I thought as much."

The colonel paused for a moment and held his breath, willing her not to deny him.

"Any such understanding, if it exists, can hardly be any concern of yours, Gerald," she answered calmly. Not a glowing endorsement by any means, Derek thought ruefully, but no denial either.

"We shall see how you change your tune once Sheldon learns who you are, my dear Fanny," the viscount drawled. "I wager you will come running to me when he gives you the cut direct. Why not save yourself the humiliation and admit that this business with the colonel is merely a passing fancy? One of your famous starts that I recall you once found so amusing, Fanny."

Derek could hold back no longer. He stepped forward, brushing past St. Ives to stand beside Lady Fanny. He cupped her elbow lightly, noticing that she looked pale, although her violet eyes blazed defiantly.

"Is everything all right, my dear? You look a little out of sorts, Fanny." He paused as she turned to gaze up at him, twin pools of deep amethyst that invited him to lose himself in them. Did he also discern a silent appeal there? Or was his overactive sense of chivalry taking over again? His use of her given name had been deliberate and produced a snort of impatience from Lord Penryn.

"There is nothing the matter with Fanny that a little common sense would not cure," he muttered to nobody in particular.

Neither Fanny nor the colonel paid him any heed. Derek was elated when her eyes never left his face, and a tentative smile relaxed her mouth. He returned her smile and felt some of the tension go out of her.

"It appears that I lack common sense, or so these gentlemen claim," she murmured, continuing to hold his gaze.

Derek's lips twitched. "Surely we already knew that, my dear," he said softly, quite as though they were alone together. "I see no reason to fall into a pother over that."

"Then all I can say is that you must have windmills in your head as well, sir," the viscount snapped impatiently. "Allow me to point out that you know nothing about this female with whom you enjoy, or so the gossips say, a secret understanding. St. Ives and I trust it is merely one of Fanny's hoaxes, since no notice has appeared in the *Gazette* to confirm this rumour."

Derek felt Fanny stiffen, and although he felt that Penryn deserved to be put in his place, preferably with a well-placed left hook to the chin, he suppressed the angry retort that leapt to mind.

"I think I know everything I need to know about Lady Fanny's past," he said mildly. Then he turned to his make-believe betrothed and with no little alarm heard himself say, "I see we have been remiss in sending out the announcement, my dear," he remarked, seeing the shock in her eyes, combined with something that looked like fear. "I will attend to that matter in the morning. That is if you agree, my love?"

A paralyzed silence followed this announcement, and Derek was certain that he had finally taken leave of his senses before Lady Fanny responded in an unusually meek voice.

"Whatever you think best, Colonel."

"Fanny!" Lord Penryn exclaimed furiously, "have you run mad? You were ever a willful baggage, but this is beyond the pale. I will not stand for it. Admit that this betrothal"—he fairly spat out the word—"is another of your Banbury tales. I forbid you to continue with this deception, Fanny, do you hear me? If you do not renounce this farce immediately, I shall have no other choice but to tell *all*."

The colonel again felt the urge to land the obnoxious viscount a facer and destroy his aristocratic profile forever, but instead he dredged up a deprecating laugh. "I fear it is too late for that, my lord," he said patiently. "The offer has been made and accepted. Has it not, my dear?"

Lady Fanny raised her eyes and held his gaze for several

moments before answering. When she did, her voice was soft but steady. "I would have been foolish indeed to reject such a charming offer, Colonel."

Derek had barely enough time to consider the enormity of what he had just done, when the viscount struck back. "More fool you, Fanny, to imagine you could escape your past," Lord Penryn said sarcastically. "You should know, Sheldon, that this woman's name is not Wentworth. She is Fanny St. Ives, sister to Freddy here, and to our dear Roger, the man who seduced your wife. I imagine you will not be so eager to hold her to this ridiculous betrothal now you know she is a consummate liar," he paused, then added in a smug voice, "and other, worse things besides."

The colonel felt as though he had been dealt a particularly savage blow below the belt. For a moment he had difficulty breathing, and when he looked down at Fanny, willing her to deny this shattering accusation, she would not meet his gaze. Suddenly he felt her tremble, and his initial revulsion was replaced by a determination to save Fanny from the viscount's vicious attack. They would settle the matter later in private, but for now he knew they must join ranks and present a united front to deflect Penryn's malicious revelation. Either that, he told himself calmly, or he must come to fisticuffs with the wretch without delay and create a scandal in Lady Palmer's dining room.

"It is hardly your place to tell me what I should or should not do, my lord," he said coldly as soon as he was able. "And as I have said before, I know all I need to about Lady Fanny's past. Now, if you will excuse us, I will escort you back to the card room, my dear," he said, addressing a strangely subdued Lady Fanny.

Lord Penryn made as if to block their passage, but the colonel drew himself up to his full height and glared at the smaller man until he stepped aside, muttering beneath his breath.

The silence was thick about them as they walked along the hall, but before they reached the door to the card-room, Margaret rushed out, closely followed by Sir Joshua.

"Oh, Fanny!" Margaret exclaimed, wringing her hands. "How glad I am to find you. Lady Wentworth has been taken ill. Only a dizzy spell, she tells me, but I do wish you

would come to her. Derek," she added, turning to her
brother, "I do believe we may have to take our leave early.
Perhaps you should order the carriage, dear."

The colonel was only too glad to get away. And later, as
he handed the ladies into the carriage and mounted his
horse, his mind could not—or did not want to—accept Lady
Fanny's connection with the scandal in his own past.

To her shame, Lady Fanny's first reaction when she
heard of her aunt's indisposition was relief, since it provided an excuse for her to make an early departure from
Palmer House. She tried to insist that the colonel and his
sister remain to enjoy the remainder of the evening, but
Margaret was adamant. How could they enjoy themselves
knowing that one of their guests was in pain?

Her emotions in an uproar, Lady Fanny had little inclina-
tion to argue, so in no time at all, she found herself handed
into the Sheldon chaise by the silent, thin-lipped colonel.
She dared not look at him and kept her eyes resolutely
lowered as she settled herself beside her ailing aunt. Once
he had closed the carriage door and mounted his horse,
Fanny relaxed, but her thoughts were not reassuring.

The colonel's confirmation of their false betrothal and
his intention to send out the customary notice to the *Gazette* had left her stunned and confused. What could have
induced him to carry their make-believe so far into the
realm of reality? It was true that Gerald had been deliberately provoking, but once that announcement was made
public, it would be impossible for either of them to with-
draw without creating another scandal.

Fanny wanted no more scandals. She would have to
make certain that no announcement appeared in the *Gazette*, much as she wished that things could have been different. But it was fruitless to daydream, particularly since
the colonel was now—thanks to Gerald's spitefulness—fully
aware of her relationship with the man who stole his wife
away. She had been surprised that the colonel had not disowned her on the spot, but was grateful for his gallant
gesture to help her save face, undeserved as it was.

Whatever his reasons for protecting her in public, Fanny
was certain that the colonel had condemned her in his

heart. And she had only herself to blame. She felt contempt for herself, for the weakness that had overridden her common sense and drawn her into accepting a role she was not fit to play, even in her wildest fantasies.

Fanny sighed and reached to settle the rug more firmly around her aunt's knees. She wondered how she could convince her romantic, kind-hearted aunt that the charade was over. The sooner they returned to Primrose Court the better.

"She is sleeping, poor dear," Margaret remarked, distracting Fanny from her melancholy meditations and reminding her that Lord Penryn's spiteful revelation would doubtless deprive her of a friendship she had come to cherish. Fanny realized that she owed Margaret an explanation.

"Oh, Margaret," she began, making sure that her aunt was indeed asleep, "something terrible happened at the Palmers' tonight, something that I have dreaded ever since Lord Penryn and my brother discovered me—"

"Your *brother*?" Margaret interrupted. "St. Ives is your brother, Fanny? I suspected as much, dear. You resemble him a little, you know. The same colouring and hair, and except that overindulgence has coarsened his features, his nose is a replica of yours."

"Why did you never remark on it, Margaret?"

"St. Ives is obviously a part of that past you ran away from ten years ago, is he not?"

Fanny was both surprised and humbled. How had she ever imagined Miss Sheldon to be an innocuous country mouse? She had turned out to be kind and generous to a fault, and had easily discovered one of Fanny's secrets. The thought of losing such a friendship saddened her. All the more reason to tell Margaret the truth now, she thought.

"Did you mention this to your brother, Margaret?"

Her friend smiled. "No, dear. Derek did not notice the resemblance and to have pointed it out to him would have uncovered old wounds that he only recently seems to be putting behind him. Thanks to you, my dear Fanny. My greatest wish is that my brother will help you to put whatever troubled you in the past behind you, too, Fanny."

When Fanny failed to respond, her throat suddenly tight with emotion, Margaret continued. "You must not mind Derek's gruff manner, my dear. He was an officer in Wellington's army—sometimes he acts as though he still is—and is accustomed to giving orders. But underneath that harsh exterior, he has the kindest heart imaginable—"

"Oh, I know he does," Fanny cut in, her voice unsteady with emotion. "Only consider this make-believe betrothal he has undertaken, at great inconvenience to himself, with the sole purpose of protecting me from further unwanted advances from Lord Penryn. And then tonight . . . Oh, Margaret, you have no idea what he said when Gerald odiously insinuated that I am playing a hoax on the colonel."

"No, dear," Margaret gently prodded, when Fanny paused to gather her thoughts, "what did Derek say?"

Fanny swallowed. "He said, as calmly as though it had truly happened, that he had made me an offer and that I had accepted. Can you imagine that, Margaret?"

"Oh, indeed I can," Margaret responded, with a smile. "What a sly thing to do." She appeared to be hugely diverted by the account. "I never would have given him credit for such quick thinking."

"I could hardly deny it in front of Gerald, who was monstrously put out when I agreed—under duress you understand—that we should send out a notice to the *Gazette*. I cannot believe I was such a lackwit as to agree to something that cannot possibly happen."

"And why cannot it happen, dear?" Margaret asked.

"How can you ask such a question, Margaret? You must know I cannot allow this pretence to gain momentum until your poor brother finds himself trapped in a betrothal he does not want."

Margaret's smile faded. "How can you be so sure Derek does not wish to be trapped? He cares for you, Fanny. I know he does, and men are notoriously evasive when it comes to matters of the heart. Only consider how many years I have been waiting for Joshua to declare himself. How do you know my brother did not devise this whole charade to avoid having to come out into the open?"

Fanny listened with growing horror. Was it possible, as Margaret hinted, that the colonel entertained softer feeling for her despite his frequent avowals of disapproval? The momentary feeling of joy that flared up in her heart withered before it did more than stir up the pain there.

"Oh, no, Margaret," she murmured in anguish, "you are mistaken. You *must* be mistaken. And in any case, it no longer signifies. You should have seen your brother's face when Penryn told him who I am and pointed out my connections with Freddy. I only wonder he did not disown me on the spot."

"But he did not do so, Fanny," Margaret remarked after a short pause.

Fanny refused to be comforted. "I know he wanted to. He was so cold and stiff, it hurt to look at him."

Margaret reached over and gently took Fanny's hand in both hers. Unbelievably, she was smiling again.

"I do believe you care for him, Fanny. Admit it, you do care a little, do you not?"

Fanny felt the emotional strain of the evening overtaking her. By some ironic twist of fate, the colonel's heart might conceivably have been within her reach. But that same fate had brought Lord Penryn and her brother to Brighton, and Gerald had managed to destroy her tenuous grasp on happiness, exactly as he had ten years ago.

Fanny felt herself crumble inside and could no longer withhold the hot tears that had threatened to spill all evening.

"C-care for him?" she stammered between sobs. "O-oh, Margaret, I l-love him."

She felt the comforting arms of her friend encircle her and draw Fanny to the seat beside her. Under these kindly ministrations, Fanny gave herself up to grief.

CHAPTER 19

The Announcement

The following morning dawned cold and windy, and Fanny was not surprised to see the low rain clouds scudding across the sky like so many overfed sheep. The change in weather was somehow fitting. She had spent a restless night. What little sleep that did come to her was disturbed by the most heart-wrenching dream she could remember. Not even those long-ago nightmares of the duke, upraised quirt in hand, had conjured up the anguish Fanny had suffered as she stumbled through dark woods, up rocky hills, and over icy streams in the wake of a shadowy man in black. Not once did that man turn around, but Fanny knew who he was. His large, broad-shouldered figure, with its tall black beaver and swirling cloak, drew her ever onwards in an impossible quest.

Yvette's arrival with her hot chocolate distracted Fanny from these lugubrious thoughts, but although the dream faded, she felt the futility of that nightmarish chase linger on.

"Milady!" the abigail exclaimed as she placed the tray on the dresser. "What be ye a-doing out of bed so early? And without your slippers, too. Here," she fussed, "put on your robe, milady. No sense in getting yourself sick again. The colonel will have me hide if you show him that long face at the breakfast table, and no mistake."

Fanny looked at her loyal, outspoken maid with affection. Yvette had been at her side through most of her life, and Fanny could not imagine being without her.

"I am not hungry this morning, Yvette," she said, slipping into the warm robe the abigail held out to her and settling into the cozy armchair beside the empty hearth to drink her chocolate.

"Blue-devilled are you, milady?" Yvette demanded, her sharp eyes fixed on Fanny's face.

"How is my aunt this morning?" Fanny enquired, evading the abigail's question. "Perhaps I should visit her before breakfast."

"Settle down and drink your chocolate first, lass," the abigail ordered, settling a cushion more comfortably in her mistress's chair. "Lady Clarissa woke up as perky as a sparrow more than an hour ago. Seems it was a bad case of indigestion that laid her ladyship low. I gave her one of my potions as soon as we got her to bed last night and that set everything to rights again."

"I am glad to hear it, Yvette," Fanny said, setting down her empty cup, "because we have a busy morning ahead of us packing our trunks. I intend to return to my aunt's house this afternoon if she is up to the journey." Before the abigail could protest, Fanny rose and opened her clothes press. "I think the dark green bombazine will be adequate this morning."

Yvette pulled out the sober-looking gown and laid it on the bed. "Are you sure you would not rather try one of the new morning gowns Madame Clochard made up for you, milady?" she said hopefully. "The lilac muslin with the double flounce is particularly fetching."

"No," Fanny responded, shaking her head. "I am in no mood for frivolity this morning, Yvette."

Fanny heard the abigail heave a theatrical sigh and glanced at her suspiciously. "As you wish, milady," she said in a meek voice that did not fool Fanny for a moment. "But I wonder if the colonel would not prefer to see you in the lilac muslin when you meet with him in his study?"

Fanny's heart gave a lurch. "Since I am not meeting him this morning, I daresay it matters little which gown I wear," she said. "Unless there is something you have not told me, Yvette."

As it turned out, Fanny wore the lilac gown when she trod downstairs later that morning. In response to the colonel's request that she meet with him—a request the abigail insisted she would have delivered after her mistress had eaten her breakfast—Fanny was shown into the study by an impassive Collins a little after eleven o'clock.

The man Fanny had chased through her dreams the night before was standing at the window when she entered, but swung round as the door closed behind her. He greeted her soberly, his rugged features set as if he anticipated an ordeal. There would be no dimples for her this morning, she thought, running her eyes over the colonel's square jaw and thinly compressed lips. No dimples today, or perhaps ever again. How different he had been only yesterday, his eyes warm and soft, his breath hot on her fingers as he carried them to his lips, as he had formed the habit of doing at unexpected moments since they embarked on their make-believe betrothal.

He had played his role too well.

Fanny felt as though her heart had suddenly ceased beat-

ing. And it was all her own fault, she thought bitterly. She
had broken her own golden rule regarding gentlemen, one
that had kept her safe from precisely the emotional turmoil
that now wracked her body and soul. Fanny was quite certain the colonel had not set out to seduce her, but without
trying this man had lulled her into enjoying his presence,
depending upon it, relishing every kind gesture, every warm
glance, wanting it, wanting so much more than he had
given her.

Yet all the while, he had disapproved of her. Even more
intensely now if she read his rigid expression aright. She
should have reminded herself of that inescapable fact every
minute of every day. She should have remained aloof and
untouchable, as she had with innumerable gentlemen in the
past. She should not have let down her guard for an instant.

But what did it signify now to speak of what she should
have done? she thought helplessly. What did it signify that
she had also disapproved of him at first sight? Fanny vividly
recalled her contempt for a man who had no charm at all.
Had she not remarked on that fact to her aunt? Now here
she was, her heart in her mouth like some love-sick schoolroom chit, distraught at the knowledge that their make-
believe understanding was at an end.

Fanny stepped forward into the room, her shoulders
straight, head high. Fanny St. Ives would allow no sign of
her inner turmoil to show, she vowed. He must never know
how much she had been drawn into this make-believe, how
much her heart had been touched.

"I understand you wish to see me, Colonel," she said,
amazed at her own coolness in the face of disaster.

"Yes, my lady," he responded, motioning her to a chair.
"I believe we have a matter still pending between us."

Fanny's heart sank, but she remained standing. This interview would not take long, not after he heard what she
intended to say. "If you refer to Lord Penryn's revelations
last night, sir, I must confirm that I am indeed Francesca
St. Ives, and that Roger St. Ives is my brother, as is Frederick. After I was banished from my home ten years ago, my
Uncle John and Aunt Clarissa took me in. It seemed natural at the time to use their name since I became their
daughter in everything but birth. I make no apologies for

that. But it was a shock to me to learn of Roger's involvement with Lady Sheldon's death. I quite understand that you wish to cut all connections with me, and if my aunt is recovered enough to travel, we shall be out of your house by this afternoon."

Fanny stopped abruptly, quite out of breath at this recital. Her fingers were icy cold, and she grasped them together to still their trembling. There was more she wanted to say, but the odd expression on the colonel's face made her pause.

"I do believe you," he said slowly, "that your brother's affair with Constance came as a shock. But it is hardly reasonable to blame you for your brother's crimes." He paused and cleared his throat, a gesture that increased Fanny's apprehension.

"As a matter of fact, my dear, that is not what I wished to talk with you about," he continued, his voice noncommittal.

When a full minute went by and he said no more, Fanny could bare the suspense no longer. "I see. You wish to hear the other, *worse* scandals that Lord Penryn threatened to reveal about me last night."

He smiled. It was only a small one, without dimples, but it warmed Fanny's heart and brought her close to tears. "Not at all," he said, picking up a paper from the desk. "I wished to show you the announcement we talked of last night before I send it off to the *Gazette*."

Fanny felt as though her legs had turned to jelly, and her heart thumped so loudly that she was certain he must hear it. She opened her mouth to speak but no words came.

At last she whispered, "Never for a moment did I believe you were serious. How could you be? After all, this whole pretense was designed to ward off Gerald's unwelcome attentions, was it not?"

"Was it, Fanny?" he said so softly that she wondered if she had perhaps imagined this entire exchange.

"I b-believe that was the idea," she stammered, quite sure that the colonel had taken leave of his senses.

"Then you cannot deny that once the announcement appears in the *Gazette*, you will have nothing further to fear from Penryn. You will be safe, Fanny. His malicious threats can no longer harm you."

Fanny stared at the colonel for a long moment, stunned. How naive of him to think that the only scandal Gerald held over her was her connection to Lady Sheldon's seducer. But how like this kind and generous man to offer her, probably against his better judgement, the protection of an official betrothal.

"No," she said clearly, "that cannot be." With sudden clarity, Fanny saw that she could not treat the man she had come to love with less consideration than he had offered her. "I cannot allow such an announcement to be published," she added, her voice more determined. "If our pretense becomes official, it changes everything, Colonel. Unless you intend to jilt me, there is no drawing back from such a commitment. Can you not see how impossible that would be?"

"Impossible?" he repeated softly. "I see nothing impossible about it at all, Fanny."

Disregarding this obvious sign of madness, Fanny pushed on. "You cannot have considered the implications, Colonel. If you send this announcement to the *Gazette*, everyone will believe that we are . . . that we are . . ."

"That we are betrothed?" he helped her out, a sardonic smile curling his lips. "Is that what you mean, my dear?"

"Of course that is what I mean," Fanny cried, exasperation giving her strength. "And that would be a worse pretense than the one we—"

"Aha! Now I see where the problem lies," he interrupted. "You do not trust me to protect you from that debauched rogue, is that it, my dear?"

"That has nothing to do with it," Fanny responded quickly.

"Then you do not see me as a suitable candidate for the daughter of an earl. Confess that you think me a paltry creature." The colonel's lopsided smile tore at Fanny's heart.

"Nothing could be further from the truth, as you must know," Fanny protested, anger making her voice shake. "I never thought to hear you spout so much nonsense, Colonel."

"Then it can only be that you have discovered I am interested solely in your fortune," he murmured, so convincingly that Fanny's heart constricted. Then he smiled, and she felt a rush of relief.

"Poppycock!" she snapped, beginning to lose her patience.

"I see," he said, the smile slipping off his face abruptly. "Then must I believe the worst, that you cannot bear the thought of becoming Lady Sheldon, my dear Fanny?" His voice dropped to a mere whisper, "I should have guessed that a woman as beautiful and accomplished as you are would not look twice at an ordinary man like me."

Fanny stared at the colonel, her mind reeling. She heard Margaret's words ringing in her head: *He cares for you, Fanny. I know he does . . . men are notoriously evasive when it comes to matters of the heart . . .* For a delicious moment she allowed herself to bask in the glow of this fantasy. Then she gave herself a mental shake. Margaret was right about evasive gentlemen, she thought bitterly. Was she supposed to believe this rogue was seriously interested in making their betrothal official without committing himself to making an offer?

Why did she not tell him that she had no burning desire to be Lady Sheldon? That is what the Lady Fanny Wentworth of six months ago would have done. Ruthlessly quash the laughable pretensions of an upstart military nobody. She had given any number of gentlemen crushing set-downs in the past, why could she not do the same with Colonel Sheldon?

Something in his eyes told her all too plainly why she could not lie to him. Something in her heart told her she did not want to.

Before Fanny could pluck up her courage to speak frankly of her marriage and divorce, there was a scratching at the door, and Collins announced Sir Joshua Comfrey.

"Morning, Sheldon. I trust I am not interrupting anything important," the baronet blurted out, plunging into the room in the butler's wake as though the hounds of Hell were at his heels. Collins gave his master a mortified glance

and withdrew with an air of offended dignity, nose elevated
in disapproval.

"Lady Fanny and I were discussing—"

"Ah, Lady Fanny," the baronet interrupted, apparently
noticing her for the first time, "I see you are blooming as
usual, my dear. Let me congratulate you once more on
your betrothal to Sheldon here. Never suspected anything
like that was in the wind, must admit. Not that I ain't
pleased as a peahen to see my old friend taking another
wife. Nothing like a loving wife and a brood of little ones
running around the old halls to make a man feel he has
done his duty to God and country, what?" Sir Joshua
grinned broadly at this witticism, and favoured Lady Fanny
with a sly wink.

Derek noted that she had blushed at Sir Joshua's compliment, but quickly turned pale and uncomfortable as the
baronet rattled on about wedded bliss. He wished she had
responded to his last question, but then again perhaps it
was better this way. Did he really wish to hear that Lady
Fanny had no desire to become Lady Sheldon?

The colonel turned to the beaming baronet. "We expected you this afternoon for tea, Sir Joshua. Has something urgent come up to change your plans?"

"You might say that, Sheldon," Sir Joshua responded
with another grin. "If you must know the truth, I cannot
wait to put my head in the noose." He paused abruptly,
then glanced uneasily at Lady Fanny. "Not that Margaret
is anything like a noose, you understand me, my lady. That
is just my manner of speaking. A simple man I am, ain't
that right, Sheldon? With simple tastes." He paused again,
then added quickly, "Not that Margaret is simple. Nothing
of the sort. She is as complicated as any other female, if
you know what I mean."

"I cannot say that I do," Lady Fanny said sweetly,
and Derek hoped she did not intend to tax the baronet's
intellect unduly. "I have heard gentlemen refer to us as
simple-minded; we have learned to ignore that. But now
you tell me that you are simple yourself, while Margaret
is not. How do you expect to go on together if you are
so different?"

"All I meant was that Margaret ain't no bluestocking

like some I could name. I cannot abide a female who puts a man in the shade by spouting Latin or Greek or some other foreign gibberish."

Lady Fanny smiled. "Margaret is fond of poetry, especially Sappho and our own Byron."

"I never heard of this Sappho fellow, and Byron is an odd kind of cove. Never could understand that Don Juan character of his, always up to havey-cavey antics with females. No morals to speak of, if you ask me. Well, I ain't Byron, nor would I want to be, but Margaret was good enough to tell me she liked the poem I wrote for her."

"As I was saying, Sir Joshua," Derek interrupted finally, "Lady Fanny and I were discussing the announcement we are sending to the *Gazette*."

Sir Joshua looked startled, quite as though the idea had never crossed his mind before. "Of course, of course, there is that to attend to. Perhaps we could send two announcements instead of one," he added hopefully. "Merely changing the names, naturally."

"Naturally," Lady Fanny murmured. "But I wonder if you have discussed it with Margaret, Sir Joshua. I am certain she would like to be consulted."

"Actually I had not thought of that yet," he admitted, guiltily. "But since you mention it, Lady Fanny, I shall send out the announcement today."

"I trust you will wait until the offer has been made and accepted, Sir Joshua," she said gently, and the colonel suddenly realized this comment might be meant for him as well. "What a pickle you would be in if the lady refused her consent. Imagine the embarrassment."

Sir Joshua stared at her, evidently the notion of rejection never having crossed his mind. "Oh, Margaret would never refuse me," he blustered, although the colonel could see that his friend's faith had been shaken. "We have had an understanding for years and years. Her brother will vouch for that, will you not, Sheldon?"

"Let me warn you, Sir Joshua," Lady Fanny cut in before the colonel could come to his friend's rescue, "an understanding is not the same as an offer." She paused, and the colonel knew without a doubt that she had spoken to him. "Furthermore, Sir Joshua, I sincerely hope you are fully prepared to go down on your knees and beg. That seems only fitting after so many years of keeping a lady in suspense."

The colonel smiled inwardly at the look of pure horror that flashed over Sir Joshua's face. "Down on my knees? That sort of farradiddle only happens in rubbishy novels read by schoolgirls with addled brains."

Lady Fanny laughed. "I hate to disabuse you, sir, but many ladies of sensibility enjoy these rubbishy novels as you call them. Margaret and I both read them. So I warn you, be prepared to prostrate yourself and tear your hair."

"Tear my hair, too, must I?" Sir Joshua ran a hand over his balding pate and sighed. A thought seemed to strike him and he glanced at his host. "Tell me you did not prostrate yourself, Sheldon," he begged, a hint of panic in his voice. "Tell me this whole kneeling business is a Canterbury Tale invented by women to . . . well, to bring us men to our knees."

Before he could think up a suitable answer to his friend's dilemma, Lady Fanny turned and swept towards the door. "I shall leave you gentlemen to work out the details of this operation in peace," she flung over her shoulder as she closed the door behind her.

"Tell me you did not do it," the baronet pleaded after the lady's footsteps had died away in the hall.

"No, I did not," the colonel admitted, "although perhaps it would have been better had I done so. Saved myself a deal of argument, I daresay."

He stood for a few moments listening to the silence in the hall outside. Then he turned resolutely to his friend.

"Are you suggesting that I do this kneeling thing?" Sir Joshua muttered, looking appalled.

"Yes, old man, afraid so. You heard what Lady Fanny said. Females expect it. And the sooner you get it over with, the better, I would say."

"Then I have your permission to address Margaret?"

The colonel felt a stab of envy at the eagerness and uninhibited joy on Sir Joshua's face. At least his friend was reasonably sure that his lady love returned his regard.

"Of course, you do, old man," he said bracingly, giving Sir Joshua a resounding slap on the back.

The relief of Sir Joshua's face was comical, but his reaction was not what Derek had expected. "Much obliged, Sheldon. You have taken a load off my mind. I will put the matter before Margaret in the next few days, and then—"

"In the next few days?" the colonel exclaimed, thunderstruck. "Are you mad, sir? If you mean to offer for my sister, do it now while you are in the mood. Leave it for later and Margaret may well decide to look elsewhere for a husband."

Sir Joshua looked alarmed, his Adam's apple jumped as he swallowed several times. "Do you think she would?"

"What is there to stop her?" Derek responded ruthlessly. "Fix your interest once and for all. Then you may rest easy. Besides," he added, seeing his neighbour's courage wilt before his eyes, "once you have Margaret's approval, I can send both announcements to the *Gazette* at the same time."

Without waiting for an answer, the colonel reached for the bell pull.

"Ask Miss Sheldon if she can spare us a moment of her time, Collins." he ordered as the butler—who had obviously been standing outside in the hall—threw open the study door.

"Yes, sir," Collins replied, a glimmer of a smile softening his severe countenance. "Immediately, sir."

CHAPTER 20

The Abduction

Lady Fanny mounted the stairs to her aunt's room in a pensive mood. Her interview with the colonel had unsettled her, and as she reviewed their conversation she knew that she could not go another day without putting him in full possession of all the awful facts. The longer she withheld the truth the more reason he would have for disowning her. She would tell him before she left Sheldon Hall that afternoon.

Hurried footsteps from above distracted her, and as Fanny reached the first landing, she ran into Margaret, who stopped abruptly at the sight of her.

"Well?" her friend demanded eagerly. "Is it settled? Did Derek finally declare himself?" When Fanny smiled ruefully and shook her head, Margaret's face clouded. "Oh, Fanny, I cannot believe I have such a nodcock for a brother. I thought he had put Constance and her shameful behaviour behind him and was ready to start a new life with you." She regarded Fanny searchingly. "I quite thought he sent for me to share the good news, but now——"

"Now I must go up to Aunt Clarissa and tell her we are returning to Primrose Court this afternoon," Fanny interrupted in a subdued voice.

"Well, I hate to disappoint you, dear," Margaret responded quickly, "but your aunt is in no condition to travel. I have just been with her, and I fear we may have to call on Dr. Mackensie again if she does not rally soon."

Fanny raised her eyebrows in surprise. "B-but Yvette assured me this morning that she was in prime twig," she protested.

"That may have been so earlier this morning, but I can assure you, Fanny, that Lady Wentworth is not feeling at all the thing at the moment."

"Then I must go to her at once."

"I will come up again as soon as I find out why Derek has sent for me in such a rush," Margaret said, turning to descend to the hall below.

At her friend's words, Fanny gave a gasp. "Oh, Margaret, how could I be so thoughtless. I forgot to tell you that Sir Joshua is with the colonel, and I suggest you prepare yourself to receive his offer, my dear. And do not be surprised if he goes down on his knees. I warned him that we females expect it."

For a moment Fanny was able to forget her own troubles as her smiling friend gave her an impulsive hug and fairly ran down the stairs. But Margaret's evident happiness only made Fanny more conscious of how far she was from reaching that same state herself.

Her aunt greeted her with a weak smile, and Fanny's heart went out to the older woman as she bent to kiss her soft cheek. "What is this I hear, Aunt?" she demanded teasingly. "Still lolling about in bed, I see."

"I am sorry to be such a nuisance, dear, but I still do not feel quite the thing. But never mind me, dear, I shall be right as rain by tonight." She closed her eyes as though this speech had tired her, and soon fell into a light sleep.

Fanny dismissed Mrs. Collins, who had been sitting with the invalid, and settled down to await Margaret's return. After twenty minutes of listening to her aunt's gentle snores, Fanny moved over to the escritoire and reached for a sheet of pressed vellum. She sat staring at the blank sheet for several minutes before taking up a quill. By the time the door opened to admit a radiant Margaret, Fanny had only listed her mother's death by suicide and was wondering how to explain the tangled events leading to her divorce and banishment. She had thought that writing the scandals from her past down on paper would be easier than telling the colonel face to face, but nothing made that part of her life less painful.

"Margaret!" she exclaimed softly, throwing down the quill and rising to clasp her friend by the hands. "Am I to wish you happy, my dear?"

The answer was obvious from Margaret's expression, her flushed cheeks, and sparkling eyes, and Fanny had to suppress a pang of envy at the happy conclusion to her friend's long ordeal.

"Did Sir Joshua go down on his knees?" she wanted to know. "And did he actually confess that he loves you?"

"After a little prodding, he did," Margaret replied with a happy smile. "You know how reluctant gentlemen are to speak of love. But Joshua was quite ready to go down on his knees without protest. Quite eloquent he was, poor man; I confess I was very moved. Of course, he did require my assistance to get back on his feet again, but by that time, we were formally betrothed, and he seemed so pleased with himself that I did not have the heart to tell him that my first action as mistress of Cedar Lodge will be to cut down on all those sweetmeats he eats."

"Have you settled on a date yet?" Fanny asked as she

drew her friend into the adjoining sitting room so they
could speak freely.

Margaret blushed. "Sir Joshua was all in favour of an
early wedding. He even mentioned Sunday a week from
tomorrow, but I told him that was ridiculous, why, it requires three weeks for the banns to be read. Men have no
idea what it takes to arrange such an affair."

"There is always a special license," Fanny said hesitantly.

Margaret looked shocked. "Not if I have any say in it.
He has waited for so many years, he may wait another
three weeks and do things properly. Besides, I have yet to
order my gown."

It was Fanny's turn to smile. "You should know that I
have reserved that embroidered white silk you liked so
much at Madame Clochard's, and I am certain she could
make it up in a trice."

Margaret looked at her in surprise. "That is very kind of
you, Fanny, but you will need it for yourself, if I understood
my brother correctly."

Fanny felt herself grow pale. "And just what has the
colonel said to put such a notion in your head, Margaret?"

"It is you who should tell *me*, Fanny," she said accusingly. "How could you pretend to me that you and Derek
had not come to an understanding? You had me calling
him a nodcock when all the time the two of you . . . Oh,
Fanny, how could you?"

"What has your brother told you?" she repeated in a
calm voice, although her heart was racing uncomfortably.

Margaret smiled. "As if you did not know, dear," she
teased. "Derek told me he has sent the announcements of
both betrothals to the *Gazette*."

"What a stubborn, overbearing man he is," Fanny exploded, rising to her feet and pacing the room. "He has
deliberately gone against my express wishes, Margaret.
There will be the devil to pay for this."

"You do not wish to marry my brother?" Margaret
asked, her eyes uncomprehending.

"Of course I do," Fanny responded forcefully. "But I
cannot. And that is an end to it."

"I cannot imagine why not," Margaret said patiently.

"He knows you are the sister of that wretched seducer Roger St. Ives. What else is there to know?"

Fanny gazed at her friend for several moments before seating herself beside Margaret on the settee. "I shall tell you," she said. "Everything. And then you will agree that Colonel Sheldon has every reason to despise me."

Twenty minutes later the whole truth was out, every sordid little detail. When Fanny at last fell silent, she could not tell from Margaret's expression whether she should abandon any hope of finding happiness with the colonel.

On the pretext that she was needed at Lady Wentworth's bedside, Fanny avoided joining the family for dinner that evening. She was not at all sure she could bear to listen to the newly betrothed couple discuss their wedding plans without bursting into tears. She was even less desirous of spending an entire evening entertaining the colonel while the lovebirds tasted the heady delights of their new intimacy. Fanny was too conscious of the shadows from her past rising like a physical barrier between them.

"You should tell him all," Margaret urged when she came up to check on Lady Wentworth before retiring herself. "I have given much thought to your early misfortunes, Fanny, and I firmly believe that my brother cares for you more than enough to forgive—"

"Forgive the scandal of a divorce? Is that what you were going to say, Margaret?" Fanny interrupted impatiently. "How kind you are, dear, but I have no hopes of it happening; and I am determined to make a full breast of everything in the morning." She glanced towards her aunt, who was dozing intermittently. "And if my aunt is well enough to travel, we shall be gone by tea-time."

Margaret looked disappointed. "Not tomorrow, Fanny, please. I need you to accompany me to Town to order my gown from Madame Clochard. Please say you will."

"What about my aunt?" she protested.

"Mrs. Collins will take excellent care of me, dear," Lady Wentworth spoke up from the bed, suddenly wide awake and cheerful. "Besides, it is not as though I am on my deathbed. All I have is a slight indisposition that will be gone by tomorrow or the next day."

The prospect of discussing wedding gowns with the loquacious Madame Clochard did not appeal to Fanny in the slightest, but upon Margaret's insistence, seconded quite adamantly by her aunt, Fanny promised to accompany her friend into Brighton the next morning. Actually, Margaret's invitation suited Fanny because it would take her away from Sheldon Hall where she was constantly reminded that she owed the colonel a confession, one that would shatter her dreams forever.

"Why the long face, dear?" her aunt asked as soon as Margaret had left them. "I believe Margaret is right, Fanny, the colonel will forgive you anything. If ever I saw an infatuated gentleman, he is one."

Fanny felt her throat grow taut. "I cannot bear to face him again, Aunt. He has already forgiven more than I could hope for. I shall have Collins deliver him a letter confessing all while we are in Brighton tomorrow." She glanced at her aunt, who appeared to be have recovered her spirits. "I hope you will feel well enough to return to Primrose Court in the afternoon, Aunt, for I can guarantee that we will no longer be welcome here."

"Do not be too sure of that, dear," Lady Wentworth said vaguely. "And do not count on returning home tomorrow, Fanny. I cannot say for sure that I will be well enough to travel." She closed her eyes and sighed gustily.

Fanny regarded her aunt sharply. Was it her imagination, or was Lady Clarissa exaggerating her indisposition? "If you are not feeling more the thing tomorrow, perhaps we should call in Dr. Mackensie to examine you, Aunt."

"That will not be necessary," her aunt snorted, opening her eyes abruptly and glaring at her niece. "Now leave me, dear," she continued in a weaker voice, as if remembering she was an invalid, "I need my rest."

Fanny smiled to herself as she kissed her aunt's cheek and gently closed the door behind her. Lady Wentworth was up to something, she was sure of it. She was also certain that her aunt would not be well enough to return home tomorrow. Fanny was determined to discover why.

Derek slipped his hand inside his comfortable hunting jacket and withdrew the letter that lay there next to his heart. That Lady Fanny had written him a letter made him jittery. Collins had handed it to him several hours ago, at the exact moment Sir Joshua had presented himself at Sheldon Hall to keep their appointment to purchase some sheep in Rottingdean. The colonel had refused to keep his friend waiting and had slipped the missive into his pocket for later perusal. But throughout the long haggling and the hearty meal at the local inn, Derek had anxiously wondered what secrets Lady Fanny had revealed.

Only when Sir Joshua went to order their horses saddled was the colonel able to read Lady Fanny's letter. It was short and to the point. Derek's mind went numb with shock and he suddenly understood why the lady had put up such resistance to an official betrothal announcement. This then was that other *worse* scandal she had wanted to reveal to him. He had not believed anything could be worse than her connection to the scandal in his own life.

But he had been wrong. He should have guessed that Lord Penryn would reserve the most damaging secret till last.

The colonel blindly paid his shot and followed Sir Joshua out into the inn yard. For the life of him he could make no sense of his companion's merry chatter about wedding plans as they pointed their horses homewards. Lady Fanny's letter had chased every other thought from his head; lying like a dead weight in his pocket, the missive seemed to burn through the fine lawn of his shirt and brand his bare chest with the appalling truth she had finally revealed: an adulteress, divorced and cast off by her husband.

Husband? The word made Derek's heart cringe. The notion that Lady Fanny, *his* Fanny, had shared a marriage bed with another man cut more deeply than the scandal implied by her divorce and adultery. And a duke of the realm no less. Fanny a duchess! No wonder she had always appeared so regal and poised, so in command of herself and those around her. So far above him in station and consequence, he thought bleakly.

Had the lady's confession not been etched on his brain, Derek would have convinced himself that he had imagined the letter and its disturbing contents. He wanted to take it out and read it again. Could he not have misread it? But every word of that cursed letter rang inexorably in his head until he thought he would go mad.

"Would you not agree, Sheldon?" Sir Joshua's jovial voice cut abruptly into the colonel's somber thoughts.

"Indeed I do," Derek responded, without the slightest idea of the baronet's original question.

"Well, I am very glad to hear you say so, Sheldon," Sir Joshua remarked with obvious complacency, "and so I shall inform your sister as soon as I see her. It is pure contrariness on her part to deny me a quiet ceremony in the chapel at Cedar Lodge together with you and Lady Fanny."

The colonel was startled. "Lady Fanny?" he repeated stupidly.

The baronet let out a huge crack of laughter that shook his stout figure and made the yellow butterflies on his chocolate velvet waistcoat appear to flutter their wings frantically. "Caught you wool gathering have I, old man? You remember Lady Fanny? The lovely lass you will be riveted to quicker than the cat can lick her ear?" When the colonel stared blankly, he continued, "I suggested that we make it a double ceremony next Sunday, Sheldon. It would be a simple matter to obtain special licenses from the bishop in Brighton. Inordinately fond of partridge is Bishop Preston and many a time have Comfrey birds graced his table, let me tell you."

"No," the colonel replied more sharply than he intended. When Sir Joshua glanced at him curiously, he added in a softer tone, "I cannot make plans for a hasty wedding without consulting with Lady Fanny." He could not bring himself to admit that there might not be a wedding at all between them. Fanny had warned him, but like a fool he had refused to consider her resistance anything more serious than her natural feminine contentiousness. Even now, Derek had difficulty reconciling himself to losing her.

Lose her? His heart went cold at the thought. But how could he justify introducing a female of her scandalous reputation into the Sheldon family tree? He envisioned his sister's horror; Margaret would never forgive him. He could not even forgive himself for dwelling on the possibility that such a match might still take place. He knew it to be an impossible dream, but could not stop thinking of the young girl Fanny had been at the time. How had so weighty a scandal fallen on her young, innocent head?

Innocent? Had she perhaps been innocent of the charges brought against her? He was suddenly intrigued by the thought. He recalled long ago rumours of dissipation and depravity linked to the Duke of Cambourne's household, but not being given to gossip, the colonel had paid scant attention. Now he wondered about the kind of father who would give his young daughter into the keeping of such a man. The thought of Fanny married to the degenerate duke, as Cambourne had been called, revolted the colonel. Had he but known her then, he might have saved her. A fanciful dream indeed, he thought ruefully. But for a moment he felt an unexpected kinship with Lady Fanny. He had had his own private hell to live through, but if he had learned anything from his wife's betrayal it was that guilt and innocence were often difficult to tell apart.

"I say, old man," he heard Sir Joshua exclaim as a travelling chaise swept past them from behind, "ain't that your carriage? Seem to have seen that long-faced coachman before."

The chaise was gone in a cloud of dust before the colonel could drag his thoughts back from his meditations. He had caught only a cursory glimpse of the coat of arms on the varnished door.

"I doubt it," he answered cryptically. "Carruthers would never spring his horses like that. Besides, from the list Margaret showed me this morning, I doubt the ladies will return in time for tea."

A good fifteen minutes later, as they were approaching the gates of Sheldon Hall, Sir Joshua, who had been relatively silent since the encounter with the chaise, gave himself a mighty slap on the thigh and reined in his horse. "I knew it," he exclaimed gleefully. "I knew I had seen that fellow somewhere before."

"What fellow?" the colonel asked, more because it was expected of him than because of any interest.

"That fellow sitting up there with the coachman," his friend explained excitedly. "It was that rogue Penryn or I ain't Joshua Comfrey. Bold as brass he was, too."

Derek came awake suddenly. "Penryn, you say? Are you sure?"

" 'Course I am. Nothing wrong with my eyes, you know."

"What the blue blazes is that scoundrel doing here?" the colonel growled. "He had better not stop at Sheldon Hall, I can tell you that," he added, kicking Ajax into a gallop.

He swept round a bend, Sir Joshua hard on his heels, and came in sight of the imposing iron gates. As they drew closer, the colonel saw his old gatekeeper standing in the middle of the lane, waving his lanky arms over his head.

The colonel slid to a halt, Ajax snorting loudly at this cavalier treatment. "What is it, Rufus?" he demanded.

"Something mighty odd happened, Colonel," the old man replied ponderously, evidently highly agitated. "Never seen the like of it in all me born days."

"And what could that be, Rufus," the colonel demanded calmly. "Not Squire Masters' Jersey bull on the rampage again, is it?"

"Oh, no, Colonel," the old man replied. "I would not be standing 'ere in the road if that nasty piece of work was loose again. I may be old, sir, but I ain't stupid. No, it tweren't the bull, no sir." This speech was followed by a gust of creaky laughter that brought on a fit of coughing.

"Tell us what brings you out in the road, then," the colonel asked with infinite patience, after the old man's cough had subsided.

"The coach, sir. Miss Margaret's coach came up the road as smart as ever I saw. But when I stepped out to wave 'er in, Colonel, bless me if Carruthers dinna crack his whip at me fancy-like and shoot by as though 'e 'ad a ferry to catch in Dover."

This witticism brought on another spasm of coughing, and it was several minutes later that the colonel was able to extract the information that there had been another man on the seat beside Carruthers.

"A fancy looking nob, Colonel, all got up in white-topped boots and a waistcoat that Prinny 'imself might not 'ave been too grand to wear. Fair took me breath away 'e did, and that I can swear to, sir."

"Thank you, Rufus," the colonel said. "Now get yourself

up to the house and tell Mrs. Collins I told you to take a glass of brandy for that cough. Do you hear?"

Rufus looked forlorn. "Mrs. Collins is bound to give me one of those evil smelling potions of 'ers, Colonel."

"Tell her I said brandy," the colonel repeated before turning his attention to his companion. "Looks as though the ladies are in trouble, Sir Joshua. Are you game to help me rescue them?"

Without waiting for a reply, Derek whirled his horse and urged him into a gallop. With any luck he might just get the chance to darken that shabster's daylights for him, he thought with savage pleasure.

Landing the viscount a facer was something the colonel had wanted to do for a long time.

CHAPTER 21

The Rescue

The coach rocked so violently as it came around a curve that Lady Fanny was thrown against Miss Sheldon, cowering in the corner. Neatly tied parcels containing their purchases in Brighton tumbled from the opposite seat onto the floor in an untidy heap. The man sitting there merely laughed and made no effort to pick them up.

"Is it absolutely necessary to proceed at this breakneck pace, Freddy?" Fanny demanded angrily. "You will founder the colonel's horses if you insist on such recklessness."

She had little hope of instilling any sense into this stranger whom she had once thought of as the dearest of brothers. There was a hardness about him that boded no good for either Margaret or herself. Fanny had known they were in trouble when they came out of the lending library to find Freddy and Lord Penryn waiting beside the coach, confirmed when the two gentlemen climbed into the vehicle uninvited.

"I cannot say I care a fig for the colonel or his horses," her brother replied carelessly. "He should have known better than to defy Gerald by sending off that ridiculous announcement about his betrothal to you, Fanny. Betrothal indeed. What impertinence. Does this half-pay soldier fellow really consider himself good enough for the daughter of the Earl of Hayle? Or have you not told the poor blighter yet that he is aiming too high for a wife? Amusing yourself, are you, Fanny? That is what I told Gerald, that you would come around once you tired of this bucolic existence and of taking tea every afternoon with a collection of rural nobodies. But you know how impetuous Gerald is; he was always the one to ride roughshod over anyone foolhardy enough to cross him."

Fanny remembered all too well this intemperate side of her childhood idol. As a young girl she had considered the viscount's brash contempt for obstacles to his will highly romantic; only later did she discover the ruthless disregard for anything but his own pleasure that lay beneath his captivating charm.

"I still say that this ridiculous abduction is going beyond the pale even for Gerald," she said with more calm than she felt. "There is absolutely no reason to subject Miss Sheldon to this shabby treatment. And as my brother, you should be the first to protest this highhanded, improper behaviour, Freddy. I marvel that you have countenanced such an outrage against your own sister."

Her brother looked vaguely uncomfortable, but answered roughly. "Cease this blathering, girl. You have only yourself to blame, you know."

"I fail to see how you can blame me for not wishing to wed a worthless pervert," Fanny challenged him. "And if you were not so spineless yourself, Freddy, you would have broken free from Gerald years ago."

"To do what?" her brother demanded sharply.

"You might have joined the army or the Church—"

Freddy's crack of cynical laughter made Fanny's heart sink. "The army is for patriotic fools like your precious colonel," he snarled. "And do you honestly see me togged up in black, visiting rheumy old biddies and dispensing counsel to idiots and half-wits in some insignificant parish out on the moors of Yorkshire?" He laughed again and for the first time Fanny felt a stab of fear.

"If you had bothered to ask me, I could have told you there will be no wedding, Freddy, and we might have avoided this unseemly dashing around the countryside," Fanny said firmly. "As you correctly surmised, it was all a hum."

Beside her, Fanny heard Margaret gasp, but she did not turn. Unfortunately she could do nothing to prevent her brother from noticing Margaret's reaction, and she saw a grin spread over his narrow face.

"Trying to bamboozle me, are you, Fanny? Well, it will not fadge, love. I am not blind. Do you think I have not seen the way your eyes glaze like a lovestruck schoolgirl's when you look at your soldier-boy? Gerald has seen it, too, and is not at all pleased with you, love. He plans to closet himself with you at some out of the way inn for three or four days until you come to your senses. By that time, naturally, that paragon of prudery will have disowned you, and no doubt you will be grateful to Gerald for salvaging your honour."

His knowing smirk chilled her, but Fanny forced herself to speak with a hint of conspiracy. "How much would it cost me to gain your support, Freddy?"

"Support?" He looked nonplussed. "What are you talking about, my dear Fanny?"

"Your support in escaping Gerald's nefarious plan, Freddy. Get us away from him, and I will pay you whatever you ask."

He was quiet for a moment and appeared to give some thought to her offer, but then his face cleared, and he laughed that humorless laugh again. "Oh, never fear, my love. Your money will find its way into my pockets all right, but it will be Gerald who will pay me, Fanny, not you. He has promised me a fair share of your fortune after it is safely in his hands."

"And you believed him?" Fanny demanded sarcastically. "You are still not a match for Gerald, Freddy, and never will be. You actually believe he will share my fortune with you? How naive." She laughed gently and sank back against the cushions as the coach lurched over a bump in the road.

Freddy glared menacingly, but while Margaret appeared cowed, Fanny's mind was working furiously to find a flaw in Gerald's plan. It was obvious that Gerald was the mastermind behind the daring scheme, and Fanny was fairly certain that in his arrogance, he had miscalculated along the way. She must discover where his overweening pride had caused him to err, and use it against him. Margaret's safety depended upon her.

Before she could devise a strategy, however, the carriage came to a grinding halt, throwing both ladies onto the opposite seat in disarray. Freddy uttered a sharp oath under his breath, jerked open the carriage door, and leapt down into the lane. Several shouts were heard, and then the unmistakable sound of a pistol exploded into the afternoon air, causing the horses to dance about nervously, jolting the carriage from side to side. Fanny heard the jingle of harness, the shouts of the coachman, the raised voices of several gentlemen, only one of which she recognized as her brother's.

Then another voice, hoarse with fury, rang out. "What in Hades do you think you are doing, sir?" he bellowed. "Get out of my way or I shall blow your ugly face away."

Fanny guessed that this threat could not have been uttered by anybody but Gerald, but it appeared that his bluster did not impress the stranger he was addressing, for all the response he got was a hearty laugh.

"If that first shot was any indication of your aim, sir," a familiar voice remarked nonchalantly, "I shall take my chances with the second. Once you get the pistol reloaded, of course, and if I do not decide to darken your daylights in the meantime."

"Come on down and fight like a gentleman," an unfamiliar voice put in with enthusiasm. "That is if you dare, sir."

"What is this ruckus about, Gerald?" Fanny heard her brother ask belligerently. "And why did you stop our carriage, whoever you are?"

The mild reply was a glaring contrast to Freddy's aggressive question. "I recognized Colonel Sheldon's carriage and wished to greet him," that familiar voice said.

Fanny listened in amazement. Then she jumped into action. "Jack!" she exclaimed in delight. "That is Jack out there, Margaret. Let us show ourselves."

"Oh, Fanny, please do not be rash. Those men are firing pistols. You might be seriously injured, dear."

Fanny made a movement towards the open carriage door, but Margaret seized her by the arm. "I beg you, Fanny, do not go outside. Let the gentlemen settle the matter between them."

"And miss seeing Captain Jack in action?" Fanny protested with a joyous laugh. "Too tame by half, Margaret. Now let me go." She could not believe their good luck. If anyone could save them, it had to be her dear Jack.

"Oh, I wish my brother were here," Margaret cried. "He would know what to do."

"So does Jack," Fanny cut in quickly. "He will mill them down before they know it."

"Well, Derek is a recognized pugilist," Margaret countered with unexpected fervour.

"That may be so, Margaret," Fanny conceded. "But he may be miles away—"

"No, he is not," Margaret interrupted, her head cocked to one side, listening intently. "Here he comes now, and with reinforcements. Cannot you hear the horses?"

Fanny could certainly detect the galloping hooves of at least two horses, but it was Margaret who stuck her head out of the window. "Oh, yes. It is Derek, and Sir Joshua is with him," she murmured, jerking her head inside and searching around until she found her battered bonnet. "And I must look like the veriest hoyden," she wailed, hastily flinging it on her head and tying the pink riband beneath her chin.

Surprised to see the usually unflappable Margaret in such a dither, Fanny stuck her own head out, only to be greeted by the sight of the grim-faced colonel bearing down upon them *ventre-à-terre.*

"Oh, dear," she muttered, suddenly conscious of her own disarray. "It *is* your brother, Margaret. Where is my bonnet?" She burrowed under the untidy heap of parcels on the floor and pulled out her new blue straw bonnet, very much squashed out of shape.

Fanny sat staring dejectedly at the ruined bonnet, and when a horseman came to a clattering halt beside the coach, she did not look up. What did it matter how she appeared? The colonel knew all her ugly secrets by now. He would avoid her, of course, and Fanny could not blame him. She had kept him far too long in the dark about her past, and had only herself to blame if he never spoke to her again.

"I trust you two ladies are unhurt."

Fanny heard his beloved voice, flowing over her like a favourite piece of music and pronouncing these prosaic words mildly, as though she were not forever fallen from grace. Margaret responded to what must have seemed like a perfectly normal question in a perfectly normal voice, but Fanny's own throat constricted with emotion, and she was unable to speak, even had she wished it.

After a tiny pause, she heard his voice again, and this time there was a quality in it that compelled her to respond.

"And you, my dear Fanny?" he said softly, wrenching her heart.

She raised her eyes to his face, and for an instant time stood still.

His grey eyes were dark with an emotion she had not expected to see there.

She nodded. "Yes," she whispered, barely moving her lips.

And then he was gone, followed by another horseman she recognized as Sir Joshua, and Fanny was left to pull her scattered wits together to face the inevitable.

The sight of Lady Fanny's anguished face wrenched at the colonel's heart as he urged his horse away from the window towards the melee of men in the lane ahead. Quickly dismounting, he surveyed the fray with professional eyes. It was immediately apparent that Captain Jack Mansford was holding his own against the onslaught of his two opponents, and had it not been for the pistol Lord Penryn was hastily reloading while St. Ives engaged the captain in a flurry of wild jabs, Derek would not have felt the need to intervene.

Stepping forward, he grasped the viscount by both shoul-

ders and swung him round with such force that both pistol
and powder horn slipped from his fingers into the dusty
lane. Face to face with his rival, the colonel could not stop
the grim smile that sprang to his lips. The fastidious viscount sported one eye half closed, a bleeding nose, and
deep gashes on his face from several punishing blows.

Lord Penryn growled low in his throat, and in a blur of
movement brought up one fist to connect with his opponent's ribs in a bruising punch. Derek grunted in surprise
and stepped back, ready to return a deadly left jab. The
viscount must have seen his intention, for he began to flail
his fists about wildly, feinting from side to side. Coolly waiting his opportunity, the colonel took advantage of an opening and landed a facer on the viscount's chin, jerking his
head back and causing him to stumble backwards. The
crunch of his knuckles against his rival's chin gave the colonel a savage sense of satisfaction.

Take that for Lady Fanny, he thought, a primitive vitality
coursing through his blood. *And that,* he added, landing
another punch on the viscount's handsome face as the man
lurched forward with a murderous gleam in his eyes.

"Damn you, Sheldon," the viscount muttered as he
reeled under a third blow glancing off his cheek. "You will
never have her, you know. She is mine. Always was and
always will be." His battered face split into a leer. "I wager
the little doxy forgot to tell you that, along with several
other ugly details of her sordid past."

The colonel felt himself go rigid with fury at the viscount's ugly accusations. "Lady Fanny has told me everything," he growled through taut lips, keeping his temper in
check with difficulty. If he let himself go, he would batter
this contemptible creature into a bloody, unrecognizable
lump.

"Has she, indeed?" Penryn sneered. "I doubt very much
that our dear Fanny has revealed all," he added, deftly
evading a blow the colonel aimed at his face. He returned
the jab, and Derek realized he had allowed himself to be
distracted when he felt the force of the viscount's knuckles
knock his head back and a trickle of blood run down his
cheek.

Infuriated at his own carelessness, the colonel placed a

savage right to his opponent's solar plexus, followed by a fulminating left to the chin that sent the viscount down for the count.

"Good show, old man," Sir Joshua exclaimed admiringly, coming up to stand beside the colonel. "But you might have left something for me. I have not enjoyed a good set-to these many months. Rotten of you to hog all the fun yourself, though. Any chance of a second round?" he added hopefully, tapping the fallen viscount with his toe. But the man was unconscious, and the colonel turned his attention to Mansford.

The captain's face showed signs of battery, but his opponent lay in the dust holding his head and moaning, evidently none too eager to continue the fight. The unholy grin on the captain's face reflected Derek's own, and in an impulsive gesture of camaraderie he flung his arms around his friend and gave him a bear hug. He had not felt this young and carefree in years.

"Glad to see you looking well, Mansford," he said heartily, thumping the captain on the back. "Aside from that lump over your eye, of course."

"At least I am not bleeding all over my cravat," Jack responded with a laugh. "But I confess I was glad to see you, Sheldon. That sojourn in the Lisbon dungeon was not exactly designed to keep me in fighting trim. That fancy looking fellow in peach velvet turned out to be a lot tougher than he looked. This other one," he gestured with his boot towards St. Ives, still sprawled in the dust holding his head, "is all bluster and no bottom."

"Jack!" a feminine voice called out from behind them. "Oh, Jack! I am so thankful to see you back in England safe and sound."

Both gentlemen turned as Lady Fanny ran towards them. For a heady moment, the colonel imagined how it might feel to be received with such obvious enthusiasm by this particular lady. But it was the captain who received Lady Fanny's warm embrace, and the captain's arms that slipped around her slender form while she reached up to kiss his rugged cheek. They stood there for what seemed like an eternity to the colonel, who remained rooted to the ground, his emotions churning violently in his breast.

"Oh, Jack, you are hurt," Lady Fanny gasped when she caught sight of the dark swelling that threatened to close the captain's left eye. She reached up gingerly to touch his face, and the colonel almost wished he had suffered a black eye himself if it might have earned him a tender caress from Lady Fanny.

The colonel tried to tear his gaze away from this painfully intimate scene, but his eyes locked with the captain's, and in a flash of intuition, Derek knew that his friend had guessed what was in his heart. Gently, Mansford disentangled himself from Lady Fanny's embrace and gave the colonel a broad wink over her shining head. Bending to whisper in her ear, he turned her round to where Derek stood.

"Now, this is the gentleman you should be thanking, lass," Jack said smoothly. "Had the colonel not come along when he did, I fear those two rogues would have made short work of poor old Jack. Your colonel here saved the day with his pugilistic skills, quite took my breath away, he did."

"Doing it too brown, Jack," Derek cut in, unwilling to allow the captain's glib tongue to distort the facts. "And what was Lieutenant Howard doing while you took on these two ruffians?"

"Oh, Timothy was holding the horses," Jack responded offhandedly. "But I was about ready to call on him when you arrived, Colonel. And as you can see, my dear," he added, addressing Lady Fanny, who could not seem to meet the colonel's eyes, "the poor man was grievously wounded for his pains."

This comment caused the lady to glance up quickly, and Derek heard Lady Fanny gasp when she saw the bloody gash on his cheek. The shock appeared to jolt her out of her inertia, for she stepped forward, pulling a scrap of lace from her sleeve. "Your poor face," she exclaimed, looking up at him with eyes full of compassion. "Let me wipe away the blood before it drips all over you."

"That cravat is already beyond repair, lass," Jack pointed out. "And I fear the colonel is in danger of swooning from loss of blood—"

"Enough of this foolish talk," Lady Fanny snapped in

something approaching her normal voice. "Give me your handkerchief, Jack. I will try to improvise a bandage."

"Take mine," the colonel said, pulling it from his pocket and offering it to her. "But I do not need a bandage, Fanny, truly—"

"We shall see about that. Do hold still," Lady Fanny snapped, gently wiping his cheek. "Oh, dear, this *is* a nasty cut."

The colonel opened his mouth to protest that it was nothing but a scratch, but he caught Jack's eye and closed it again. After all, was not the gentle touch of Fanny's fingers on his face what he had wished for only a moment ago?

Jack turned away to help Lieutenant Howard, who was trying to get Lord Penryn, rather the worse for wear, back on his feet, but not before giving the colonel another speaking wink.

Derek looked down at Lady Fanny, standing on tiptoe and balancing herself by lightly leaning on his arm as she mopped the blood from his face. How beautiful she was, even more so without her bonnet and her fair hair escaping its chignon and drifting in rebellious tendrils about her face. He had a sudden desire to see her with her hair loose about her shoulders, or spread wantonly across his pillow. The colonel pulled his mind firmly away from such erotic daydreams. There was so much he needed to say to this woman if only she would listen. So much he needed from her if only she would consent to give it to him.

"Fanny," he murmured, and she raised startled eyes to his. In that brief unguarded glance he read uncertainty, wistfulness, yearning, and a deeper emotion he dared not name. Then she shuttered her gaze and all he could read was resignation and a hint of unhappiness that tore at his heart. "Fanny, my dear," he repeated, "there are things we must discuss."

She regarded him for a moment, then returned to her task. "Have you read my letter, Colonel?" she asked bluntly.

"Yes." He felt her flinch, but her fingers on his cheek were steady.

"Then there is nothing else to say, is there?"

Her voice was so matter of fact that the colonel was

momentarily distracted. Then he noticed that she had gone pale and that her fingers trembled before she removed them abruptly from his face.

"I think you should travel home in the coach, Colonel," she said coolly. "I know Margaret will want to call in Dr. Mackensie to look at your injury."

The colonel brushed away these diversionary tactics impatiently. "We must talk, Fanny," he said urgently. "I insist upon it."

This brought a fleeting smile to her pale face. "I am glad to see you have lost none of your autocratic temperament, Colonel. But you forget that I am not a woman to be bullied, sir."

"I am not bullying, Fanny," he replied urgently. "I am begging. Please let me talk to you."

Lady Fanny sighed and turned away, and Derek imagined her shoulders drooped. "I do not need to have a litany of my sins read to me, Colonel," she said briskly, "and I can think of nothing else you might say to me."

"Nothing at all, Fanny?" he murmured softly.

She paused and cast him an enigmatic glance over her shoulder. "Nothing that you *could* say, Colonel, under the circumstances." Leaving those ambiguous words hanging in the air, Lady Fanny walked away, and the colonel was left to follow her graceful figure with his eyes, vowing that he would have his say come hell or high water.

CHAPTER 22

Magic Moon for Lovers

The coach was halfway up the driveway to Sheldon Hall before Lady Fanny realized she was still clutching the colonel's bloody handkerchief. Her eyes blurred as she looked at it, and her fingers closed instinctively on the soiled linen.

The colonel had read her letter. He knew all the scandals

she had kept hidden for so long. Everything. She shuddered. Yet it was also a relief to have everything out in the open. At least she would not have to lie to him again. In truth, she should be grateful to Lord Penryn for forcing her to make a clean breast of her secrets. Perhaps now those frightful nightmares that had started all over again when Gerald came back would go away.

Yes, he had read her letter. So now he knew exactly the sort of female Lady Fanny St. Ives was. Or at least what she was reputed to be by those who should know. By those whose testimony—false as it had been—passed for truth before the courts that had branded her adulteress. She had not even known the meaning of the word when the duke had shouted it at her; she had been unable to believe that Gerald had actually confessed that she had seduced him into sinning against his cousin.

"But we did no such thing," she remembered crying out to her enraged husband, first indignantly, and then—as she began to realize that no one believed her—in desperation and anger.

Still no one had believed her. And the colonel would not believe her either, she had told herself as she wrote that revealing letter to him. Why should he? She was not exactly a model of propriety. Had not the colonel disapproved of her from the moment he laid eyes on her? His elegant lip must have curled instinctively at the sight of a lady wielding a sword stick against three ruffians on a French wharf.

No, Fanny thought, there was no earthly chance that the colonel would believe her innocent when three gentlemen had sworn she was guilty. The duke must have known her innocent, and Gerald certainly did. More than likely Freddy was also party to the plot to ruin her, since he had made no move to defend her. The word of these gentlemen had condemned her.

Yes, the colonel knew everything there was to know about Fanny St. Ives, except that she loved him. And he never would. Yet, in spite of learning all her sins, both real and trumped up, he still wished to talk to her. He had *begged* to speak with her. Fanny had been astounded at the sincerity in his voice but hardened her heart against him. How could he possibly have anything to say that she would want to hear?

Fanny sighed and bent to help Margaret pick up the last few parcels from the floor of the coach. At least dear Margaret would have her beautiful wedding gown, and be wed to the man she loved and bear his children in the tranquil haven of Cedar Lodge.

"You are very quiet, Fanny," her friend murmured. "Is anything the matter, dear?"

Everything is the matter, Fanny thought fatalistically, a lump forming in her throat, but she could not say so to Margaret and spoil her joy. Her own tenuous dreams of happiness might tumble about her ears, but Fanny St. Ives would bear up as she always had and laugh at the world that threatened to overwhelm her.

"I was thinking that I have brought you and your brother nothing but trouble since I set foot in Sheldon Hall," she said after a pause. "Had I not been with you, Lord Penryn would never have abducted us, and the colonel would never have been wounded. Your brother would not have embarked upon this make-believe betrothal had Gerald not come to Sheldon Hall looking for me. Had I not—"

"Oh, what a bag of moonshine!" Margaret cried out, grasping Fanny's hand and squeezing it comfortingly. "It was Derek's idea to publish the announcement of your betrothal, my dear Fanny. And I know my brother has every intention of honouring it, so cease this worrying."

"He may have once, Margaret, but not any more."

Margaret stared at her. "You are talking in riddles, Fanny."

"You advised me to tell your brother everything, and I did so in a letter this morning. He admitted reading it, just now in the lane. I cannot imagine why he is still speaking to me. I cannot understand why you are still speaking to me yourself, Margaret, after . . . after—"

"Because we love you, Fanny," her friend said serenely, "and I for one do not believe those unkind things Lord Penryn said of you. Even I can see he is a scoundrel of the worst kind. You can be sure Derek has not been taken in by his lies either."

Fanny suppressed the urge to burst into tears. She had

never had a friend like Margaret, and this sincere expression of trust overwhelmed her. "I will treasure your friendship forever, Margaret," she said shakily.

"As I will yours, Fanny, and look forward to calling you my sister-in-law, dear."

The colonel deftly secured Lady Fanny's gloved hand and steadied her as she descended from the carriage. Her face was somber and she did not glance up at him as he escorted her up the shallow steps and into the hall, where Collins was wringing his hands in distress at the sight of his master's bloody cravat.

" 'Tis nothing to throw a fit about, Collins," he said reassuringly. "A mere scratch. Please ask Mrs. Collins to prepare a room for Captain Mansford in the West Wing. The captain will be staying with us for a sennight or more. Lieutenant Howard will be joining his regiment in Brighton tomorrow."

He felt Lady Fanny stiffen. "I cannot permit you to inconvenience yourself on Jack's account, Colonel," she said, dropping her hand from his arm. "He will stay with us at Primrose Court."

Derek smiled, recognizing an evasive tactic when he saw one. "But you are here, my dear," he pointed out gently, "and may be for many years to come," he added recklessly.

"Years? I cannot stay here forever," she responded, startled.

"Why not? Unless of course you are not comfortable at Sheldon Hall."

"You are being absurd, Colonel," she began, but ceased abruptly when Margaret appeared to escort Lady Fanny upstairs.

The colonel watched them go, arms linked companionably, and it suddenly struck him that his sister must already be privy to Lady Fanny's secrets. He slid his hand inside his coat and fingered the letter that had revealed so much about Fanny's past but nothing at all about her present and future. He wondered what his very proper, strait-laced sister thought of her lovely friend's scandalous history. How two such different females could be friends the colonel could not imagine, but it was evident that they were.

Derek wondered what his sister might be able to tell him about the real Fanny; not the regal Lady Fanny Wentworth she paraded before the world, sword stick in hand, carefree smile on her lips, but the Fanny he had kissed on the dim stairs at the Blue Parrot Inn, a gentler, more tender Fanny, who had stolen his heart away.

Abruptly suppressing these disturbing thoughts, the colonel spent the rest of the evening playing host to his three male guests until it was time to dress for dinner. He was disappointed when Margaret appeared in the drawing room without Lady Fanny, who pleaded her aunt's indisposition to have a tray sent up.

"It appears her ladyship is avoiding me," the colonel murmured into his sister's ear when the party gathered in the drawing room after dinner.

"You are teasing again, Derek," she chided, a faint blush telling him he had hit the mark. "Fanny is worried about her aunt who—"

"Who runs down the servants' stairs as sprightly as any gazelle when she believes no one is watching," the colonel interrupted laconically. "I saw her myself only yesterday, my dear, so do not try to bamboozle me. This indisposition of hers is all a hum, Maggy. Confess it, Fanny and her aunt are playing Canterbury tricks on me, is that it?"

His sister looked alarmed and glanced up at him guiltily. "No, Derek. Fanny truly believes Lady Wentworth is feeling poorly. She would be most put out were she to discover that—"

"Then whose idea was it to play this charade?" the colonel broke in gently. "Not yours, I trust, Maggy?"

"Oh, no. Lady Wentworth wished to prevent Fanny from dashing off to Brighton so impetuously. And I must confess I took part in the little charade, as you call it, Derek, because I thought Fanny was making a mistake she would regret."

The colonel regarded his sister searchingly, wondering what lay behind that calm facade of hers. "And what mistake was this?"

Just then Sir Joshua interrupted them with a request for a tune on the pianoforte. The alacrity with which his sister acquiesced to this request suggested that she was glad to escape further questions regarding their elusive guest.

Margaret's revelation of Lady Wentworth's little deception intrigued the colonel and made him wish he had quizzed his sister on other secrets she may have shared with Fanny. The more he thought on his predicament, the more Derek decided it was high time he came to a real understanding with the woman who seemed so determined to avoid him. If she refused him, at least he would know where he stood. On the other hand, if she accepted him . . .

The colonel gave his fantasies full rein that night, and as he floated between sleeping and waking, he came to admit that his future happiness lay in the hands of a certain lady of scandalous reputation, whose innocence appeared to him far more compelling than her guilt.

Fanny awoke the following morning feeling more confused than she had in weeks. Things had come to a head so suddenly and with such violence that she had been forced to take a long hard look at herself. She believed what she had said to Margaret yesterday in the carriage. She had brought upheaval into the placid life at Sheldon Hall, but this should not bother her, for she was accustomed to causing a stir wherever she went.

What she had not told Margaret, however, was that her own life had been changed forever by the Sheldons. Fanny had suddenly realized this truth as she stood in the dusty lane yesterday, staring up at the blood running down the colonel's cheek. It came as a shock to her that this man had risked his life for her, even after reading that infamous letter.

The thought humbled her. Humility was a new experience for Lady Fanny Wentworth and it opened her eyes to her own foolishness. How wrong she had been to mock the colonel's lack of polish and charm. She had measured him with the wrong yardstick and found him wanting. Only when Fanny had seen him next to Gerald had she discovered that her youthful infatuation with the viscount had had no real substance to it at all. When she had seen him lying in the lane, his handsome face mashed by the colonel's fists, she had felt nothing but pity. The colonel's gashed face, on the other hand, had torn at her heart, and it was all she could do not to throw herself into his arms.

Yes, she was no longer the Lady Fanny Wentworth who had faced up to three ruffians on the wharves of Calais. And she had the colonel to thank for that. Perhaps it had all begun with that clandestine kiss at the Blue Parrot. Or had it been his concern for her on the cliff that rainy afternoon? After all, in spite of her protestations, he must have truly feared she would jump to her death. Then he had stepped in to rescue Jack, and to save her from Gerald's persecutions. And above all there was that announcement he had sent off confirming their betrothal to the whole world. How would he extricate himself from that?

The appearance of Yvette with her morning chocolate steered Fanny's thoughts into more immediate concerns.

"How is my aunt feeling this morning?" she enquired, wondering if her abigail was privy to the real extent of Lady Wentworth's indisposition. "I trust she will be able to leave her bed today."

Yvette looked at her mistress sharply, but she answered mildly. "From what her abigail tells me, Lady Wentworth is much improved, milady."

Fanny's thoughts had already veered to another subject. "I wish to have a long talk with Captain Mansford this morning," she remarked. "Do you know if he has been down to breakfast yet, Yvette?"

"Oh, yes, milady. Captain Mansford and the young lieutenant rode off with the colonel early this morning," she replied. "Collins says the gentlemen went off to visit Cedar Lodge. Something about sheep, he said. Collins expects them to take their nuncheon with Sir Joshua, or so I heard him tell Mrs. Collins."

Fanny took it as further proof that she had left her old self behind when she did not instantly fly into a miff at taking second place to these anonymous sheep. Had the colonel not *begged* for an audience with her? Fanny had woken up that morning with the intention of granting his request. Now it seemed he had left her to kick her heels until the afternoon when she might well lose her nerve.

As it turned out, Fanny did not see any of the gentlemen until she and Margaret came down for dinner to find Sir

Joshua in the drawing room. The colonel had invited him to
dine, the baronet announced as soon as he saw the ladies.

"And how could I refuse the opportunity to see my
dearest Margaret again?" he exclaimed in his jocular fashion, clasping that lady's hands and bestowing a resounding
kiss on them that brought a blush to her face.

"Tell us all about the sheep, Sir Joshua," Fanny demanded unexpectedly. Any topic of conversation was pref-
erable to the newly awakened lover in Sir Joshua blathering
on about his happy state, she decided, avoiding Margaret's
amused glance.

"I was not aware that you were partial to the woolly
creatures, my lady," he replied, looking mystified. "But I
am glad to hear it because I confess that sheep are my
great passion. That is second only to my dear Margaret. I
am only too happy to oblige, my dear Lady Fanny." Settling himself in a comfortable chair, a glass of sherry in his
hand, Sir Joshua proceeded to inveigle the ladies with far
more stories about his experiences with sheep than Fanny
would have considered possible.

They were interrupted by the colonel and Captain Mansford, neither of whom could divert Sir Joshua's flow of
information on the trials and tribulations of raising sheep
in Sussex. Even after the party repaired to the drawing
room, the baronet continued to dazzle the company with
the diseases, fatal or otherwise, that were peculiar to flocks
in that part of England. Then Margaret had the happy notion of suggesting a stroll on the terrace.

"Tonight is the full moon," Margaret explained, "and
hereabouts the country folk consider it lucky to watch it
rising. My mother always claimed that she felt Aphrodite's
presence most strongly when the moon was full."

Fanny caught a look of disbelief on Jack's face, but he
merely grinned and begged to be excused from moonlit
pilgrimages to pagan goddesses. "I for one have no wish
to be skewered by a stray arrow from Cupid's bow."

Fanny did not miss the sly wink Jack sent in the colonel's
direction, and instantly racked her brain for an excuse to
avoid a tête-à-tête in the moonlight with a gentleman who
must be wishing her in Jericho.

CHAPTER 23

Aphrodite Prevails

"Pay no attention to disbelievers, Fanny," the colonel heard his sister say in a low voice as she slipped her arm through their guest's and guided her out onto the terrace, where the day was mellowing into twilight.

Jack's wink had disconcerted him. Here was the perfect opportunity he had wished for to fix his interest with Lady Fanny, and suddenly he felt as though a million butterflies were cavorting in his stomach. The lady had not looked too happy either and the colonel wondered whether she, too, felt uneasy at the mention of the goddess of love. Yet it was definitely love he felt for Lady Fanny, an emotion worlds removed from the blind infatuation he had felt for Constance. The very thought of spending the rest of his life without Fanny made him break out in a cold sweat.

What confused him most was the realization that he loved a female who was far from perfect. Lady Fanny did not fit the ideal he had carried in his head for so long, and he suspected she never would. But the colonel wanted no more to do with insubstantial ideals; he wanted Fanny. He wanted her with all her flaws—those very flaws and foibles made Fanny what she was. He would not have her any other way.

If he knew anything about his sister—although Derek was not so sure anymore that he knew as much as he had imagined—he would have sworn that she felt the same way about Lady Fanny. She had known, as had his little Charlotte, that Fanny belonged at Sheldon Hall, with him, as his wife. The suddenness with which this impetuous female had taken over first his thoughts, then his heart, had paralyzed him. Derek had not been able to accept his feelings. But Margaret had known what was in his heart before he did himself, as she always had, he thought with a glow of affection.

Margaret was setting the stage for him, but the sequel was up to him. The colonel joined Sir Joshua in following the ladies out into the mild May evening. The air was redolent with the scent of roses and, as he watched, the two ladies paused on the brick path beside the rose-bed.

"Sir Joshua, do you have your pocketknife with you?" his sister enquired, turning to the baronet. "I have a fancy for that white rose." She pointed to a perfect pale bud, which Sir Joshua hastened to cut for her.

"Which one would you care for, Fanny?" she asked her guest, who surveyed the multitude of blossoms with a bemused look. "I feel it is only proper that we should carry a small token to Aphrodite on this her special night."

The colonel moved up to stand beside Lady Fanny, casting a glance at the profusion of roses. His eye was caught by a deep scarlet bloom half-unfurled and promising to reach its full beauty in the morning.

"Allow me to cut this red one for you, my dear," he murmured, pulling out his own knife. "It cannot match your beauty, of course, but no mere flower can come close to that." He reached over, brushing her arm with his sleeve, and deftly cut the blossom. Before handing it to Fanny, the colonel raised it to his nose and took a deep breath. "Delicious." His eyes held hers over the blood-red petals of the flower until she dropped her gaze, a blush tinting her cheeks.

Charmed by this unusual display of modesty, the colonel offered his arm, and they strolled together in companionable silence.

"I had the distinct impression that you wished to escape me again just now, my lady," he said after a while.

"Why ever would I wish to do that?"

"Perhaps because you wish to avoid hearing what I have to say to you?"

"Now there you mistake the matter, Colonel. I fully intended to give you a chance to have your say, but you went racing off to ogle sheep instead."

He laughed. "I was not ogling sheep, my dear," he protested. "It so happens that Sir Joshua is the local magistrate, and he requested our testimony against Lord Penryn and your brother before deciding their punishment."

Lady Fanny looked at him in surprise. "I trust Sir Joshua was not too harsh on those misguided scoundrels," she said. "They received so much punishment at your hands and Jack's that—"

"I would have ordered them drawn and quartered for their unspeakable impertinence," he interrupted sharply. "Sir Joshua merely fined them and forbade them to show themselves in the neighbourhood again. Too lenient by half if you ask me. They are gone now; we made sure of that, so you have nothing more to fear from them." He did not add that he had paid her brother's shot at the White Hart Inn himself to keep St. Ives out of the hands of the bailiff.

She stopped abruptly and faced him, amethyst eyes brimming with emotion. "If I live to be a hundred," she said in a low voice, "I shall never be able to repay you for all the kindnesses you have shown me, Colonel."

The colonel gazed at her for a full minute, telling himself firmly that he could not, should not take this beloved woman in his arms and kiss her till her head spun. Twilight was falling, but it was still light enough to see the swans down by the lake settling themselves on the verge for the night. Of his sister and Sir Joshua there was no sign.

"Let us take the rose to the goddess, my dear," he suggested, his voice husky. "Perhaps she will give us an answer to this dilemma."

She made no protest when he placed her hand in the crook of his arm and slowly walked her towards the lake. The swans made warning sounds as they passed by into the trees, dim with lengthening shadows. As they neared the grotto, Derek was not surprised to see his sister emerge clinging to Sir Joshua's arm. Her dreamy expression and Sir Joshua's fatuous grin told him that Margaret had been thoroughly kissed.

Impatient to enjoy his own moment of passion with the woman by his side, the colonel suffered a momentary twinge of alarm when Lady Fanny stopped short and glanced at him.

"Perhaps it is time we returned to the terrace," she suggested.

"Not unless you wish to incur Aphrodite's wrath, my dear Fanny," his sister chided as she came abreast of them. "You have not yet offered her the rose. And Sir Joshua assures me that the moon will appear at any moment now, so we intend to watch for it from the terrace."

Derek felt Lady Fanny waver, but then acquiesce. In truth, he had rather looked forward to lifting her in his arms if she had vacillated, and carrying her into the shrine of the goddess.

She mounted the steps slowly, and Derek was conscious of the rustling of her silken garments tantalizing his senses and arousing his desire.

The time had come to grasp at happiness. The colonel followed Lady Fanny into the pink twilight of the grotto. He felt his blood sing as he came to a halt behind her and watched her place the scarlet rose on the small altar at the feet of the pink marble goddess.

Yes, he thought, excitement rising in him like a tidal wave, the time had come.

Lady Fanny was achingly aware of the man standing close behind her. He had not touched her yet, but he would as soon as she turned around. She felt it in her very bones.

Fanny stood very still, staring up at the goddess and soaking in the soothing atmosphere of the shrine. She still could not quite bring herself to believe that the colonel desired to speak with her concerning anything but the official breaking of their betrothal. The necessity of bringing this connection with the man she loved, tenuous though it had been, to a conclusion had depressed Fanny all day.

Aphrodite seemed to have a satisfied smile on her face, Fanny noted, and let herself believe for an instant that the Sheldons' grandmother had been right about the goddess. Was she really watching over lovers, or was this wishful thinking? If this myth was anything more than mere superstition, an extension of Fanny's own desires, surely the colonel's presence at the grotto confirmed that he had other things on his mind besides her scandalous past. Were they standing here as lovers? The possibility made her heart beat faster. There was only one way to find out. Fanny took a deep breath and turned around.

The colonel was standing so close to her that her skirt brushed against his Hessians. The size of him looming over her disconcerted her for a moment.

"So?" she began in a breathless voice. "I presume you wish to talk to me about ending our make-believe betrothal, Colonel?"

A flash of surprise crossed his face, and then he laughed. "For an intelligent woman, my dear Fanny, you are astonishingly obtuse." He gazed down at her intently, and what she saw in his eyes convinced Fanny that perhaps her fears had been unfounded.

"After you read my letter, I imagined you would not wish to have anything to do with me."

He smiled, and Fanny was treated to a quick flash of dimples. "Your imagination is seriously impaired, Fanny."

"But you *did* read the letter?" She could not believe he had been unaffected by the scandals it revealed.

"Of course, I read your letter, my love. Several times, in fact."

"Then you know I have the most scandalous reputation a female could possibly have—"

He reached out and grasped her by the shoulders, and Fanny felt the warmth of his hands through the thin silk of her gown. "I know all this, Fanny," he said, his voice rough with emotion. "But that letter speaks only of the past, of all the unfortunate events in your life that brought you here to Sheldon Hall. I have scandals in my past, too, my dear, as you well know. Do you imagine you would be standing here with me now had none of that occurred?"

Fanny looked up at him, bemused by his intensity, but basking in the warmth of his eyes. She had never thought of her past in quite that light before. Perhaps it had been her destiny to run into the colonel in Calais, to come to Sheldon Hall, and . . .

"Let us put the past behind us, Fanny," he said unevenly. "It is the future I need to speak to you about, my love. Our future here at Sheldon Hall. Our future *together*." He gazed at her fiercely, and Fanny felt his hands tighten on her shoulders.

"God, you are lovely, Fanny," she heard him mutter hoarsely, and then she was in his arms, his hands tight around her, his face buried in her neck, his breath uneven against her skin. For a moment that seemed like a lifetime, he held her thus, then Fanny felt the heat of his lips climbing her neck to nuzzle her ear, and sliding across her face to cover her mouth. Then he was kissing her, his mouth hot and wet over hers, sending tremors of ecstasy radiating over her entire body.

Senses spinning, Fanny felt her knees go weak. Of their own accord, her hands groped blindly at his coat, inching their way up the lapels to tangle in the dark curls clustering above his collar. Never had she imagined the erotic sensation touching a man's hair could give her. She had never done so before, even in those childish forays with Gerald behind the laburnum bushes. And naturally Cambourne had never kissed her like this. All she remembered were two dry lips pressed briefly to hers solely, she now understood, as a concession to her innocent expectations and the social conventions her husband had long disregarded in his private life.

There was nothing tentative or reluctant about the colonel's kiss. It seared away any doubts she had about his intentions, and ignited a deep, devouring need in her for more of him, for all of him. Fanny moaned softly in her throat and pressed closer to the solid planes of his body, seeking to mold her softness to his strength, matching her need to his.

His response was immediate and unequivocal, his arms compressing her so tightly against him that she imagined she felt every ridge and curvature of him imprinted on her body. It was still not enough to satisfy the passion boiling in her, so when his tongue teased her lips, Fanny opened to him eagerly, revelling in the heat of him as he entered her mouth and explored her softness with tender thoroughness.

Her passionate nature demanded more of this delightful experience, but Fanny ran out of breath. The colonel must have sensed her distress for his arms relaxed instantly, and he raised his head.

"What is it, love?" he demanded softly, in a voice that was far from steady.

"I cannot breathe," Fanny gasped, taking a deep breath

and expelling it slowly. "You have quite taken my breath away, Colonel," she added with a spontaneous giggle. "I swear I am quite giddy."

His arms tightened around her again, and Fanny snuggled against him, seeking the comfort and warmth she had found there a moment before.

"Derek," he murmured. "Please call me Derek, my love. And perhaps now you will never run away from me again, Fanny," he added, his breath warm against her neck.

"I cannot recall ever running away from you," Fanny whispered against his chest.

"But you did try."

"Oh, yes, I certainly tried. I wished to save you from getting entangled with a scandalous female. One you heartily disapprove of," she reminded him.

"All that is in the past," he said, his lips moving warmly against hers. "And if you can forgive me for being such a pompous jackass, I can certainly forget you were ever scandalous, my love."

"Are you saying that we can approve of each other now?" Fanny teased his mouth with her tongue, and was gratified to feel his arms tighten about her.

"I love you, Fanny," he said fiercely, gazing down at her with such intensity that Fanny felt a surge of desire race through her.

She smiled shakily. "That is not the same thing," she said. "I love you too, Derek, but I also approve of the man you are, even though I may not always agree with you. You are kind, and strong, and honourable, and of course, prudent," she added with a gurgle of nervous laughter. "You are the man I wish I had met ten years ago, before I became the managing, opinionated, headstrong female I am today. A female who has made a fortune in Trade, do not forget." She paused and reached up to kiss the tip of his chin. "I am afraid you will want to change all that, Derek."

"What if I tell you I love you just as you are, Fanny?" His gaze was steady, and Fanny's heart lurched. "Ten years ago I would not have been able to say so, my dear. I demanded the perfect wife, and thought I had found her." He paused, his countenance clouding. "But today," he grinned unexpectedly, and Fanny reached up to pull him down for a brief, fierce kiss, as if she needed to erase the memory of Constance from his mind. "Today I know there is no such thing."

For the next few minutes, Fanny luxuriated in the colonel's renewed passion, returning his deep kisses with an abandon that left her dizzy. Abruptly the colonel broke their kiss and raised his head.

"Marry me, Fanny," he whispered roughly. "Marry me, sweetheart, and let me take care of you."

Ecstatic at hearing these precious words from a man she had, until an hour ago, despaired of having, Fanny hesitated. Some deep perversity in her nature made her waver on the very brink of fulfilling her dreams.

"Are you sure you wish to wed a female who dabbles in Trade?"

To her surprise, his mouth quirked into a crooked smile. "I daresay you were too giddy to hear me just now when I said I love you the way you are, Fanny. I am not asking you to change, my love. I'm only asking you to marry me."

"But you do not approve?" she insisted.

He shook his head. "No, I cannot approve, but I will not bully you about it, love." He pulled her closer and placed his cheek on hers. "I am confident that once our family begins to grow, you will be tempted to spend more time with us than with grubby tradesmen, agents, and other riffraff."

Fanny's heart skipped a beat. "Our family?" she demanded in mock astonishment. "You put me to the blush, sir, and surely you are premature. I have not yet agreed to marry you."

"Oh, but you will, Fanny my love, you will." His laughter bubbled up from deep in his chest and warmed Fanny's heart anew. "Even if I have to go down on bended knee to convince you, my dear."

"I can think of only one way you might convince me, Derek," Fanny said primly, "and it does not entail kneeling."

"Tell me at once and I shall do it."

Before Fanny could reply, a shaft of moonlight cut through the trellised wall of the grotto and illuminated their faces. The grotto came alive in a seductive pink glow all around them.

"The full moon," she cried, regret in her voice. "We have missed watching it rise with Margaret and Sir Joshua. Whatever will they be thinking?"

The colonel laughed again, a rich, exultant male sound that held promises of delightful things to come. "If my sister has the sense she was born with, I expect she has better things to do, my love," he whispered against her mouth. "Now tell me the secret to your heart, Fanny."

"Just kiss me again, Derek," she moaned, straining to reach up to him.

"I only kiss females who agree to marry me, my dearest Fanny," he teased, holding his lips just out of reach.

"Of course, I will marry you, you wretch," she promised, savouring one of the sweetest moments of her life. "You must know I will, Derek. Now kiss me again. Please!"

The colonel did not make her beg any longer, and Fanny was dazzled all over again by the half-tender, half-fierce assault he made on her willing lips.

Behind her, Fanny could have sworn she felt the smile of the goddess glowing in the moonlight.

The Barbarian Earl by Nadine Miller

The unscrupulous Earl of Stratham has offered his illegitimate son Liam a generous inheritance—if Liam marries the noble Lady Alexandra Henning. But an arranged marriage is an affront to Alexandra's romantic sensibilities—unless Liam can find the way to her heart—and perhaps open his own as well....

0-451-19887-5/$4.99

The Scottish Legacy by Barbara Hazard

Clear-headed Lila Douglas never believed in love at first sight—until she fell hopeslessly in love with her dashing second cousin, Alastair Russell. Ever since, she's dreamed of future meetings that end with happily ever after. But can her romantic fantasy withstand reality—not to mention a most unexpected rival?

0-451-19888-3/$4.99

To order call: 1-800-788-6262